W9-CYB-147

"How . . . how did you find me?" was all she could manage to say.

She paled, then flushed as her heart began to pound.

Miles Raven smiled at her, a smile so sweet, it would melt the heart of an alabaster saint.

Which she was not. She was a real woman of flesh and blood, a woman—one of many?—whom the handsome scoundrel before her had carelessly seduced and played false.

"I was desperate to find you, Gillian," he explained. "Come home with me, love."

Miles reached out and caught her trembling hands, bending the full intensity of his silver-blue gaze on her.

She struggled to free her hands, but he wouldn't let them go, so she gave up and let them rest there while she fought against drowning in the compelling pools of his eyes.

"Nay, I can't. I *won't*, Miles. I won't let you hurt me . . . !"

Dear Reader,

This month brings another exciting first from Harlequin Historicals. A time-travel story. But *Across Time,* by author Nina Beaumont, is not an ordinary time-travel. It is the story of a young woman catapulted through time into the body of her ancestor, the evil Isabella di Montefiore. Don't miss this passionate tale of treachery and desire.

And just in time for the new year comes another daring love story from DeLoras Scott, *Spitfire.* When the headstrong daughter of a wealthy rancher runs away to find her *bandido* lover, gunslinger Lang Cooper is sent out to bring her back.

For those of you who enjoyed *Beloved Deceiver,* we have a new book from Laurie Grant, *The Raven and the Swan.* Awarded a former abbey for his loyalty to the Tudor crown, Miles Raven is shocked to find himself the protector of an innocent young orphan who seems determined to wreak havoc on his well-ordered life.

Readers of contemporary romance will surely recognize the name Muriel Jensen. In *Trust,* the author's first historical romance, the sparks fly between a woman with a notorious past and an ambitious businessman in turn-of-the-century Oregon.

Keep a lookout for next month's titles wherever Harlequin Historicals are sold.

Sincerely,

Tracy Farrell
Senior Editor

Please address questions and book requests to:
Reader Service
U.S.: P.O. Box 1325, Buffalo, NY 14269
Canadian: P.O. Box 1050, Niagara Falls, Ont. L2E 7G7

THE RAVEN AND THE SWAN

LAURIE GRANT

Harlequin Books

TORONTO • NEW YORK • LONDON
AMSTERDAM • PARIS • SYDNEY • HAMBURG
STOCKHOLM • ATHENS • TOKYO • MILAN
MADRID • WARSAW • BUDAPEST • AUCKLAND

If you purchased this book without a cover you should be aware that this book is stolen property. It was reported as "unsold and destroyed" to the publisher, and neither the author nor the publisher has received any payment for this "stripped book."

ISBN 0-373-28805-0

THE RAVEN AND THE SWAN

Copyright © 1994 by Laurie A. Miller.

All rights reserved. Except for use in any review, the reproduction or utilization of this work in whole or in part in any form by any electronic, mechanical or other means, now known or hereafter invented, including xerography, photocopying and recording, or in any information storage or retrieval system, is forbidden without the written permission of the publisher, Harlequin Enterprises Limited, 225 Duncan Mill Road, Don Mills, Ontario, Canada M3B 3K9.

All characters in this book have no existence outside the imagination of the author and have no relation whatsoever to anyone bearing the same name or names. They are not even distantly inspired by any individual known or unknown to the author, and all incidents are pure invention.

This edition published by arrangement with Harlequin Enterprises B. V.

® and TM are trademarks of the publisher. Trademarks indicated with ® are registered in the United States Patent and Trademark Office, the Canadian Trade Marks Office and in other countries.

Printed in U.S.A.

Books by Laurie Grant

Harlequin Historicals

Beloved Deceiver #170
The Raven and the Swan #205

LAURIE GRANT

combines a career as a trauma center emergency room nurse with that of historical romance author; she says the writing helps keep her sane. Passionately enthusiastic about the history of both England and Texas, she divides her travel time between these two spots. She is married to her own real-life hero, and has two teenage daughters, two dogs and a cat.

To Beverly Shippey, Anne Bouricius, and my friends on Prodigy, with thanks for their information and views on convent life.

And as always, to Michael.

Prologue

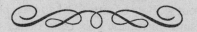

"Oh, *there* you are, Dame Ancilla. And about time! I paid my money to die in peace and comfort, not in loneliness and squalor."

The young novice smiled and tried not to wrinkle her nose—for the old woman was much disinclined to bathe—and answered calmly, "I know that it must seem like a long time to you, but I looked in on you just before Chapter meeting, and you knew I must attend it."

"Hmph! And since when are novices allowed to attend Chapter as if they were the same as professed nuns?" Mistress Elizabeth Easington asked in her querulous fashion. "Bah, what does a young thing like you know about nursing, anyway? You should be out having babes, and save the convent for when you're too old to be anywhere else!"

The young woman looked away, afraid the fretful old woman would see warning of the trouble in her eyes. Just this morning the prioress had announced the news they had all been dreading—Kyloe Priory was to be dissolved by order of King Henry VIII, just as other convents and monasteries all over the kingdom were being closed. The nuns, many of them old and unable to remember any other way of life, would be homeless.

Apparently Mistress Easington noted nothing amiss, though, for she went on: "And you've a passionate mouth on you, wench, made for kissing, not lisping prayers day and night!"

Dame Ancilla gaped at her for a moment, startled by the old woman's words. In the years she had spent behind these walls, she had rarely given her face a thought. A nun did not worry about worldly beauty. She had been promised to the convent since birth, the only child of her parents to survive the rigors of infancy in the north-country climate. Before she had been old enough to enter the community as a postulant, she had been a boarding pupil here.

Her hand flew to her mouth in uncharacteristic self-consciousness. She'd always thought the old woman could see but poorly. What did she mean, a passionate mouth? For one impulsive moment she wished she had a piece of silvered glass to use as a mirror.

"Ancilla," the old woman mused. "I'll vow that nunly name covers up a pretty, feminine one, doesn't it? Well, girl? What were you christened?"

The infirmary faded before the young Benedictine and the years went rushing away as she strained to remember the way her mother and father had said her name, their voices full of love. It was a thing she had not thought of since the ceremony in which she had asked the convent to accept her as a novice.

"Ancilla was a saint, a holy martyr," she said, fighting the memory. "And it's time for your bath, Mistress—"

"I didn't ask how you got your religious name, did I? Are you deaf, girl?" the old woman snapped. "Come now, make a dying woman happy—what is your real name?"

"Gillian. My name is—*was* Gillian," she corrected firmly. "And you're not dying, at least not today. I'll put some water on to heat."

"Such a managing wench," the old woman complained. "I'll warrant you even tell the Prioress what to do, and when."

Dame Ancilla was about to retort that no one needed to tell the gentle, loving Mother Benigna what to do, when suddenly the heavy oaken door creaked and a draft of February air preceded Sir Herbert, the priory's priest.

"Father?" began Dame Ancilla, wondering why he wore the vestments he only donned when saying the Mass or delivering the sacraments.

"Good morrow to you, Dame Ancilla," the red-faced, corpulent priest murmured, nodding curtly toward her, his small black eyes disappearing into the folds of flesh as he smiled in his smirking way. "Mistress Easington, I've come to give ye the Eucharist, aye, and extreme unction, too, if ye want it—ye're always saying ye're dying, after all. Best take advantage now. I shan't be here after today. No sense in my staying, with what's about to happen to this place!"

The priest had clumsily announced the very news that the prioress planned to break gently to the old pensioner!

"What d'you mean?" the old woman asked, anxiety flooding her face. "Stop trying to shush him, Ancilla," she added sharply, swiveling on her cot to face the young nun. "I can see he's let the cat out of the bag!"

"Oh, did ye not hear?" Sir Herbert went on in his blundering fashion, oblivious to the old woman's alarm. "The community's to be dissolved. The priory's been given to a Sussex knight, with all occupants to be gone within a month. I will need to scurry to find a new living, so there's no sense dallying here, much as I am dedicated to serving the spiritual needs of Kyloe Priory," he added pompously.

You mean to the soft living and the handsome table you sit down to in the vicarage, and the harlot who lives there, thought the young woman, annoyed with the babbling priest.

"But they can't put me out, they can't! I've paid my corody! I'm to live here the rest of my life!" Mistress Easington's voice rose to a screech.

"Tush, my daughter, King Henry can do as he wants," Sir Herbert said, unaware of how absurd it sounded to call the old woman "daughter" when he was half her age. "Now, do you want the sacraments or not? I must be away!"

"My heart..." murmured the old woman, clutching her bony chest and falling limply back on the pillows.

Once it became clear that the last rites were not going to be necessary after all, the priest beat a hasty retreat. It took hours for Dame Ancilla to get old Mistress Easington calmed, though. The frater bell, announcing midday dinner, had been ignored as the young woman dealt with the old woman's hysterics and prayed that the poppy syrup she had administered for her pain would take effect.

Finally, as she became heavy-lidded, Mistress Easington admitted that she could go to York and live in her sister's house, though she expected her family would not be happy to see her.

At least you have somewhere to go, thought Dame Ancilla. She had nowhere, and no one; in any case, she could not imagine any other life but that of a Benedictine. She was only weeks away from taking her final vows! She decided she would follow the other, older nuns when they left Kyloe, and hope that they found a permanent refuge from King Henry's greed.

Chapter One

Sir Miles Raven swore colorfully as he reined in his horse above Budle Bay, seeing the rain begin to fall in ever-increasing droplets and feeling its chill as several drops managed to find their way down his neck between his hat and his fur-trimmed cloak.

Didn't spring ever reach the north? It was now late April, and it felt colder than Sussex in January. And now the very thing that had delayed him from coming a month ago—roads made impassable by thick mud and swollen streams—seemed bound to delay him from reaching Kyloe Priory this afternoon.

There was no help for it. He'd have to seek shelter for himself and his horse. Morosely he turned his attention from the narrow bay, which at low tide was little more than an apron of mud flats speckled with waterfowl searching for food. The fog rolling in made it difficult to see, but he thought he could make out some sort of dwelling perched on the headland above the wild, lonely bay.

It would have to do. He clucked to Cloud, his gray stallion, and the horse wheeled around and plunged into the rain, now falling in sheets.

Rock walls lined the dirt road leading to the house built of freestone. He spied a barn off to the right. Even in his haste to escape the icy rain, however, he noticed a general air of neglect about the place. The glass in the windows was clouded with dirt; a boarded-up window on the second story looked like a patched eye. Another pane, on the first story, was broken. A pile of unburnt refuse lay in the front yard. A sow, seemingly oblivious to the rain, rooted among the rubbish.

No one came at his first knock, nor the second. He might have given up had he not heard through the broken window a child being hushed somewhere in the house, but once he knew for certain that the dwelling was inhabited, he set up a pounding that would have awoken the dead. He was not going to get soaked in this downpour while whoever lived here stayed snug in their home! Did the north-country folk believe in no duty of hospitality?

At last the door opened a crack, revealing a squinting eye, and a moment later Miles heard the bolt being drawn back. Then a weasel-faced man was facing him on the threshold.

"Good day to you," Miles said, when it seemed all the man could do was stare. "I am Sir Miles Raven. Might I ask the favor of shelter from the weather for myself and my horse? It's a cursed chilly rain."

The man continued to study him as if trying to find the words to refuse his request.

"I assure you, the barn will do quite well for both of us," Miles said stiffly. "As soon as the rain lets up, I intend to press on in any case. I need to reach Kyloe Priory before nightfall if at all possible."

"Now, there's no need t'be testy," the man said in a rumbling Northumbrian accent, his mind apparently made up at last. "Certainly ye're welcome t'coom in, sir. 'Tis just that we don't get t'see many fine gentlemen from th'south! George Brunt's the name. Ned'll take yer horse t'th' barn, won't ye, lad?'' the man said, referring to a curious-faced boy whose small, narrow features proclaimed him the man's son. Suddenly the man was all affable hospitality, ushering Miles into the dimly lit hall and over to the fire.

Miles looked around as he lowered himself onto the settle and saw that while the exterior was neglected, the house's interior was in a state little short of squalor. Dust lay thickly over every horizontal surface. Ancient cobwebs festooned the corners of walls that had not been whitewashed in the past decade. A piece of broken crockery adorned a carpet little better than a rag.

"Mag!" his host roared, after he had taken a seat on a rickety chair to the right of the settle. A moment later a nervous-faced woman appeared, a thin toddler clinging to her dirty apron. "Some wine for Sir Miles, our neighbor-t'-be at Kyloe Priory, who's coom seekin' shelter from th' storm!" Brunt's tone was hearty, as if he was the knight's social equal and Sir Miles was a welcome though not unusual sort of guest. Miles intercepted a look between his host and the man's spouse, however, which was full of tension. Why did his visit make Brunt so nervous?

Brunt did not seem inclined to talk while they waited for the wine. At least the fire was welcoming, thought Miles, feeling his chilled body begin to thaw as the heat from the hearth penetrated his damp clothing. Without waiting for an invitation from his silent host, Miles stood and removed his cloak, draping it over another chair to his left. If he wasn't going to be offered dry clothing, at least some of the moisture could drain out of the cloak.

The wine, eventually brought in crude pewter goblets by the woman, was little better than vinegar. Miles could not conceal the involuntary wrinkling of his mouth at the sour taste, but his host did not seem to notice. Brunt drank deeply and became more talkative.

"Don't drink too much wine, m'self. Ale's what I drink, most days. Just kept that in case some quality visitor coom t'call, such as th'abbot was wont t'do. I guess we won't have t'worry much about th'abbot coomin' any more, will we?" he asked with a chuckle and slapped his knee, looking to his guest to confirm the humor of his remark.

"An abbey has been closed nearby?" Miles asked, more out of politeness than out of any real interest. He was still trying to keep from puckering as he drank, though the wine's warmth did feel pleasant spreading through his body.

"Belford," his host said in confirmation. "And good riddance t'th' Cistercians and all the rest, *I* say. Damned leeches! Always coomin' round t'demand their rent of a sheep a year. Dunno th' name of the gentleman that received Belford of the king, d'ye?"

"Nay, I hadn't heard." He would have to inquire, since it seemed they were to be neighbors.

"And ye're th' new master of Kyloe, eh? Ye gave those dames their quittance? Good for ye, I say! Places like that give lazy women an excuse t'live useless lives, pretendin' t'pray when all they want is a reason t'get out o' their God-given duties o' cookin' and bearin' a man's children!"

Miles was certain that Brunt made sure his wife escaped none of her God-given duties. He forbore to argue the point, even though he knew the lives of most religious women were full of hard work as well as hours spent in prayer.

"Yes, Kyloe is mine now, though I confess I had not sought it. My late father had applied to the Commission of Augmentations for one of the many properties it had to sell, but he died before he could claim it."

"And you inherited it." Brunt nodded with wine-induced sagacity.

"Not precisely. My brother, Thomas, is the older son, but as the heir, he had enough to manage with Ravenwood in Sussex and wanted me to have my own land."

"I don't imagine he wanted t'coom clear t'th' north, anyhow," Brunt opined.

No more than I did, Miles thought, absently watching the droplets of water draining from his cloak onto the hearth. He thought his brother was trying to give him a purpose in life, a centering place far from the empty glitter of court with its superficial, greedy inhabitants.

Such as Lady Celia Pettingham, a dark-eyed beauty who had led him a merry dance when he was newly come to court, then cut him from her life without a qualm when she found another suitor who was more than the second son of a merchant made a gentleman by the last king.

When Miles had mentioned something about his new estate, and a plan to start a stud there, King Henry immediately invited himself north, "for the grouse season, you know, my Raven, and to look over the grand colts you'll get from your magnificent gray stallion."

Now that Miles had risen in the royal favor, it was amazing how quickly Lady Celia's interest in him had been rekindled, but Miles ignored her renewed smiles. He'd marry well some day, and ally himself to a powerful noble family who could advance his fortunes, but he'd been burned once by Lady Celia. Once was enough.

He wondered why he had told Brunt as much as he had. The wine must have loosened his own tongue, as well. Fearing the man might become emboldened to pry further into his life, Miles took hold of the conversation. "And have you lived here long, Brunt?" He was curious. Though the house and grounds were in a state of disrepair now, the property looked as if it had once been an elegant and comfortable manor and certainly beyond the means of his rustic host.

"Here at Mallory Hall? Aye, sir, all my life, though not in the house itself until a few years agone. I was th' shepherd, before Sir William and his lady died of the sweating fever. As there were no heirs except the church, th' abbot said I might live here, protecting the place for the abbey, as its bailiff," Brunt finished.

Oh, ho! No wonder the man was so eager to see the monks banished from the nearby abbey. Their departure made this erstwhile shepherd effectively master of the manor!

"The gentleman had no family?" he questioned, allowing the skepticism to show in his voice just to see what results it would produce.

"Nay, not a one," Brunt insisted, a defiant glare in his eye although his tone remained cheerful. Miles noted, however, that Brunt was unable to meet his eye for more than a second or two before pretending great interest in his wine.

"Anyway, he was the son of a knight who died at Bosworth, fighting for Richard the Usurper," Brunt added, in a tone laced with contempt for any who had followed the fallen king over fifty years ago.

Miles did not doubt that had Richard Plantagenet triumphed at Bosworth, Brunt would be expressing the same disdain for any Tudor supporter. He was the sort of man who would give lip service to whomever was in power while concentrating only on his own advantage.

Had his own father been any different? If he had not fought for and donated money to the Tudor cause, the senior Thomas Raven might have died a merchant rather than a knight, and his sons would not now be two of Henry VIII's "new men."

An hour later the rain ceased, and Miles, somewhat drier now, was able to continue on his way to his new property.

Each time the prioress coughed, the young nun was sure it would be her last, for the spasms that shook her wasted old body were much more frequent now, and the scraps of linen came away blood-soaked rather than merely tinged with red. It would not be much longer now, though beyond Mother Benigna's last breath Dame Ancilla dared not think.

She shivered in the cold of the chapel, tucking the blanket closer around the prioress's bony shoulders before poking up the coals in the brazier. They would have been warmer in the infirmary, which had its own fireplace, but the prioress had insisted she wanted to die in front of the altar. Believing Mother Benigna's remaining life could be measured in hours rather than days, Dame Ancilla had reluctantly helped her make the move.

They were the last two Benedictines in Kyloe Priory. The others had left a month ago, accompanied by the ever-complaining Elizabeth Easington, twenty-four hours before the day the new owner of the property was due to arrive. Even then the prioress had been too weak to make the journey.

Her health had begun to decline the day she had made the announcement that the convent was to be closed. Eventually it had become obvious that those who planned to find another convent would have to go on without her.

Mother Benigna could not be left alone to die, of course, and Dame Ancilla had volunteered to stay with her. She could not have done any less, for she loved the old prioress who had always been so kind to her, but she had watched the departure of the others with great unease. They promised to send a message as soon as they knew where they

would be settling, but no other convents had as yet sent
answers to their requests to join. Were there any still oper-
ating in England? The nuns had no way of knowing, but it
was certain they could not remain at Kyloe with Sir Miles
Raven due to take possession.

Daily, as Dame Ancilla nursed the failing old nun, she
had expected the arrival of the Sussex knight who now held
title to the priory, but he did not come. Perhaps he had been
held back by the torrential spring rains that had been falling all over England. But the weather had not prevented the
looters.

Once the servants of the priory, such as the shepherd and
the steward, had been discharged and the other nuns had
left, the nearby villagers and farmers had viewed Kyloe
Priory as deserted. They had lost no time in creeping up to
the convent singly or in pairs, intent on seeing what they
could carry off.

The king's officials had long ago taken away the chapel's treasures, the silver chalice, the jeweled pyx and the
golden candlesticks given by Henry VI, but the scavengers
were after more practical items, prying the glass from the
windows and loose stone from the wall while their wives
sought any bedding and cooking pots that the Benedictines had left behind.

They obviously felt they owed no loyalty to the priory's
unknown new owner. Yesterday, however, when the young
novice had surprised a man and wife in the cloister, their
arms laden with pallets from the dorter, they had had the
grace to look ashamed.

"Oh! I thought all th' ladies had left th' priory!" the
man had said. "W-wull ye be needin' these, Dame?" He
gave her a sheepish grin.

"No, I am sleeping next to the prioress, who is dying—
which is why I've not left. But those things are not yours,"

she added, unsmiling. "The convent's goods belong to its new owner now, and stealing is a sin."

The red-faced, sullen couple left without expressing any concern for the prioress's condition, probably because of my stern reproof, Ancilla thought ruefully, wondering why she bothered to defend the rights of the man who was about to evict her. *Perhaps if I had been kinder, they would have offered aid. I just hope they left the last of the loaves of bread and the chicken broth, in case the prioress feels well enough to take some nourishment.*

But the dying woman had taken nothing all day, dozing between intervals of coughing. Sometimes she lay awake, staring at the altar with a glazed, unfocused gaze. At these times the young woman would read aloud from the Book of Offices, her eyes often leaving the illuminated gothic script and reciting from memory.

The prioress seemed fretful and kept mumbling, "The cabinet... Go look in my cabinet, daughter." She meant the locked cabinet in her office, in which all the priory's important papers were kept.

"I will, Mother. Later, when you're breathing more easily," Dame Ancilla said, repeating herself minutes later when the prioress asked her if she'd done it. The dying were so worried about trifles when they knew their time was short. She had seen it before.

It was now late afternoon. After the storm, the sunset streamed in blood-red through the high clerestory windows, bathing the altar in a fiery glow.

"Look, Ancilla," whispered Mother Benigna suddenly, startling the young nun with her intensity. "Our Lord comes...for me...." With amazing strength she half sat up on her pallet, pointing toward the sunlit altar.

"What do you see, Mother?" Was Christ standing there, beckoning in welcome to the old woman?

She was never to know, for suddenly the prioress began to cough and then sputtered as bright crimson blood erupted from her mouth and drained onto her snowy wimple. She did not struggle any further, however, just continued staring in rapture at whatever she saw on the altar.

Frantically Dame Ancilla searched in her pocket for the small jar of chrism, or consecrated oil, that she had found in Sir Herbert's abandoned cottage. Her voice choked with tears, she murmured the Latin words that commended a dying soul to its Maker.

Feeling her touch, the old nun turned her head to look at Ancilla. Mother Benigna's eyes were full of a peace that was at odds with the shocking scarlet stream staining her wimple, and though she was past speech, Ancilla could feel the abbess trying to convey her farewell and thanks. And then, after a deep, sighing breath, she was gone.

The young woman was left alone with her panic.

Gone was the dazzling brilliance from the altar. In the fading light, Dame Ancilla lit the last of the precious beeswax tapers and straightened the prioress's body, crossing the hands over her breast and wiping away the blood that stained her lips and chin.

As she worked, she tried to pray aloud, but finally gave in to the sobs that threatened to tear from her slender frame if she did not give them voice.

She felt like an abandoned child. She had maintained a brave, composed front as long as the prioress lived, but now she felt terror seizing her. How was she to see that the prioress was properly buried? She did not even know if there was a shovel left in the gardener's shed, now that the looters had taken so much of the priory's goods. If there *was* a shovel, had the ground thawed enough that she would be able to dig even a shallow grave in the Benedictines' graveyard beyond the cloister wall?

* * *

Standing in the doorway of the nuns' chapel, Miles caught sight of the lit candles, and his mouth twisted wryly. So even thieves had a shred of religious feeling left, he thought, having already noted the missing glass, hinges and other evidence of pilferage.

His entire body ached with fatigue and the chill of the drenching he had endured this afternoon. He had hoped to find some food left in their kitchen and a bed for the night, but if what he had seen thus far was any indication, local scavengers had already picked the place clean.

As he peered through the shadowy chapel, he thought at first that the nuns had left their habits piled up in front of the altar. It was not until he heard the sound of sobbing that he realized the chapel was not deserted as he had thought.

His eyes adjusted to the gloom, and he saw that there was a black-robed figure kneeling on the stone flags in front of a pallet upon which lay another similarly clad form. The Commission of Augmentations had assured him that all the nuns had had homes and family, even if they were only distant kin, to go to! He had not wanted to be in the position of evicting religious women; such would not be the case, he had been promised.

Not only were they not all gone, but apparently the one on the pallet was ill. Fool he was to have believed the commission's words!

A sneeze gave away his presence just as he was wondering how he should speak to the kneeling nun.

The sound made by the intruder caused Dame Ancilla to choke off her sobs and whirl around, thinking it was another of the local farmers who had come to see what he could make off with from the convent.

Surely, out of common decency, whoever had come to steal could be pressed into service to help dig a grave in the hard, cold ground, she was thinking as she turned. Surely he would take pity on her plight.

But the man standing in the doorway was no north-country farmer. Even straining through tear-blinded eyes, she could see that he wore the clothes of a rich gentleman. On his head was a hat with a stiff, turned-up brim adorned by a large, drooping feather. A coat with slashed, padded sleeves and edged with fur made the tall man seem even more massive than he actually was. Underneath the coat he wore a black velvet doublet, which was slashed to show a white linen shirt beneath. Short breeches came halfway to his knees, and fine leather riding boots revealed a goodly amount of powerfully muscled legs covered in dark hose. She could see little of his face in the shadows, except that it was angular and possessed a thin, hawkish nose.

"I beg your pardon if I startled you, dame," the man said, stepping forward into the circle of candlelight as he spoke.

Some dim corner of her mind registered his deep, mellifluous voice with its accent unfamiliar to her northern ears. It was velvet-edged, a voice made for nighttime, not the fading daylight.

It was his eyes, however, that held her attention as he removed his hat from black, windswept hair and made her a respectful bow. In contrast to the inky darkness of his hair, his eyes were the palest shade of blue that is still blue before it is said to be gray. Their silvery hue reminded her of a Northumbrian stream racing through the Kyloe Hills, swift, penetrating—and just as cold.

Unconsciously, she shivered.

"I am Sir Miles Raven, the new owner of this property, dame."

She was suddenly furious, realizing that here was the cause of all the misery and anxiety Mother Benigna had endured for the last weeks of her life. Though old, the prioress had been well enough until the day the message had arrived that this man now owned the convent and they would have to leave. From that day the prioress's health had begun to fail, and now she lay lifeless on the pallet behind Dame Ancilla.

"You thought all the nuns would be gone," she interrupted, her tone icy. "Well, I am sorry to inconvenience you, sir, but two of us are left because one of us was dying. The Prioress of Kyloe is now dead," she continued, her voice a lash as she stepped aside to reveal the old nun's body on the pallet. "If you will be so kind as to help me bury her, I will then be on my way so that you will not continue to be discomfited."

Her heart pounded and she felt the blood rush to her cheeks as she faced him. She was not aware that the weeks of uncertainty about her future and the last days, in which she had scarcely slept or eaten, had taken their toll of her, too. All at once there was a roaring in her ears, and Sir Miles' surprised face faded as everything went black.

Chapter Two

Miles leaped forward, but he was too late to catch her, and she collapsed in a black-and-white heap. He knelt, staring at the young nun who only a moment before had been so scornful and defiant. With her head and neck swathed in the concealing folds of her white linen wimple, she reminded him of a wounded swan.

Reaching beneath the tight, starched wristband, he felt a sluggish pulse beneath her fingers, but the skin was cold. She breathed; he could see the slight rise and fall of the heavy cloth over her bodice. But oughtn't he to loosen the wimple that bound her head and neck so tightly? He was aware that he was also curious to see what lay beneath. The snowy line that framed her neck and brow totally concealed any hint of hair.

Nuns cut their hair as a sign of their sacrifice of worldly vanity, but did they keep it unnaturally short all the rest of their lives, or let it grow out again? The pallor of her complexion had given him no hint as to whether her tresses were brown, red, yellow or black.

As he removed the linen wimple, he was rewarded with the sight of a cap of honey-blond curls limply plastered to the girl's clammy forehead. Absently he smoothed the curls away from her face. What beautiful hair she must have had before it was cut! He pictured it long, streaming down her back in a golden, silken river or spread over a pillow....

Marry, but he must be crazed by his drenching, he thought wryly, to be thinking of a nun that way! Or perhaps he was but suffering from the effects of denial. He'd been too busy of late, with his shipping business in London and the arrangements for remodelling his new estate, to take advantage of the willing courtesans who frequented the king's palaces. As soon as he solved the problem represented by the dead prioress in the chapel and the young nun who had been nursing her, he would have to seek out a woman. Surely the villages of Northumbria had whores!

Still, even as Miles chastised himself, his fingers sought the petal-soft skin of her cheeks, stroking it, feeling it warm beneath his touch.

He couldn't leave her lying in the cold chapel near the corpse. He would have to find somewhere he could light a fire. Miles scooped up the unconscious nun, cradling her head against his chest.

Although she was nearly as tall as he, Miles was astonished at how slender a body had been concealed under all those folds of black cloth. Had she been starving since the other Benedictines had left? Was she not only a wounded swan, but a dying one?

As he carried her toward the chapel's entrance, he must have missed the moment when her eyelids flickered open. One moment she was lying limp and boneless in his arms, the next thrashing and struggling as if she were truly a wild swan—but a swan with a voice.

"Put me down, sir, immediately! I say put me down!" she demanded stridently, and when he hesitated, dumbfounded at her sudden revival, reached up as if she would have struck him in the jaw.

"In faith, you are alive! Nay, 'tis not necessary to strike, there you are," he said, fending off the blow and setting her on her feet, but with an arm at the ready if she staggered. "I didn't mean to frighten you, good dame, merely to carry you to where you might lie down in comfort."

"You'd be hard-pressed to find such here, now that our good neighbors have carried off all that was not nailed down," she began, then clapped a hand to her bare head. "My veil and wimple! What have you done with them?"

"You needed to breathe freely," Miles explained, while pointing to the articles of cloth on the floor, "so I removed them. I assure you I intended no harm."

Unconvinced, the young nun darted a glance full of accusation and suspicion at him, then walked over and picked them up.

"Is there nowhere fit to stay the night?" Miles asked, wondering if he was going to have to sleep before the altar, rolled up in his cloak. And he could hardly do that in the company of a nun!

"Naught except for the infirmary, and only because I've kept it locked. Between the king's men and the looters, I fear they've left you but a shell of a building," she added, and Miles heard a tinge of satisfaction in her voice.

"'Tis no matter, I intended refashioning it as a manor house in any case," he responded, unruffled. "The infirmary, then. I'll take you—"

But when he would have taken her arm, she whirled away from him, eyes blazing.

"Ho! Why so prickly, dame? I meant but to help." Distracted, he stroked his small pointed beard and mustache. This nun had none of the meek, mild nature he'd always assumed common to women in convents.

"Thank you, sir, but I need no such help. As I said, I need but aid to bury the prioress and I'll be on my way."

She did not answer his question about her temper, he noticed. And though two spots of hectic color had appeared on her pale cheeks, she looked anything but strong.

"'Tis impossible, good dame, at least till morning. Night has fallen," he said, indicating the west-facing windows, behind which no setting sun shone through the stained glass.

She gazed where he pointed, then gave him a wide-eyed, dazed stare. "Oh... I remember now. The sun was setting as she took her last breath. I..." Her eyes, of a deep blue, filled with tears, but she impatiently wiped them away as if she had no time for such weakness.

"How long have you been alone with a dying woman, dame? And how long since you last ate?" he asked. For all her defiance, the Benedictine looked as if a good wind would carry her off.

"I don't know," she said with a vague gesture. "I've been so occupied with trying to ease Mother Benigna's suffering...."

"Then we'd best get some food into you, and some wine, to put color back into your cheeks." He saw her flush with returning self-consciousness and look away as if the thought of him assessing her made her nervous.

"All that's left is a half a loaf of bread in the infirmary. The thieves even took the sacramental wine. And the livestock were all sold to pay for the dames' journey."

He shrugged. "Then I'll share mine. I brought some cheese and tarts and a skin of wine with me. With your bread, surely we can contrive not to starve at least until the morrow."

She nodded, then gestured for him to follow.

The infirmary was not luxurious, but it had a fireplace and stout shutters to keep out the cold. The walls were whitewashed and adorned only by a large crucifix facing the four narrow beds. One of those beds, the one nearest the fireplace, had rumpled sheets and had obviously been the prioress's. The stone floor was bare even of rushes; Benedictines evidently did not want to make being ill too easy.

Miles went out to the stable where he'd left Cloud, and when he'd seen to the gray's comfort, he returned with the food and wine. He found the nun had managed to kindle a fire and had sliced the bread at a small table.

The nun's eyes grew large as she saw the things he spread before her. At first she pretended not to be hungry, but after biting into the fruity sweetness of a tart, she gave up the act and began to eat as if she had not done so for days.

"Have you given any thought as to what you shall do?" he asked, to slow her eating. After long self-denial, it couldn't be good for her to eat so hurriedly.

"Do? Oh, you mean on the morrow, after you bury the prioress. Why, I shall leave."

"And where will you go, dame?" He hoped she would tell him of a nearby home and family waiting to receive her so that his conscience could be at rest.

Her clear blue eyes fought free of his and stared into the fire. "I shall find out where my sisters have gone—the other nuns of this community. They left to join another convent," she said.

He did not know why the thought of her leaving should cause him to wince, but it did. In spite of her self-reliant stance and harsh, scornful words earlier, there was something about the enormous blue eyes—the same blue as the Virgin's robe, he thought, forgetting he had put aside such popish nonsense—that reminded him of untouched innocence. Few women at court displayed such a quality, even as maidens, now that Anne Boleyn had made worldly sophistication a required trait. He knew he would feel as if he was turning a lamb out into a wolf-infested world if he let her leave without telling her what he knew. Surely brutal honesty was the best course.

"Dame, homeless monks and nuns are wandering all over England. It would be a waste of your time to roam the roads trying to find another religious community, for the few that are left are overrun with refugees like yourself. And even they will be closed ere long—I know this for a fact. It's best that you accept it, so you can start a new life. Have you family hereabouts who could take you in?"

She was still avoiding his gaze, but her profile was turned to him, and he saw tears well up again. "Nay, there is no one. My parents are dead."

"No brothers, no sisters, no other kin?"

"Nay... I was the only child living...."

The wind whistled around the priory, causing a flicker in the flames as a draft came down the chimney. He saw her stiffen her shoulders, heard her try to hide the tremble in her voice.

"Well, then," he broke in briskly, determined to stave off her panic. "No need to fear, just take the pension money you were given and use it to pay for lodging in one of the villages. Nuns are well-educated, and a woman with your learning could teach young children, or be a companion to a gentlewoman.... Perhaps you might even marry," he added with a bracing optimism.

He thought her reaction to his last words might give some hint of a sweetheart left behind, but she seized on something else entirely.

"Pension money? I don't know what you mean."

"Aye, pension money. The funds the commission has allotted each displaced religious person to enable him—or her—to resettle, now the monasteries and convents will all be closing."

"We received no pension money, Sir Miles."

"Of course you did. I made sure that it was sent, since I would be taking over the property. 'Twas sent in a lump sum in the care of your priest, Sir Herbert, to be dispersed to all of you. It amounted to several pounds apiece."

She sank limply in the straight-backed chair, a look of despair settling over her features like a black shroud. "No wonder the fat swine of a cleric was in such a hurry to leave," she said.

"You're saying that the convent's priest absconded with your pension money?" he asked in blank disbelief. He had heard of the abuses documented by the king's investigators in several religious houses but had thought them the exception rather than the rule.

"My lord, all I can tell you is that Sir Herbert left as soon as Kyloe's closing was announced, and he never mentioned receiving any funds. Sending money intended for the nuns to that man, Sir Miles, is comparable to asking a weasel to guard a dovecote," she concluded with a wry attempt at humor that did not reach her eyes.

No wonder she was so afraid! With no money and no relations, she truly had no options. "I shall see the rascal traced, and your money recovered, if that is possible," he promised.

She shrugged slender shoulders. "Thank you," she murmured tonelessly. It was clear that she knew there was little likelihood the dishonest priest would ever be found.

"And until then, of course, I will consider your welfare my responsibility," he added on an impulse, determined to banish the fear clouding the eyes that now turned on him with an expression of disbelief mingled with suspicion.

"Why should you?" she challenged in her north-country burr. "'Tis not your fault the priest was a thief. Are you salving your conscience for buying Kyloe Priory, Sir Miles?"

The mulish, defiant glint had returned to her eyes now that her stomach was getting full, he noted. "Nay, for 'twas not I who bought it, but my father," Miles said, surprised to feel on the defensive. For the second time that day, he explained how his father had died before taking possession of the new property and that his elder brother had given Kyloe to him. "I suppose I said I would assume responsibility for you because you have no one else. Because 'tis the right thing to do."

"Nay, I can't let you do that." The deep blue eyes locked with his in a challenging stare.

"What are you going to do, then, sell your body?" He heard her gasp at his crudeness, but went brutally on. He was weary and longed to have the matter settled so that he could get some rest. "I can't see that you have any other choice, with no money and no family. How else shall you earn your bread, unless you mean to turn thief, that is?"

"Of course I didn't mean to sell my body or take to thievery," she retorted, affronted. "I'm a nun."

"Not any more, you're not. Like it or not, King Henry has abolished that way of life in England. See here, lass, you're going to have to face reality. I . . . I'll be needing a housekeeper, once the priory has been rebuilt into a manor as I plan. Why not take the position, at least until you have something else you want to do?" He hadn't known until the words were out that he was going to say them, but to cover up his surprise at himself, he added teasingly, "And shouldn't I know your name, if you're going to eat your supper and mine, too?"

She looked down at the crumbs that remained, mostly in front of her. "Oh! I . . . I ask your pardon, sir . . . I did not mean to be so greedy. I'm Ancilla. Dame Ancilla."

"I didn't mean your name in religion, mistress. I meant your real name. Perhaps you should start thinking of yourself that way. It's best that you begin today, I think, to leave such things behind you."

She looked at him as if wondering if he could steal her soul by knowing her real name. He waited, saying nothing.

"'Tis Gillian. My name in the world was—is—Gillian Mallory."

"Of the Mallory family who supported Richard Plantagenet?" He had heard of the old northern baron who had fought so fiercely for Richard, only to be slaughtered alongside him. Then he thought of the manor house he had departed. Could it be...?

Gillian Mallory nodded. "My grandfather died at Bosworth Field with *King* Richard," she said boldly. "He left my grandmother heavy with his babe. My father was her only child, and she never remarried. The Mallorys were stripped of their barony and left with one poor manor in Northumbria. I assume your family fought for the Tudor?"

"Yes, Thomas Raven received his knighthood on the field. He had been but a wealthy merchant before."

"So he saw a chance to better his lot by betraying the rightful king," she said disdainfully. "You must be one of Henry's new men about whom we've been hearing—the ones who have encouraged him to abandon his wife and his church."

The cheek of her, to attack what she supposed to be his politics when he owned the roof over her head! She had nerve, he'd give her that. "Mistress Mallory, I've ridden through a cold, drenching rain today, only to find a dead nun on my property and another that I cannot, in good conscience, simply turn out onto the road to starve. Could we possibly revisit Bosworth Field another day?"

She had the grace to flush and hang her head. "Forgive me, Sir Miles. I did sound like an ungrateful wretch. Feelings still run high, here in the north. We were loyal to King Richard to the last, you know. I did not mean to sound unappreciative of your offer."

"Then you will accept?"

Gillian nodded warily. "As you have pointed out, I haven't any *honorable* alternatives. Perhaps, however, you should allow your lady wife to interview me before we make any final arrangement?"

"I am not wed, dame—that is, Mistress Mallory, so you see the decision is entirely up to me. I say you have the position for as long as you desire."

Pleading fatigue, Miles left her soon after that, taking some blankets and linens from an unused bed and saying that he would be in the dorter.

The nuns' dormitory echoed with a cold emptiness and had been picked bare of all but one lumpy pallet. He'd slept on worse on campaign with the king, he told himself. He'd just roll up in the blankets and think of the way he wanted to transform this ruin into a manor house he could show with pride to a lady of good family who would someday be his wife.

It was a face, not a building, however, that danced before his closed eyes—a heart-shaped one, first framed by a white wimple, whose owner possessed the most disdainful deep blue eyes.

Chapter Three

She thought she was visiting her childhood in a dream, for her father had always lovingly stroked her cheek as he put her to bed, telling her what a good child she had been that day and how proud he was of her. Gillian smelled the fire in the grate and felt its radiant heat warming her. Stirring slightly under her covers, she savored a feeling of warmth and security that she had not known for a long time.

All at once she realized why those feelings were so foreign to her. She remembered the prioress hemorrhaging and dying in her arms, and the coming of the man who had caused it all. And a part of her knew she was remembering *his* touch yesterday, and not that of her father so many years ago.

Gillian padded over to the shuttered window and opened it. Dawn. The late winter sun was just rising. Exhausted, and lacking the discipline of the bells that had divided her sleep for so many years, she had slept through the night. She dressed hurriedly in the chill air, pulling on the serge habit but leaving off the wimple and veil. *You are no longer Dame Ancilla, Benedictine novice. You are Gillian Mallory.* The draft stealing around her short, uncovered curls felt decidedly odd.

There was still some bread and wine. Perhaps she should see if Sir Miles was up and about and just waiting on her to break his fast.

He was not in the dorter. Could he have left, thinking better of his offer of employment? She was irritated at the tiny quiver of panic that thought engendered. She should be glad if he was gone!

But no, of course not, she chided herself, this was to be his home. Where else would he go, except perhaps to buy food? But when she checked the stables, a gray stallion, obviously his, trumpeted a greeting. He was somewhere on the convent grounds, then; probably already out digging the prioress's grave.

But when she would have gone out beyond the rectangle of buildings, she found her feet pausing at the door of the prioress's office.

Just once more she would step inside that door, remembering the many times she had stood within this room, receiving the prioress's blessing or reproof, which had both been rendered in a warm, loving manner. Surely if she closed her eyes, she could feel the prioress's presence.

This room, like the others, had been picked clean, except for the massive oaken cabinet that was built into the wall. The farmers and their wives hadn't yet figured out how to deal with that. Unable to budge it, they would doubtless soon be back with axes, sure the Benedictines had forgotten sacks of gold there.

Then she remembered Mother Benigna's words, words she had thought just the fretful whimpers of a dying woman, worrying about trifles. *The cabinet . . . go look in my cabinet, daughter.*

Now, as her eyes adjusted to the early-morning gloom, the words seemed to take on an importance they had not had just twenty-four hours ago. Perhaps she should see what was in the cabinet that had been so important to the dying woman. Perhaps there were records that would indicate family who should be notified of her death. But she couldn't open the cabinet, not without the key the prioress wore on a ring of keys at her waist.

Had Sir Miles already buried the prioress? Would he have thought to remove the ring?

Gillian flew down the cloister toward the chapel, her sleeves and skirt flapping behind her.

She saw with relief that Mother Benigna still lay at rest in the chapel, her face serene and wiped free of blood, her hands folded on her breast and holding the crucifix that had swung at the end of her girdle. There was no sign of the ring of keys.

Gillian gave a small cry of vexed frustration and began to run again, this time in the direction of the nuns' graveyard beyond the walls.

He had stripped to his shirt and was chest-deep in the newly made grave, a shovel flinging clods of earth on either side in a steady rhythm. He must have found the implement where she had hidden it under some moldy straw. As she drew closer, still unseen by him, Gillian could see the play of muscles beneath the bleached linen shirt and the damp patches between his shoulder blades and at the center of his chest.

"Ah, Mistress Mallory. You're up. I trust you slept well and are feeling stronger?" His face was ruddy from his exertion.

She had always been taught to keep her eyes modestly downcast around men, but now, stripped of her veil and wimple, she felt exposed, vulnerable. And surely that made it necessary to meet those compelling, probing pale blue eyes—if only to keep him from penetrating her soul. She forced herself to notice details about him, the unruly hair

that brushed his forehead, so black that it held blue high-
lights, the high cheekbones, the mustaches that met the
beard that edged his chin, emphasizing the arrogant, com-
manding set of his mouth. Only then could she try to ignore the voice of black velvet that wrapped itself in clinging
tendrils of smoke around her senses.

"Well enough, Sir Miles. But I need to know if you took
the keys from the prioress's waist?"

Her tone must have sounded accusatory, for he quirked
an expressive brow at her as he answered. "Aye. Surely you
didn't expect me to put them in the ground with her? I'll be
needing to open some of those doors, now that 'tis my
property."

He was reminding her she had no right to question him,
for he was lord of this place! She clenched a fist within the
concealing black sleeve. "Naturally. I just needed to get
into a cabinet in Mother Benigna's office, to see if she left
aught of import behind."

"Ah . . ." He stood the shovel in the hole beside him and
unfastened the belt at his waist, bringing up the ring of keys
she sought. "I had wondered about that cabinet myself. I
merely hadn't got around to trying all these yet." He extended them to her.

"Thank you. I'll return them shortly. And you needn't
worry—I only look for any documents that might pertain
to myself." She allowed her tone to be stiff, for his remark
still rankled.

He eyed her, hands still on his waist. It seemed for a long
moment as if he would say something about her coolness,
but he said only, "I will be ready to bury the prioress soon.
Surely you'll wish to be present to see that I do it properly." *Since you think I am naught but a heretic and an
opportunist,* his voice implied.

"I'll be there," she said, and with a whirl of black skirts, left him, feeling his eyes bore into her back.

Gillian returned to the graveside just as he was clambering out of it, so that his first sight of her was of her black skirts and sensible, thick leather shoes. It gave her a wicked sense of triumph to come upon him that way, on his hands and knees as if he was a suppliant. Perhaps it was because she no longer had to feel like a beggar dependent on his good will.

"I find I do not need your offer of employment, Sir Miles, though of course I am grateful for it," she began as he straightened and dusted himself off.

"Oh?"

"Aye. I found out why the prioress was so insistent, as she was dying, that I should look in her cabinet. There I found this." Out of her sleeve she brought out a roll of dust-dry, crumbly parchment. "Do you read Latin?"

"You'll have to tell me what it is," Sir Miles said, with a meaningful glance at his dirt-encrusted hands. He did not deign to answer her question about his Latin.

She unrolled it so that he could see the fading Gothic script and signatures at the bottom. "'Tis my parents' will. It says that Mallory Hall, our home, was to be in the trust of the Abbot of Belford as long as I remained in religion and to become the abbey's land only after I died. It was to be returned to me if I should ever leave the convent." She raised her eyes triumphantly to his. "Possibly the abbot no longer holds his position, and in any case, willy-nilly, I am no longer a nun. Therefore Mallory Hall is mine. I thank you for your kind offer, Sir Miles, but I am no longer homeless, but the owner of a fine manor."

He swallowed, and for the first time did not seem to want to meet her eyes. Could he have liked having her at his mercy so much?

"My congratulations," he said with an ironic twist to that arrogant mouth. "But perhaps there is still a bargain to be made here, though 'tis you who would be doing me the favor rather than the other way around."

"I don't understand."

"When you accepted a post as my housekeeper, we still had not touched upon what we should do in the meantime while the priory is being refitted as a gentleman's manor. We could hardly have lived here while the reconstruction is being done."

She waited, and with a glance at her, he went on.

"So now you are in the position to rent me lodgings. Mallory Hall is no great distance from here, perhaps an hour's ride or less. 'Twould be ideal for me to live there, paying you rent, of course, until my new house is ready."

How very certain the arrogant knight was that she'd take him in merely because he thought it convenient, she raged. Over the long years in the cloister she had achieved peace and a sense of herself. Now it seemed she would no longer be a nun, but her own mistress. She could not have him there, under her roof, destroying with his bold gaze the serenity she had fought to develop!

"Perhaps 'twould be ideal for you, but not for me. I fear you will have to make other arrangements, Sir Miles."

His mouth tightened and he made an exasperated sound. The pale blue eyes narrowed and became slivers of ice.

"Do you imagine that the faithful Mallory retainers have been holding this land for you, just keeping the manor house shining like a jewel and longing for your return?" His contemptuous tone stung her.

A pox upon him for being so cool and mysterious! "My parents always had good servants. And I mislike riddles, Sir Miles. What do you know of Mallory Hall?" she asked.

"I stopped there on my way here, but I think you should see for yourself," he said, refusing to explain. "And since you have no mount, and it's a long walk over hilly and boggy ground, I will take you there, and be present while you meet your 'good servants.' If all is as you expect, by all means, send me on my way, and I'll find somewhere else. If not, I will stay as your tenant and lend you whatever aid your prickly little soul will accept while I am there," he said, his gaze daring her to object.

"Very well," she said, and did not allow herself to be drawn to the bait by his insults. She would be hanged if she would beg him for details, even though his words made her uneasy. "I suppose there can be no harm in that."

"Nay, there isn't. Look you, Mistress Gillian—I know you don't like me. You see yourself as part of the old aristocracy and me a rich upstart and the source of the priory's misfortune, rather than King Henry. But I think we could do one another a mutual service. Let us lay the prioress to rest and be on our way."

She nodded in token acceptance, vowing that she would soon show Sir Miles Raven she'd have no trouble as mistress of Mallory Hall!

It took little time to ready the prioress for burial. Gillian dressed her in the habit of fine wool she had only worn on feast days. Then the shrouded body was lowered into the deep grave, and she watched woodenly as Sir Miles shoveled the clods of earth upon her.

Sir Miles left her alone at the grave for a time. "Goodbye, Mother Benigna," she whispered. "Thank you for being so good to me. Pray for me, Mother, as I begin a new life. I will admit I am afraid of Sir Miles, though he seems to make an honorable offer . . . but more afraid of what he hints I may find at my old home. Guide me, Mother."

When he returned she was oddly touched to see that Sir Miles had fashioned a cross out of two sticks he had lashed together with a bit of rope to mark Mother Benigna's grave. She felt tears sting her eyes.

Mounted pillion behind him on his great gray stallion, Gillian could not resist a look back as they rode out beyond the stone wall that enclosed Kyloe Priory. This place had been her home since she was a girl of ten. She loved every stone of it, every inch of cloister walk, every blade of grass in the garth, but even if she returned when it became this man's country house, it would not be the same. The stones would be broken apart and refitted, the lead roof melted down and shaped to a new use. No doubt the chapel, which had echoed with the Benedictines' plainsong, would become Sir Miles Raven's great hall and ring with worldly laughter. The stone floors, worn smooth by nuns' sandaled feet, would be covered over with rushes, or more likely Turkish carpets, which Sir Miles' wealth could purchase.

It was not a long ride out of the Kyloe hills to Budle Bay, but because it was mostly downhill, Gillian was forced to cling to Sir Miles' waist and found herself very aware of the powerful muscles concealed beneath the layers of shirt, doublet and fur-trimmed jerkin. This Sussex knight was no soft gentleman, for all that he frequented a pleasure-loving court.

Sir Miles' deep voice broke into her reverie. "'Tis a beautiful day. I'm beginning to believe 'tis possible for spring to come to the north, after all."

She looked around her as they descended onto Buckton Moor. After yesterday's downpour the sun shone strongly, as if to prove Northumbria was capable of a more gentle season after its harsh winter. The moorland that would be ablaze with purple heather and yellow gorse in summer and fall was now showing the fresh green of spring growth. In the distance a pair of red deer, feeding on the new grass, lifted their heads to watch them pass, then went on grazing. Meadow pipits shared the sky with larks, while from a nearby bush a cuckoo announced his presence with monotonous but musical notes.

"Ah, that bird's song proves the season," Gillian said. "My father always told me that cuckoos winter far away in Africa, but return to England in the spring."

"To lay their eggs in the nests of other birds, the lazy creatures," Sir Miles added with a chuckle.

Nothing could have prepared her for the difference between the way Mallory Hall looked now and her childhood memories of the manor's stately beauty. She gave a gasp of dismay as she viewed the broken glass in the window that had once been her mother's pride, the rubbish lying in the mud that had once been an immaculately manicured green lawn, and the chipped and peeling paint of the trim around the door.

Sir Miles must have felt her distress, because he said in low, comforting tones, "'Tis naught which cannot be put right, Mistress Gillian, and I'll see that 'tis done."

Even as she was sliding down from her perch on the gray's rump, the door opened to reveal the thin, ill-dressed figure of a woman, a year-old child clinging to her, his thumb firmly stuck in his mouth.

"Good morrow, Sir Miles ... Dame?" the woman said, staring at Gillian in her incomplete habit. Then, calling over her shoulder: "George! 'Tis the gentleman who visited yesterday and a nun ... I think!"

The man must have been watching their approach from one of the upstairs windows, because he joined his wife at the entrance a moment later. Though he greeted the knight pleasantly enough, he seemed suspicious of the purpose of Sir Miles' return.

"Ah, Sir Miles! I was just wonderin' if ye found all in order at th' priory! And might this be one of th' good dames of Kyloe?" he added with forced heartiness.

Sir Miles, who had dismounted, allowed the ghost of a smile to play about his lips as he turned to face the other man. "Yes, all was in order if one turns a blind eye to the plunder of anything portable. George Brunt, Mistress Mag Brunt, allow me to present the former Dame Ancilla."

As she returned their nods, Gillian wondered why Sir Miles had not given her real name.

"She'll be havin' t'find a new line o' work, won't she, th'times bein' what they are? Oh, say, Sir Miles," George said, darting a nervous glance from Gillian to the tall knight, "I hope ye wasn't countin' on me offerin' employment t'her. Me wife an' me, well, we ain't in such a position...."

"No, 'tis not what I had in mind, Brunt. Not at all." As Brunt and his wife exchanged puzzled looks, Miles reached inside his doublet and pulled out the weathered parchment with its dangling wax seal. "This former nun is Mistress Gillian Mallory, daughter of Sir William Mallory, the late owner of this manor. This will verifies that she is the sole heiress to this property in the event she leaves the convent. As she has been forced to leave it by the suppression of Kyloe Priory, she is returning to Mallory Hall as its owner."

Brunt's mouth dropped open, revealing a set of blackened and missing teeth. He stared at her with beady brown eyes gone cold with hatred. "Now see here, Sir Miles, you can't just be showin' up with some girl in a habit and expect to foist her off as th'heiress t' this property! How are we to know she is who ye says she is?''

Out of the corner of her eye, Gillian saw Sir Miles's hand grasp the hilt of his sword, heard his voice change in timbre from its agreeable, melodious tone to one that was icy and threatening. ''You may be sure because a *gentleman* is telling you it is true, and if that is not sufficient—''

She did not know what he intended to use as further persuasion, but spoke up before the situation could escalate into violence. ''Master Brunt, I don't blame you for your understandable surprise, but I can prove I am indeed Gillian Mallory, daughter of Sir William. I was their only child, though my mother had two stillborn babes after me, both sons. She had pale blond hair, the shade that is known as silvergilt, and she was Anne Egremont before she married my father.''

''Thass true, George,'' Mag Brunt said softly, her worried eyes never leaving Gillian's face.

''Hush, woman,'' Brunt growled. ''Anyone hereabouts might know th'same.''

Gillian spoke again. ''Do you remember the time the snowstorm struck during the spring lambing and I helped you carry a dozen newborn lambs down from the hills, Master Brunt? I do.''

She watched the pugnacious glint fade from his eyes as her words struck home, to be replaced by something harder to read. The man looked at his feet, his shoulders hunching in defeat.

''I guess ye are indeed Sir William's daughter. I . . . I ask yer forgiveness, Mistress Gillian. I'd grown t'love the manor as my own, and when the abbot left, I thought 'twas good as mine. I hope ye'll give us a few days t'be packin' our goods. . . .''

"But I didn't intend that you leave, Master Brunt," Gillian said, coming toward the thin-faced man. "That is, unless you want to. I'll be needing a steward—might you be willing to accept that position?"

Brunt looked at his wife, who was gazing at him anxiously. It was plain that she feared his pride would not allow him to accept. After a moment, he nodded, giving Gillian a faint smile.

"Ye're very kind, Mistress Mallory. I alwus said ye was, even when ye was but a girl, helpin' me with th'lambs, didn't I, Mag?"

His wife nodded quickly, visibly relaxing.

"Then you will accept?"

"Gratefully, mistress. We have three mouths t'feed, and one more on th'way," he added, nodding toward the slight swell underneath his scrawny wife's apron. "'Tis not a time t'be on the road seekin' work. I'll…look after Mallory Hall as if 'twere indeed my own."

Gillian glanced at Sir Miles and found him studying Brunt intently. Feeling her gaze, he turned to her, a sardonic quirk to his brows.

She felt her face flame as she guessed his thoughts. *So Sir Miles scorns my kindness to this family! Thank God, we have not all been drenched with the jaded cynicism of the courtier!* "Nay, 'tis I who am grateful that you will remain on, and assist me in the running of this manor," she said kindly, giving Brunt and his wife an encouraging smile. "Having been removed from worldly affairs for seven years, I will be leaning heavily upon you for advice. With your help, I feel sure we can restore Mallory Hall to its former comfort. Mag, I hope you will take the position of housekeeper and cook—at least until I am able to hire some additional help for you. 'Tis a lot to ask, for I know you will need to tend to your little ones, as well. Oh yes, I should tell you Sir Miles will be staying on as my guest, until his new home is built at Kyloe.''

Miles was just quick enough to catch a look of surprise in Brunt's eyes before the man lowered his head respectfully to Gillian. Had Brunt thought once the knight left he would be free to take advantage of Gillian's naïveté? Perhaps Brunt would bear watching. He was glad he would be around to do it, at least for a while.

Chapter Four

There was a moment of awkward silence as Gillian, with Sir Miles just behind her, stood looking at George Brunt and his wife, standing on the threshold.

"May...may I come inside?" Gillian asked at last, breaking the frozen tableau as she walked toward the stone steps of the porch.

"Of course! I beg yer pardon, mistress, ye shouldn't need t'ask!" Brunt said, quickly stepping inside and ushering her in. Sir Miles, not waiting to be invited, followed, and was conscious of Brunt giving him a measuring look before turning to Gillian.

For Gillian it was like stepping back in time. Facing her just inside the entrance was an enormous carved wooden screen, which shielded the hall from drafts. One could enter the hall by either end, passing the pantry or the buttery.

Evidence of neglect and careless housekeeping was everywhere in the hall, but she was careful not to betray her displeasure. The Brunts had suffered enough of a shock in one day, going from masters to servants in a few moments' time. The dust that lay thick on the carved wooden mantel above the fireplace and the cobwebs that decorated the hammer-beamed ceiling could be swept away. The novice mistress had certainly taught her how to clean; she, in turn would convey her standards to Mag Brunt by example. Gillian couldn't imagine being an idle lady of the manor, content only to give orders while sitting at her embroidery frame!

For now, she decided, she would concentrate on enjoying the memories of the past as she walked from room to room. There was the settle at which her father had enjoyed sitting with her mother in the evening before retiring. She could remember seeing him watching Anne, her mother, with an adoring look on his face as she twirled her distaff or sewed his shirts. There was the long trestle table at which the entire household ate, for the Mallorys were not such grand folk that they ate in the great chamber, leaving the servants in the hall alone, except on occasions when they had visitors from court.

Gillian had been told that King Richard himself had once visited here, in her grandparents' time, when he was still only the Duke of Gloucester. What a great to-do there must have been, readying the manor house for him! She could imagine tapestries being taken down and the dust beaten out of them, and new hangings being made for the beds. An enormous amount of poultry, sheep and cattle must have been slaughtered to feed such an entourage. It would be hard to convince anyone now that this house had ever been fit to house such a guest!

There was an oriel off the hall in which was set a prie-dieu. Gillian stepped into this, noting that while the crucifix still hung in its central place above the altar, the statue of Mary and a relic box containing a bit of the robe of Thomas à Becket had been removed. She asked Brunt about them.

"I, ah, took th' liberty of removin' them, mistress, now that His Majesty has condemned all such Popish nonsense. Never fear, they're in a safe place."

"I would like you to put them back," Gillian said evenly. "I cannot believe King Henry would disapprove of the Mother of God or the saint to whom even the second Henry bowed. In any case, I will take the responsibility."

Brunt nodded, the picture of compliance.

Behind him, Miles listened in approving silence to Gillian's note of command. Perhaps she would do well, after all.

Next, though she longed to run up the stairs that led into the great chamber, she retraced her steps out of the hall and went out to the kitchen. Here again, she would have to teach Mag more stringent standards of cleanliness. Dirty pots stood on a waiting table, while a breakfast platter or two sat nearby, coated with congealed grease and half-eaten crusts of bread. A greasy-haired lad snored in the corner by the fire, while a scorched haunch of venison on the spit filled the area with its smell.

Brunt went over and kicked the lad awake. "This here's Jack, my oldest boy. Make yer curtsy t'yer new mistress, lad, Mistress Gillian Mallory. And mind the venison so it don't burn!"

The boy jumped up with a start, gaped at her, then pulled on his forelock in an addled gesture of respect before turning the venison over the fire.

"That won't happen again, mistress. Jack's a bit simple and I suppose I've been too soft with him."

Gillian looked away. She had seen how thin the boy was, how covered with bruises his arms were, how fearful he had looked. George Brunt was anything but soft to him! Jack wore much the same cowed look that Mag Brunt had when she gazed at her spouse.

The parlor led off of the kitchen, and this had become a repository for broken furniture and bits of harness and tools. It had been her mother's withdrawing room, the place where Lady Anne had embroidered and written letters while Sir William went over his accounts of the home farm and Mallory Hall's tenants.

At last, she climbed the staircase and went down the corridor to the large chamber on the end. The great bed that her parents had shared still stood in the center, but it was unmade, the blankets ragged, the linens gray with lack of washing. Obviously Brunt and his wife were using this chamber for their own; a small trundle bed on which rested a forlornly dirty rag doll proclaimed the fact that their youngest son used it, too.

"We'll remove our things this very afternoon, mistress," said Mag, speaking up before Gillian could. "I know ye'll wish t'occupy this room."

"Actually, I believe I will have you put Sir Miles here, and I will take the smaller chamber next door, which used to be my mother's room."

Behind her, the knight had begun to utter a protest. "Really, Mistress Gillian, by rights this chamber should be yours. I will do very well in—"

She raised a hand to forestall his words. "Actually, Sir Miles, I'm not being polite. I am not used to such a vast amount of space to call my own, for my cubicle in the dorter was very small and austere—only a thin curtain provided any privacy." She gave a little laugh. "Give me time to adjust to the change in my state, I beg of you. I fear I should not sleep a wink in such a huge chamber."

"Very well, though I fear 'tis not chivalrous of me to accept," Sir Miles said with a laugh, looking about the room. Then she saw his eye light on the small door at the side of the room, and he turned to her inquiringly.

"That leads to the chamber next door," she said. She did not add that her parents had rarely slept apart from each other.

He impaled her with that compelling gaze, and all at once she knew that she should have chosen a chamber at the far end of the hall, or even used the parlor for her bedroom. She could not change her mind now, or she would be acknowledging the thought she had read in Sir Miles Raven's eyes.

Let him try the door! He would find it locked from her side, aye, locked and barred, as it never had been in her parents' day. He would find out that she was no lady of easy morals, such as he must be used to finding at court!

George and Mag Brunt still stood behind them, nervously awaiting orders. Pulling her attention away from Sir Miles with difficulty, she quickly toured the rest of the chambers, finding the four smaller rooms empty except for a couple of rickety beds and some odds and ends of furniture.

"Master Brunt, you may have the pair of rooms at the far end that face west for yourselves and your boys. Perhaps we will eventually build a gatehouse cottage to give you more privacy and space. Now then, Mag, would it be possible for you to prepare a light repast for our midday meal? There wasn't much food left at the abbey, and I would imagine Sir Miles is hungry. I know I am."

After a quick, silent meal of cold mutton washed down with ale and a rather lumpy barley loaf and some cheese, Gillian arose and motioned to the anxious woman who stood as if waiting to be condemned for the poor food.

"There," Gillian announced with determined cheer. "I feel less like my belly has an aching hole in it, and more equal to an afternoon of hard work. Mag, would you show me where you keep your brooms and rags? Perhaps you would also have an old dress I could borrow, something you are about to throw away? I imagine I will get rather dirty."

Seeing Mag's alarmed look, she sensed that the woman probably only had two garments to her name. Quickly she said, "Never mind. It won't matter if this habit is ruined, for I wasn't going to be wearing it any longer, anyway."

"But mistress, ye needn't—" began Mag.

"Nonsense, there's a great deal of work to be done before supper to make the great chamber suitable for Sir Miles and the rest inhabitable for you and me. I imagine the hall and parlor will have to wait till the morrow," she went on briskly. "The sooner we begin, the sooner we'll have our tasks done and can relax over supper." Inwardly Gillian smiled, hearing in her voice the prioress's authoritative tones.

She went to the room that was to be her chamber, where she tucked her hair up into a simple cap she found in her mother's brassbound trunk.

Gillian had left Sir Miles lounging on the bench in the hall, his long legs stretched out in front of him. She knew he was amused at the way she had taken control. Probably she would not see him until supper.

The next thing she knew, however, he had joined her upstairs. He was stripped to his shirt and netherstocks, and without a word began wielding a broom and a dust rag.

He ignored her protests, and after a moment Gillian shut her mouth. There was too much to do, and besides, it was vastly diverting to see him meekly moving furniture around at her orders. George and Mag, uneasy at first at the assistance of an obvious gentleman, never mind a lady of quality, in such menial work, eventually took their lead from Gillian and accepted his presence. Soon the dust was flying, and mice that had made their homes among the dry, dirty rushes were scurrying for the cracks in the wainscoting as the rushes were swept outside to be burned.

About midafternoon, Mag went back to the kitchen to begin preparations for supper, but Gillian and Miles scarcely noted her absence as they worked in companionable silence. George was apparently arranging their few belongings into the Brunts' new chamber down the hall.

"There, that'll do for a start, until we can bring tapestries and such from the large chest in the parlor. Of course, you'll be able to see the mural of the nativity better once that wall is washed, and the other walls need a fresh coat of whitewash...."

"Hold, Lady Whirlwind!" said Miles with a grin. "Leave something for the morrow!"

Gillian was totally unaware of the smudge that covered most of her nose, or the fact that several honey-blond curls had escaped from the white linen cap, which was more gray than white now. Her face was rosy with the afternoon's exertion. She looked tired—but very desirable. Miles caught himself wondering what she would do if he kissed that smudge away.

Dolt! As if you had any right to be imagining such things about that innocent young woman who is your hostess, he chastised himself.

He thought of Celia and smiled at the contrast. Faced with a similar situation, that fine lady would not be dusting and cleaning, he knew. She would have languidly draped herself on the settle, propped herself up with cushions, content to call out orders until the work was done. She'd have made sure everyone at the manor knew how disgusted she—daughter of a marquis—was at finding herself in such disappointing surroundings.

"We *have* done a great deal today, haven't we?" Gillian was saying. "Still, so much remains to be done!" She listed aloud what she would tackle next, not knowing he had ceased listening to but not gazing at her.

* * *

Dinner was a simple affair, but Mag was obviously trying to improve on their hurried midday meal. The venison that had been cooking over the spit, its burned portion carved away, was served, along with a trio of well-roasted chickens, a lark and pigeon pie and a loaf of crusty bread. To wash it down, there was wine—the same sour vintage Miles had been served the day before—but once she tasted it, Gillian asked if she might have ale, as she had at lunch.

Mag said they'd be in the kitchen if Gillian required aught else.

"I should have insisted that Brunt and his wife dine with us," Gillian murmured. She had felt a sense of camaraderie with Mag after working shoulder-to-shoulder with her all afternoon. She remembered mealtimes of her childhood, when the lower part of the table was filled with family servants.

"Nay, mistress. Mag chose aright. Try not to forget who is master and who is servant."

Though his words had been said in an advising way, she felt resentful. She went on eating with eyes downcast. *Try not to forget where I have just come from, where humility and self-abasement were virtues, you condescending popinjay.* Aloud she said, "I know you do not think I should have made Brunt my steward."

Their eyes met across the table in the flickering light of the candles in their sconces.

"No, I don't. 'Tis hard for me to imagine that a man who has thought himself the owner of such a place could so easily allow himself to be dispossessed and then serve the very one who dispossessed him. I believe he bears watching, but I may be wrong. I hope I am."

"What an awful place court must be if everyone there is so cynical and suspicious," she blurted, then realized she sounded like a peevish, cranky child. But he had spoiled the heady, exhilarated sense of accomplishment with which she had come to the table.

He studied her for a moment, taking a sip of his ale, then put down his pewter tankard. "I said that I hoped I was wrong, but in any case I will be here long enough to detect if he is untrustworthy," he said evenly. "And if court has made me cynical, it has also made me a survivor. There are plenty there who thought their position sure, only to fall through lack of care. Queen Catherine of Aragon, for example. And now Queen Anne."

The news that the woman who had brought about "the Great Divorce" was no longer riding high diverted Gillian from her quarrelsomeness. "Anne Boleyn no longer leads King Henry around by the nose?" she asked with great interest. At the priory Nan Bullen had been an oft-discussed villainess, the source of their misfortune.

"Aye, when I left London her position was precarious, for she has offended not only the king but almost everyone else except for her adoring circle of young men. 'Tis unfortunate that she miscarried of the babe in January, for 'twas male."

Although she would have liked to hear more, Sir Miles seemed disinclined to say anything else about it. As soon as he had finished eating, he bid Gillian a good-night and excused himself from the table.

She sat there for a few moments longer, wishing he had not departed so soon. There was much she had wanted to know about his plans, but perhaps it was just as well to wait until both of them had adjusted to their new surroundings. There would be time later to find out just how he planned to transform Kyloe Priory into a comfortable home, whether he planned to raise sheep there and how much time he would be spending at court.

* * *

The next morning as Gillian broke her fast, Mag told her that Sir Miles had left word not to expect him for supper, for he had gone to Berwick to hire workmen for the priory and would have to stay the night.

She was aware of a faint pang of disappointment, which she immediately suppressed. With Sir Miles out of the way, she could get that much more done. She would direct that supper be served late and continue with her efforts until it was ready rather than stopping to tidy up beforehand.

And so she did, still wearing the old serge habit, sweeping and dusting until her muscles ached. She was aware that the erstwhile owners of the place were surprised and a little dismayed at her energy, for it kept them hopping, as well, but she didn't care. Mallory Hall was *hers,* and it had languished long enough under their ignorant neglect.

Though she had intended to work straight through until supper, Mag insisted she stop and have a bite to eat in the hall, where she had laid out some cold chicken, crusty bread, winter apples and a pitcher of ale.

"Just set yourself down awhile, mistress. I'm goin' out t'th' barn to take Brunt his midday meal, but I'll be back soon."

Gillian heard the kitchen door shut and assumed herself alone in the house, but a few moments later had the uncomfortable feeling of being watched. She swiveled in her chair just in time to catch sight of two small heads disappearing from the door to the kitchen.

"Who's there?"

There was no answer, just a sound of scurrying feet and muffled exclamations of fright.

"Please come out and say hello," Gillian called encouragingly. "I won't hurt you, I promise."

She waited, and then a lad of perhaps nine years peered cautiously around the door frame. His small, narrow features told Gillian he was Brunt's son. He was no simpleton like Jack, his elder brother, though; intelligence shone in his eyes.

"Hello," Gillian repeated, smiling and beckoning. "You must be Ned. Sir Miles told me of you, of how you helped him with his horse the first day he came here. Is there someone with you?"

Shyly, the boy came forward, pulling the same dirty-faced toddler she had seen clinging to Mag's apron the day before.

"My, aren't you a big lad," she said in soothing tones to the wide-eyed toddler, who was hanging back. "What's your name? How old are you?"

Hesitatingly the boy held up two fingers.

"He's Harry," Ned proclaimed.

"Ah! So nice to meet you both. I saw your brother yesterday, but I was beginning to think that both of you were naught but figments of my imagination, for I heard no sounds such as boys are wont to make, nor did I catch sight of you. I was always told that boys are noisy creatures."

Ned looked wary. "Don't tell Mum or me da that ye seen us, wull ye, lady? He said that ye might put us out if Harry cried or we made too much noise. Ye wun't, wull ye?" His small narrow face puckered anxiously, and Gillian's heart twisted with pity for the two skinny lads and displeasure at their father for worrying them needlessly.

"No, of course I shan't put you out, not even if you make the noise expected of young lads! But ye mustn't call me lady, for I'm a knight's daughter, not a knight's wife, so I'm just plain Mistress Gillian, all right?"

Ned nodded. "I heard ye wuz a nun," he confided in an awed tone.

"Yes, so I was—or very nearly, at least—but the king is closing the convents and monasteries and I am once again a lay person." She was charmed by the lad's open interest.

"Does that make ye happy, or sad?"

Gillian was silent for a moment, considering. "That's a very good question, Ned Brunt," she told him solemnly. "At first, I was frightened, for I had not lived out in the world for many years. A long time, is it not? And now that I have had time to think about it . . ." She paused, as an unbidden image of the dark-haired, pale-eyed Sir Miles Raven came to mind. "I don't know how I feel. Have you ever felt excited and scared at the same time?"

Again, Ned nodded. Clearly no one had ever talked at such length to him before. His small dark eyes glowed adoringly at her as he began to chatter away, dashing artlessly from one topic to the next.

When Mag returned from the barn, she found Harry seated on Gillian's lap, blissfully chewing on an apple, with Ned seated next to her, talking as if he, too, had previously been under a vow of silence.

"I'm so sorry, mistress! I told them not t'bother ye, truly I did—it won't happen again, I swear it!" Her eyes were dilated with fear.

Gillian was amazed. Did the woman really expect her to be angry? She held up a hand and spoke reassuringly. "In that case, I assure you I will be quite disappointed. Your children are charming, Mag. Please don't make them feel that they must be abnormally quiet!"

Mag sighed with relief, a cautious smile lighting her worn features. "Ye're very kind, mistress."

"As for this habit, the lad can't hurt it. I'm about to discard it for good, once I'm done with the day's cleaning. Tomorrow I shall look in my mother's wardrobe and see what is still wearable."

Chapter Five

Miles was gone two days. In the border town of Berwick, he found an excellent master mason, a canny Scot named Angus MacDougall, who introduced him to a likely gang of workmen.

"So ye waud transform a nunnery intae a hoose, waud ye?" MacDougall said. He had originally been lured from his beloved highlands by his English wife, who would not leave her ailing mother in Berwick. "Then ye'll be needin' hard-workin' men. Happen me wife's brothers are needin' wark. Eatin' us oot a' hoose an' hame, they are, but they're good lads."

It was dusk as Miles rode into the yard of Mallory Hall. He was buoyed not only by his sense of accomplishment in beginning the work at Kyloe, but also by the unexpected feeling of anticipation as he contemplated seeing Gillian at dinner.

The image of her had ridden with him all the miles to Berwick and back. In his mind's eye he saw her, still wearing the nun's habit and the cap that hid her short blond curls from view, her face attractively flushed from the hard work she had done and with the excitement of her plans for refurbishing the house—until he'd quelled her pleasure with his heavy-handed advice about the Brunts, he reminded himself. Her face had fallen and the golden lashes had swept low over her eyes as if to hide tears. He resolved to be more tactful and gentle with her and remember how drastically her life had just changed.

Gillian was actually a very resilient creature, he thought. Within one day after losing the only mother figure she had known for most of her life, she had been thrown into a bewildering and demanding new way of life. Rather than wallowing in her grief and fear, as some women might have done, she had been trying to rise to the challenge of being the new mistress of a manor that would need all her determination if it was ever to be restored to its former state of comfort.

He realized he was eager to tell her the story of finding his Scots mason in Berwick and of the ideas he and MacDougall had tossed about regarding Kyloe Manor.

Gillian greeted him at the door, having apparently heard Ned run excitedly out to take Sir Miles' stallion to the barn.

His mental image of her had not prepared him for the transformation that had taken place in his absence.

Gone was the heavy, thick black Benedictine robe that had swathed her slender figure in its concealing folds. The gown she wore was not new; he guessed that it had been her mother's. The velvet was threadbare, and he noted a discreet mend here and there, but nonetheless, what an improvement! The blue of her gown was the color of speedwell blossoms—or of her eyes, he noted. He appreciated the way the soft folds of velvet outlined her tiny waist. The narrow fitted sleeves, the style of the previous reign, complimented her slender shoulders. The low, square neckline was filled in by the snowy white of her chemise. An old-fashioned gable hood, such as the type Queen Catherine used to wear, covered all but a few of her honey-blond curls, but it framed her face enchantingly.

If she had reminded him of a wounded swan before, when her head and neck had been swathed in the confining white wimple, she was that much more the swan now, in all the glory of her full plumage.

"Mistress Gillian, worldly clothes become you well," he told her, sweeping off his stiff-brimmed hat and giving her a courtly bow.

She was not worldly enough to hide her pleased smile at his compliment, or the glow in her eyes.

"Welcome back to Mallory Hall, Sir Miles. I'm certain the gowns are very outmoded to one used to the latest fashions at court, but I believe they'll do very well until I can have some new ones made up. One hardly needs fashionable gowns here in the north, after all. But I had forgotten how soft fine lawn chemises and velvet feel against the skin, after so many years of rough linen and wool!"

Miles had to look away from her shining blue eyes, and pretended great interest in brushing some mud from the tops of his boots. His mouth had gone dry with the picture Gillian had unwittingly painted of lace-trimmed, sheer undergarments caressing the curves beneath the soft velvet of her gown. Why hadn't he availed himself of the services offered by the comely tavern wench in Berwick who had made it very clear she'd love to have him in her bed? Perhaps if he had, he'd not now be so tormented by Gillian's innocent chatter!

"But come in, you must be tired from your journey," she was saying, apparently oblivious of his internal struggle. "I'll have Mag and Jack bring up hot water for a bath, then supper will be ready. Mag's outdone herself making something special."

Indeed, he thought a short time later, when he was savoring the soothing warmth of the water that bathed his saddle-weary muscles in the great oaken tub. What a wonderful wife she'd make some lucky man someday! She'd greeted him cheerfully, not complaining about the additional day he had stayed away or of how hard she'd worked in his absence, though the evidence, as he'd passed through the hall, was everywhere. Instead, she had provided for his comfort without delay.

He smiled again as he thought of her obvious pleasure in her "new" garments, imagining her going through the wardrobe, trying on first this gown, then that one, watching herself in the silvered oval glass that hung on the wall. He would have to send word to his mother at Ravenwood to send some bolts of fabric, he decided, visualizing various colors of silks, brocades and velvets. That would be a fitting way to thank her for letting him stay at Mallory Hall until his house was built.

Supper was even more enjoyable than she had promised. Brunt's wife had indeed outdone herself, serving spring lamb flavored with chervil and onions and an eel and onion pie made with raisins and butter. The wine he had brought from Berwick to replace the sour vintage previously served complemented the tasty food and brought a becoming flush to Gillian's cheeks.

She listened attentively to his tales of Berwick, chuckling at his imitation of MacDougall's Scots burr. Her interest was obvious as he told her how he and the mason planned to transform Kyloe Priory, asking questions here and there that showed a lively intelligence and curiosity. She agreed that Cloud was a fine stallion with which to start a stud.

Gillian seemed to feel no dismay at the thought of her former convent home being so changed, he thought, and said so.

"If it can no longer be a community of religious, I would much rather it be an inhabited house, where folk live in happiness and comfort, rather than an abandoned ruin," Gillian said.

"Well, there's nothing dog in the manger about you, Gillian Mallory."

"Ah, you mean I am generous when I really stand to lose nothing I could keep, anyway," she said, her eyes sparkling in amusement. "I'm not sure if that was a compliment, Sir Miles!" She laughed, her dark gold lashes swooping low on peach-blushed skin.

"I assure you, Mistress Mallory, I meant only praise," he murmured.

Was she flirting with him? Gillian had a way of looking directly at him that was distinctly un-nunlike. Where had she learned to do that? Not in a convent, he'd warrant! Was it a talent instinctive to females in the presence of a man? Did she even know she was doing it? If she did, did that mean she was as attracted to him as he was to her?

Surely the wine he had quaffed was making him reckless; before he could think better of it, he found himself uttering a sigh, then a testing remark.

"But the Kyloe Manor I envision will be dreadfully large for just myself and a few servants to rattle around in, won't it?"

Her response was immediate and unconcerned. "I expect you'll spend most of your time at court, in any case, Sir Miles. None of you new men can quite resist the lure of Tudor favor, can you? No doubt you'll eventually take a wife to give you an heir. I wonder if you'll pick some court favorite who entreats you to take her back to the glitter of court as soon as she has done her duty? Or perhaps a more practical lady who'd be so grateful to have your name she won't mind being stuck up here bearing your babes while you follow Henry Tudor from palace to palace?''

His eyes narrowed. *The minx! She had thrown a probing remark right back at him!* He gave an exaggerated wince. ''Mistress, you wound me with your cruel estimate of my character! Do I seem to be merely a court sycophant to you?''

She faced him across the table again in that direct way of hers, but her words were enigmatic. ''Time will tell.''

''And who says I shall wed a lady from court?'' he dared, still trying to provoke a revealing response.

Had there been a spark in those eyes? Their limpid blue was shadowed now, unreadable.

''Indeed, no one. Who says you need ever marry at all?'' she parried. ''You are not the heir to Ravenwood, after all. Perhaps you would prefer to remain free of encumberment and a nagging wife who would question your movements.''

Damn, she was a cool one! If given the opportunity, she'd probably win a debate with Henry Tudor himself!

He shrugged. ''Perhaps.'' Celia came to mind. Certainly *she* would have been the type who would beg to return to the glamour of Henry VIII's palaces once she had borne him a son. She'd leave the babe behind with a nurse, never looking back.

Perhaps Celia was more ruthless than most, but wasn't she typical of the wealthy, ambitious sort of woman he still sought to wed, one who would help, not hinder him, in his quest for power? He wondered what Gillian would think of him if she knew his thoughts. He was dangerously attracted to her, aye, he'd admit that to himself, but he and she occupied different worlds. It was not just a matter of faiths, or even comparative wealth, but of goals so divergent that they would make one another miserable—even assuming Gillian wished to wed! He had learned from a chance remark that she had never taken final vows. Perhaps, though, despite that fact and her unintentional charm, she intended to keep a vow of chastity and live out her life alone.

Miles would have been interested to know of the stab of pain that had lanced through Gillian's heart at her first carefree-sounding mention of the fact that she expected him to marry and bring a wife back to Kyloe Manor and populate it with his children. It was a sensation relieved only slightly by his hint that he might not wed a lady from *court*, then fanned by his cool agreement that in fact he might not wed at all.

Why are you thinking about it at all, she chided herself, you who had been on the brink of making an eternal vow to a heavenly bridegroom? *Do you use a vain king's actions to justify yourself in caring for this courtier, a creature of the Tudor who will think of his own welfare first and foremost?*

Yet hadn't he put himself to considerable trouble on her behalf? a voice argued within her.

Aye, and look what he gained for it! Comfortable lodging within easy riding distance of the site of his new home, and they had never even discussed what rent he was to pay her. Perhaps he thought the privilege of having Sir Miles Raven living in her home was payment enough!

When she spoke again, her voice was cool and controlled. "Will you be riding out again tomorrow, Sir Miles, or would you have a few hours to look over the manor and its tenant farms with me? It's difficult to make heads or tails of what few records George Brunt has kept, as he's barely literate. I shall be needing ready funds if I am to make needed improvements here at the Hall."

"Nay, I don't need to go right back tomorrow. Angus will need a day or so at least to get his crew organized, so I'd only be in the way. I'll put myself at your disposal with great pleasure, mistress. Perhaps you had better show me what records there are tonight, so we'll be better prepared on the morrow when we talk to your tenants."

Supper over, he followed her into the parlor and watched as she showed him Brunt's records, or rather, the aggravating lack of them. Brunt had kept count of his sheep by the medieval method of tally sticks, which meant making notches on a number of sticks to correspond with the size of his flock.

If the number was accurate, the size of the flock had shrunk to a quarter of what it had been when she had left to go into the convent, she told him. What had happened to the flock? Murrain? Wolves? Thieves? A combination of the three, from Brunt's poor management?

Of the rents taken in, the only records were in Gillian's neat, convent-trained hand, written down yesterday from what Brunt had been able to report to her.

There were five farms, excluding the home farm, that owed rents to Mallory Hall of varying amounts according to their size, but even combined, it was not a large income.

"He tells me none of them are in arrears, and each pays quarterly," Gillian told Miles, standing in back of him while he sat at the desk looking over her figures by the flickering light of a candle she had moved over to aid him. "Yet he could not show me a single penny taken in from them. He says the money has gone to maintenance and the feeding of his family! Yet his family lives so poorly, and if he's made repairs I would hate to see what Mallory Hall would look like otherwise!"

He raised an eloquent eyebrow at her.

"I . . . I know. You told me not to trust him, and it seems you may have been right," she admitted. "But what can I do now?"

He wanted to erase the troubled furrow from her lovely brow, at least until he got to look over the land tomorrow.

"You need not change courses yet, mistress," he told her, turning to the figures so that he would not have to be tormented by the way she was nibbling her underlip in worried concentration. "Perhaps Brunt merely thought you would try to reclaim any coin left, since the manor has been yours legally since the convent was closed. He doesn't know you well enough to know that you would feel honor bound to leave that money his, wouldn't you?" He saw her nod. "Yes, I thought so. He may have a miserly hoard somewhere. We'll check with the tenants tomorrow and see what they say about having paid. From now on, you'll be paying him wages and taking in the rents yourself, so he may find he has no choice but honesty."

He smoothed the fingers of one hand over his mustache and beard and went on. "Having just passed the Easter quarter day, 'tis a long time until the next rents. I said I would be grateful to be your tenant, but I never meant to let it go at that. Shall we say five pounds per month, payable at the first of each month?"

His offer fell so hard upon the heels of her thought that he was taking advantage of his situation here that at first she felt ashamed of her earlier resentment, and then he began to wonder if he could read her mind.

"Don't hesitate so, Mistress Gillian," he chided her mildly. "'Tis not as if you have too many sources of ready coin, unless you want to sell off sheep and reduce the size of your flock still more. It'll be months before a kitchen garden can begin to put food on the table. And there is much that needs repair and refurbishment, as you mentioned." *And if I am paying you rent, perhaps I can manage to keep our relationship on a businesslike footing.*

"'Tis a princely sum," she murmured, her eyes downcast for once, giving him no clue as to her thoughts. "You are well-to-do, for a second son."

"I invested some of my inheritance in shipping," he said. "The ships have done well."

If she thought of sneering about a knight soiling his hands in commerce or his family's recent merchant origins, she gave no sign. "I see." Then, walking away as if their consultation was at an end, she said, "You are always pointing out what few choices I have, Sir Miles, and offering your resources as my only logical means of survival. 'Twould be churlish of me to refuse out of false pride, I know. So I will accept your offer, at least for the time being."

He realized she would have liked to refuse his money, just as she wished she did not need his help. It rankled her to take either.

Be patient, my little swan, he thought. Accept gracefully what I do to help you for the short time we are together. By then you will be standing on your own, God willing, and can attract a man worthy of you—if there is such a creature.

Chapter Six

Miles realized as he stood by his stallion in the stable yard the next morning that he was actually *whistling*. And why not? he thought with a grin. 'Twas a fine day, almost mild enough to be Sussex, with just a hint of briskness to the spring wind as it blew down off the hills. A faint line of clouds was visible in the distance, nestled among the rolling Cheviots, but nothing to trouble them today.

Mag had told him as he broke his fast that her mistress would meet him there, for she had eaten earlier. He would have to talk to her about getting another mount soon, he thought, eyeing the ancient cob that stood placidly at the mounting block, switching its tail as if it was in no hurry to go anywhere. It wasn't a suitable mount for the mistress of Mallory Hall, and besides, she was borrowing it from her steward.

"I know the cob doesn't look like much, but I tried him yesterday—just to see if I remembered how to ride, you know—and he really goes very well," she said suddenly beside him.

She had apparently unearthed her mother's riding dress. It was of dark green wool and hugged her slender figure lovingly, showing off a tiny waist. She wore a hood of matching green with a short veil. Mag had packed a lunch since it was such a mild day, she told him, explaining the small, cloth-covered basket she bore.

The cob stood placidly while Miles assisted her into the sidesaddle, which must have been a relic of her parents' time. Gathering up the reins and settling her skirts around her, she looked at him with an impish smile.

"I must confess I would really prefer to ride astride," she said. "I used to, on my pony, when I was a girl. My father called me a shameless hoyden, but he laughed when he said it, so I suppose he didn't think it was so bad."

He could picture her, her skirts pulled up around knees browned by the summer sun, the wind streaming through sun-streaked blond tresses as she galloped her pony over the hills. It was an image that couldn't help but make him smile.

"How did they ever settle you down enough to make a proper nun of you?" he teased.

"I fear I was the novice mistress' cross to bear for many months," Gillian admitted. "But at least I wanted to be there, unlike some of the girls who were there because of some vow of their parents' or because they were the fourth daughter or some such nonsense. 'Twas out on these hills that I first felt the call to be a bride of Christ." A wistful look stole over her features, and then it was vanquished by a pleasurable sigh. "But I *am* glad to be on horseback." Clucking to the cob, she cantered out of the stable yard, with a bemused Miles following.

They headed up the slope in back of the house and barn, and soon they were in the midst of the Northumberland hills, scattering the flocks of grazing sheep. It was a raw, bold land, free of the pretty little dales and thatched cottages of the south, its wind-whipped hills bare of any plant life taller than heather and gorse. Because there were no trees to block the horizon, the sky seemed to go on for-

ever. Reaching the top of the tallest hill, Miles felt the buf-
feting of the wind and was energized by its force.

He glanced at Gillian, and saw her with her face turned
toward the sun, her eyes closed, drinking in its radiance,
untroubled by the wind's brisk edge. No wonder the people of the north were so lacking in self-doubt, so contemptuous of their soft southern countrymen!

Descending the slope, they came to the first of the farms,
its sturdy stone barn and farmhouse without adornment
save for a scrubby rosebush climbing the side of the house.

A black and white dog in the yard announced their arrival with shrill barks. Evidently word had already spread of
the changes at Mallory Hall, for the farmer who came out
of the barn seemed unsurprised when Gillian introduced
herself.

"Oh, aye, Mistress Gillian, I mind when ye wur but a wee
lass riding in front o'yer father on quarter day, and I'm
glad t'see ye back at t'Hall."

"I remember you, too, Tom Small," Gillian returned his
greeting, "and that your wife made the best buttermilk in
the north country."

"She still does, and she'll be pleased to serve ye some.
Bess!" he called in the direction of the farmhouse.

"And this is Sir Miles Raven, new owner of Kyloe Priory. He'll be staying at Mallory Hall while his new manor
is being built there."

The man eyed Miles silently, giving a respectful tug on his
forelock, but otherwise he accorded Miles none of the
warmth of the greeting he had given Gillian. It was evident
he remembered Gillian and her parents with affection, but
had a different opinion of her companion. No doubt Brunt
had already blackened him in this man's eyes as no more
than another one of the king's courtiers taking advantage

of the suppression of the monasteries and convents to grab land.

It was the same at each of the farmhouses they visited, the farmers and their wives greeting Gillian with enthusiasm and expressing sympathy for the plight of the evicted nuns as well as joy that a Mallory was again in control of the Hall and its farms. They were silent and reserved toward him. Apparently he would have to prove himself a good neighbor and landlord before they would unbend enough to smile at him.

Each of them swore they had paid the rent to Brunt at the Easter quarter day, but none ventured an opinion as to what the former shepherd had been doing with the moneys he had collected. When Gillian asked about the diminished size of the flocks, they cited the causes he and Gillian had already thought of, and the fact that Brunt had occasionally taken sheep in payment when they could not pay the rent in cash.

"Not that his own flocks are in any better case," opined Jock, the shepherd at the home farm, whom Gillian and Miles came upon in the midst of a pen of bleating sheep, where he was inspecting the lambs and ewes for traces of scab. His sheepdog, a black and white collie, sat panting just outside the gate. "For a former shepherd, the man has grand ideas and no sense about sheep. He says the Cheviot breed, here—" he held up a typical white-faced ewe by her shoulders "—doesn't have a fine enou' fleece, so he spent good money bringin' over a dozen Merino rams from Spain! Well, any fool would know that sheep bred for a dry, hot country like that wouldn't do well here in the north! Sure enough, they sickened and died, though not before they'd bred the ewes with lambs that weren't much more hardy than their sires. Then he decides that Cotswold sheep are the kind to have, and brings up a dozen o'them. Well,

beggin' yer pardon, Sir Miles," he said, nodding respectfully at the knight, "it makes no more sense to bring a
southron sheep up into these hills, that are used to lush
grass and soft livin'!"

"What do you think is needed to bring the flocks back
to their former size, Jock?" Gillian asked.

"Black-faced Highland sheep," came his quick reply.
"Thick wool, they mature quick, make good mutton, and
are hardy enough for this weather."

"I'll have to see about getting some, just as soon as it can
be afforded," promised Gillian, but the shepherd's attention had already been stolen by a nervous-looking ewe that
kept circling the pen as if looking for something.

"She's missing her lamb," commented Jock. "We've
already been out lookin', th' dog an' me, but found nowt.
Didn't see any lambs friskin' about alone, did ye, out on th'
hills?"

Gillian shook her head, but promised they'd keep an eye
out for it on the way home.

"Aye, best be on yer way soon, mistress," Jock suggested, cocking an eye at the sky. "Them clouds is coomin'
up fast."

To Miles' eyes, the clouds seemed scarcely more ad-
vanced in their course than they had been this morning, but
Gillian seemed to take the shepherd's warning quite seri-
ously.

"It still looks fair to me, but Jock's right that the storms
build rapidly in the Cheviots. Perhaps we had better head
home," she said, turning her horse's head.

Miles was aware of a feeling of regret that the weather
would bring their outing to a premature end without their
having time to sample the picnic lunch. After sharing her
all morning with her tenants, Miles had looked forward to

sitting down on a sunny hillside with Gillian and eating before returning her to the Hall and her responsibilities there.

The missing lamb, however, became an unwitting ally to Miles' secret wish. They were nearly home when they came upon the lamb behind an outcropping of rock, bleating piteously because its leg was caught in a wolf trap.

"Poor thing," Gillian cooed, jumping off her horse and holding the struggling little creature while Miles worked to pry open the rusty jaws of the trap. "How stupid to put a trap where sheep are apt to stray! I'll have to speak to Brunt about this, as well as many other things, I can see that!"

Then, of course, they had to ride back to the home farm to deliver the lamb to its mother, describe to Jock where and how they had found it and listen to his praise and thanks while watching him splint and bandage the lamb's leg. By that time Miles had no trouble believing the shepherd's warning about the weather, for the skies had turned leaden and lowering, and the wind smelled of rain. Jock offered them the shelter of his cottage, but Gillian, after a speculative look at the threatening clouds, refused with thanks.

"I think we can make it to the Hall in time to avoid getting soaked," she said. "That is, if Sir Miles is not averse to a gallop home?" Giving him a challenging look, and without waiting for his reply, she touched her heels to the cob's flanks and galloped off.

Fortunately, it was possible to travel between the hills most of the way to the Hall, so Sir Miles was not loath to touching spurs to Cloud and setting off to catch up to her. He had no wish to repeat the experience of being wet to the skin as he had been the day he arrived at Mallory Hall.

Now the borrowed cob proved his worth, for he seemed little daunted by the race against the rain. Soon the gray stallion had pulled even with him, though, and they raced along, their hooves pounding out a thundering rhythm. Miles glanced at Gillian, who was laughing and clearly enjoying the run as much as he. Soon her hood was snatched away by the wind and her curls floated free in the wind, but she didn't seem to mind.

One moment they were dry, the next enveloped in a drenching downpour that virtually obliterated the path before them in sheets of rain. Forced to pull their horses to a halt, they stared ruefully at each other for a moment, then peered through the rain, trying to see how close they were to the Hall.

"I guess we should have stayed with Jock!" he shouted to her, his remark nearly drowned out by a clap of thunder that caused his stallion to curvet nervously.

A zigzag of lightning was briefly visible on a distant slope. "It's still rather far to home," she called. "We'd better seek shelter! If I remember correctly, there's a bothy around here somewhere, over that hill, I think." With a gesture that indicated he was to follow her, she put her heels to the cob and took off down the slope.

She was right. Moments later their mounts were tied in the lean-to and Miles and Gillian were stepping into the rude dwelling.

It was apparent that Jock used the bothy at such times as lambing season, for the shelter was equipped with a crude fireplace, flint and dry tinder, a few blankets and a pile of rough linen sacking. While Miles went to work trying to kindle a fire, Gillian seized a sack with a grateful sigh and rubbed it over her short curls.

"I'm sorry, I should have known better than to try to make it home with the storm so close," Gillian said, just as Miles succeeded in striking a spark that ignited the tinder and was nursing the tiny flame with encouraging breaths.

"Or perhaps we should have taken the lamb to the Hall and sent it back later."

"It's no great matter," Miles said, and found that he meant it. "We can have our picnic now, can we not?"

She laughed. "I must look like a drowned rat." She made a face as she ran her fingers through her dripping hair.

"Yes," he agreed, but softened it by saying, "but so do I, do I not?"

Had she no idea how beautiful she was, even with her hair plastered against her skull, showing off the delicate line of her cheek and jaw? Her face, innocent of the cosmetics without which no lady was seen at court, was only more lovely with the beads of moisture clinging to it.

"I'll get our lunch. Just don't let the fire go out, all right?" Gillian said, going out to the lean-to and bringing in the basket.

Luckily, Mag had wrapped the food in an oiled cloth, so it had not been much affected by the rain. Gillian spread out one of the blankets before the fire, then put out a loaf of bread, a big hunk of cheese and a skin of ale. Moments later they were sitting on the dirt floor, hungrily eating the humble fare.

Conversation was minimal as they ate, the only sound being the downpour on the roof, which showed no signs of letting up.

"My tenants seem like good people, do they not?" Gillian asked, breaking the silence at last.

Miles agreed. " 'Tis obvious they remember the Mallorys with affection, which should be to your benefit. I don't believe they'll cheat you, mistress."

"I intend to be a good landlord to them," she said. "As soon as I can purchase new rams, I'll lend them out, and their flocks will improve, too. And there must be other things I can do to better their lot."

"You've already done so a hundredfold, just by taking over Mallory Hall," he said dryly. Silence resumed as Miles wondered if Gillian thought he was needling her again about allowing Brunt to remain.

The luxury of King Henry's court was worlds away from this place. The universe seemed reduced to this small bothy, with its faint, lingering odor of sheep and the sound of the pouring rain outside. Miles had stripped off his soaked jerkin and sat in his damp shirt and breeches. Then Gillian sneezed, and he realized how uncomfortable she must be in her wet wool.

"You're soaked through," he commented. "Why don't you hang up your riding habit on that hook before the fire?"

She looked at him, her eyes hard, her tone suspicious. "Are you suggesting that I sit here in my shift, Sir Miles? Do you think because I just left the convent that I am a fool? Surely the rain will stop soon, and we can return to the Hall."

"Don't get your back up, mistress!" he said, stung by her too-accurate distrust. "I meant you could wrap yourself up in one of those blankets over there. I only thought you might get lung fever if you sat around in those wet garments."

"Oh!" she cried, coloring. "I'm sorry, I hadn't thought of that... I... What a silly shrew you must think me."

"Nay, Mistress Gillian, never that," Miles assured her, while thinking just how right she was to mistrust him.

Still hesitant, she stood, taking a deep sighing breath, then presented her back to him, for she would have been unable to undo the vertical row of tiny buttons that fastened her riding dress. Then, her back still to him, she stepped out of the green velvet dress.

He tried not to watch, but before he could turn his head away, the image of her graceful form, with its slender, straight back, gently rounded buttocks and womanly, curving thighs, all too visible beneath her damp shift, had burned itself into his brain before she gathered the ugly gray blanket around her.

Pulling the shutters open, Gillian gazed for a moment into the cloudburst. "It shows no signs of stopping—"

Just then the lightning cracked, so close that it sounded as if the bolt would reach inside the window and pierce her, and outlined Gillian with its transient brilliance. She gave a little cry of fright and hurled herself away from the window and into Miles' arms.

"Hush, little Gillian, it's over, you're quite safe," he heard himself saying. She turned her startled face to him as if she couldn't believe what she had done. He had been surprised, too, but was astonished by what he did in response.

Miles lowered his mouth to hers, giving the lie to his promise of safety. Suddenly she wasn't safe at all.

Gillian had dropped the blanket when she jumped away from the window, and there was nothing but his moist shirt and her damp shift between them as he pulled her into his arms and her soft breasts met the unyielding hardness of his chest. He drowned in the sweet honey of her mouth. Her hardening nipples became twin points of fire as she yielded to his tender assault.

All at once the storm inside the bothy was raging just as fiercely as the one outside. While one part of his fevered brain marveled that she was not resisting him, he brought them both over to the outspread blanket. Kicking aside the remainders of their picnic, he pulled her down with him.

He could not get enough of her quickly enough. Reaching inside the lace-trimmed chemise, he cupped one warm, rounded breast while using the other hand against the nape of her neck to hold her mouth firmly in contact with his. Using the pressure of his jaws, he coaxed her lips open, and his tongue plundered the inner sweetness of her mouth.

The lightning cracked again, farther away this time, and then his stallion neighed in the adjoining lean-to.

Gillian jerked away from his touch as if she had suddenly awakened, and stared at him, her breath coming raggedly and her breasts heaving.

"Oh, heavens! What have I done? What came over me?" she cried. She grabbed for the blanket she had dropped only moments ago and wrapped it around her as if it was armor against him. Her cheeks still flushed, her eyes bright with passion, she backed uncertainly away from Miles as if she was not sure he would not follow her and assert his will over her.

It was difficult for a moment not to do just that, but he forced himself to remain where he was. "You did nothing, Gillian. You were frightened by the lightning, and what followed is all my fault. There can be no excuse for my behavior, mistress. I am sorry—it shall never happen again."

By unspoken consent, they withdrew to opposite sides of the bothy. Gillian, swathed in the blanket, took up a position by the window again, while Miles lounged on his side, looking everywhere but at her.

Gillian could not tell what he was thinking but at first she didn't care. It was no longer hard to catch her breath, but her breasts still perversely ached for his touch, and there was a raging, unsatisfied feeling in the pit of her belly. Her pulse raced, as if her heart remembered his bold invasion of her mouth and the way his hands had felt as he had touched her.

The feel of his skin on hers, his weight against her, the molding of his hard, masculine body to her softness... These were sensations she had never imagined existed while she had been immured in her convent, serene in her vocation. She had never known what some of the other girls had been so resentful about leaving behind in the world, or what they had been so eager to return to when the news of the convent's closing had come.

She had felt like a bird soaring in flight, weightless, as if she was heading for the sun and that to be consumed in its fiery heat was the greatest of all pleasures.... Mother of God, was this what old Elizabeth Easington had meant when she had commented on the sensuality of her features? Could it be that she was created to enjoy a man's love—*this* man's love, that it wasn't wrong for her to want a man as she knew now she had wanted Miles moments ago?

He could have taken her, she realized. Had he pulled her into his arms and begun kissing and caressing her again in that persuasive way, she would have been returning his kisses within a few heartbeats. She would have allowed him to do exactly as he wished, for his will would have been hers.

The fact that he had not done so indicated that he was a much finer person than the vain, shallow courtier she had initially assumed he was. And didn't it mean that he saw *her* as someone more than just the sort of woman one might seduce without a qualm? Dare she think that he had stopped because he was coming to think of her as someone he could love in an honorable way—in holy wedlock?

She was still wondering whether she was reading too much into his actions when, after the rain ceased, they returned in heavy silence to Mallory Hall.

Chapter Seven

Miles was gone when she arose the next morning, leaving Gillian no opportunity to satisfy her curiosity as to how he really felt about her. No doubt he had gone to supervise the remodeling at Kyloe.

He had left her his first month's rent, however, which she put to good use, sending her steward into nearby Ross to purchase victuals to add to the scanty supplies in the kitchen. She told Brunt to buy a milk cow, if he came upon a good one, and a half-dozen hens to add to the trio of chickens and a scrawny cock already in the yard.

Sir Miles did not return for five days. By the end of that time Gillian was sure she had imagined the entire incident in the bothy, or at least the possibility that he had restrained himself because of any deep feelings he had for her. He was merely a gentleman in whom chivalrous feelings were not entirely dead. He realized that he had no right to be seducing her, that was all. She must not humiliate herself by revealing that she ever hoped it meant more.

Having convinced herself, she was therefore unprepared when he rode into the yard on the sixth morning leading a black palfrey with obvious Arab blood and announced it was hers.

Unknown to Gillian, the mare was the very image of the mount he had pictured for her. Miles had not had any intention of buying Gillian a horse when he had ridden to Berwick; he had gone for supplies, but having spotted the horse for sale, he was unable to pass without stopping to buy it.

She felt suffused with warmth as she stared at the mare, who returned Gillian's regard with ears pricked forward. It was the most beautiful horse Gillian had ever seen, but surely Miles' gift of her signified that perhaps she hadn't been imagining the affection he felt for her.

"Oh, Miles, I don't know what to say!" Gillian's eyes shone as she approached the mare quietly so as not to startle her. A moment later she was patting the palfrey's proudly arched neck and feeling her snuffling breath against her other arm as the mare searched for treats.

"Her name is Sultana, which is Arab for Princess," Miles, still astride Cloud, told her. "She's three years old, and trained to a sidesaddle as well as a regular—"

He was interrupted by the sound of hoofbeats coming up the lane. As they watched, a man on a cantering bay appeared.

"Were you expecting someone, mistress?" Miles asked, his eyes narrowing as he watched the approaching horseman.

"Nay," she said, puzzled. Then, as the man's features became visible, she added, "I don't know him, Miles."

"I do," came his short reply. It didn't sound as if he was pleased to admit the acquaintance.

The man was tall, solidly built, and his fleshy face possessed a pallor that proclaimed he did little outdoors. His clothes were those of a prosperous gentleman. When he swept off his flat-brimmed hat with its curling ostrich plume, his hair was thinning and brown.

The stranger bowed with studied elegance. "Good morrow, my lady," he said with an agreeable smile. "I had heard I had a new neighbor, and as the day was fine, decided to ride over and offer any aid you might require—"

"Mistress Gillian Mallory, may I present Sir Oliver Lang, late of His Majesty's court?" intoned Miles from behind her.

Perhaps Sir Oliver had not really looked at the man standing behind Gillian, but at the sound of Miles' voice, he appeared startled and stared at Miles over Gillian's head.

"Ench-chanted, M-Mistress Mallory," he stammered hastily, then looked at Miles.

"I am pleased to make your acquaintance also, Sir Oliver," Gillian said, then noticed that he was paying no attention. His hostile eyes were trained on Miles.

"Ah, Sir Miles Raven! Well met! I had heard you had taken possession of a northern property just as I have."

"So you're the one who bought Belford."

"News travels fast in the border country. Your property is nearby, I take it? Could it be that you are on the same errand I am, greeting our fair new neighbor and offering your service?" His tone of bluff bonhomie failed to match the suspicious look in his eyes.

Gillian was aware of the tension that stretched between the two men as a palpable thing, and not knowing its source, nonetheless sought to dispel it.

"Sir Miles is a guest at Mallory Hall while his house is being rebuilt at Kyloe," Gillian explained.

"I see! You are fortunate to have so comely a hostess, Sir Miles!"

Miles made no reply, just nodded.

Why did she suddenly feel that she had somehow made things worse? Gillian glanced from one man to the other, but received no clue. An awkward silence ensued, until Sir

Oliver's eyes lit upon the black mare whose reins Gillian held.

"That is a fine piece of horseflesh, Mistress Mallory! Is she yours? You are to be complimented on your judgment!"

Gillian remembered that her father had always liked to talk horses with other men, and hoped the ever-popular topic would be common ground for the two men who still eyed each other with barely veiled antagonism.

"Sir Miles has purchased her for me—is she not beautiful? In fact, he had just arrived with her before you came! Was that not kind of him?"

"Um...yes, excessively!" Sir Oliver's dark eyes gleamed as if he had somehow gained an advantage.

"'Tis merely that Mistress Mallory had no mount of her own," Miles said quickly behind her. "It was not fitting that she borrow her steward's swaybacked cob."

"Certainly not," Sir Oliver agreed with oily affability.

Gillian felt as if she had somehow blundered into a trap. "Would you...care to come in for a cup of wine, Sir Oliver? I was just about to offer some to Sir Miles, as soon as we put the horses away."

Sir Oliver hesitated, looking at each of them. "Nay, I thank you, mistress," he said at last. "Another time. Perhaps you would go riding with me, if I were to stop in again?"

"That would be pleasant," Gillian said out of politeness. Before she saw him again, she wanted to find out why Miles disliked this man so intensely.

"Until next time, then, Mistress Gillian," Sir Oliver said, sketching a bow. "Good day to you both."

She waited until they had unsaddled Miles' stallion and seen both horses comfortable in their stalls.

"I sense that you and Sir Oliver are not friends," essayed Gillian, feeling that she was treading on dangerous ground.

He turned to her, his eyes an icy blue. "Nay, that we are not. And why did you feel you had to tell a virtual stranger everything you know, mistress? It was none of his business to know where I was staying while my house was being built!"

She winced at his sudden truculence. "Why, Sir Miles, can it be that you are ashamed of your humble lodgings? It must be quite a loss of status for a man used to Greenwich, Richmond and Hampton Court!" Having thrown these words at him, Gillian whirled away and started to the house, her back rigidly erect, her head held at a defiant angle.

She had not gone two steps when he stopped her with a none-too-gentle hand about her wrist.

"Nay, mistress! Accuse me not of false pride! Can't you see 'tis merely that I sought to protect your reputation?"

Gillian stared at him, openmouthed. "If your taking lodgings with me will tarnish my reputation, why then did you ask to do it? 'Twas your idea, was it not?"

"Aye," he admitted grimly. "But I had no idea when I did it that such a vicious gossip as Lang would be our neighbor. You have no idea how that man's tongue has ruined lives and sabotaged careers at court. Can't you see that such a tale carrier will show you in the worst possible light? As if that naive confession that I was staying here were not enough, you had to tell him that I bought the mare for you! Why didn't you just tell him you were my paramour and be done with it?"

Without conscious thought, she slapped him full in the face, turned and ran into the house, leaving Miles alone with his fury.

He had not meant to insult her, God knew. He had been sorry the moment the words had left his mouth, but saints, the guileless chit needed to know what the blackguard was capable of! Perdition, why did Lang have to move so near? Miles had thought to leave such backstabbing scoundrels in the south!

He didn't want to have to explain the full reason for his anger at Lang's knowledge of their living situation and his gift of the mare. Sir Oliver knew Lady Celia Pettingham very well; in fact, he had wooed her diligently before Miles's arrival at court, and began again as soon as he heard that the lady had rejected Miles. Now, knowing how Miles had once cared for Celia and still coveting her for himself, Lang wouldn't hesitate to tell a luridly exaggerated version of the truth to Miles' first love.

Or would he? Would Miles' knowledge of Lang's clandestine affair with Queen Anne be enough to buy his silence?

Indeed, he hadn't meant to find the queen and her lover in that very compromising position. Over a year ago he had stepped into a supposedly vacant closet at Greenwich to avoid the importuning of an old merchant who wanted a favor of the king. There he had found the dark-eyed queen locked in a heated embrace with Lang, her skirts pushed up around her thighs. Sir Oliver's hands were busy caressing white flesh that was only Henry Tudor's to touch.

Both had reacted to his unexpected intrusion with gasps of dismay, knowing his discovery could bring disaster. Miles had merely shut the door on the shocking scene and strode rapidly away.

Lang came to him within hours with a purseful of gold and promises of favors if he would only keep silent. Miles had dismissed him with a contemptuous laugh, giving no indication of whether he meant to inform King Henry or not.

He had not intended to, of course. Adultery with the queen was worse than folly, but he was not the sort of man to capitalize on it. Sir Oliver Lang would hang himself eventually, but Miles would not tighten the noose.

Not long afterward Miles was set upon by footpads on the Strand as he returned to the Raven lodgings one evening. He had beaten them off easily, but when it happened again within the week, he began to suspect that Lang had hired assassins, having tired of the suspense of not knowing if Miles would maintain his silence.

Now, as Anne Boleyn's grasping hold on Henry and her crown was failing, Sir Oliver had obviously found it prudent to hie himself northward and inspect his new property, far from the intrigues of court.

Miles had to assume Lang had not learned from his mistakes, however. Today he had seen the enmity that remained in Sir Oliver's eyes and knew the other man resented him for the sense of obligation he felt toward Miles for his life. And now Lang was living nearby, and in a position to do irreparable harm to Miles and to Gillian Mallory.

Too much time had gone by for Miles' knowledge of Lang and Anne Boleyn to carry the same damaging weight. Adultery with the queen was treason, and if Miles now told what he knew, he would be questioned as to why he had not come forward sooner. Concealing treason was a crime.

Miles slammed his fist against the side of the barn in helpless frustration. How Lang would enjoy telling Celia about Miles' winsome hostess and misrepresenting the gift of the Arab mare as a gift from a lover.

What did he care what Celia thought? He did not love her now. Yet something in his gut told him that, allied with

Lang, she could be dangerous to him and therefore to Gillian.

All the way home he had told himself that the mare was merely a gift of friendship—even an indirect acknowledgment that Gillian had been right to refuse to make love with him.

Gillian, however, had not given him a chance to present the gift of the mare in that way. Before he could explain, he had seen the glow in her eyes.

It was the glow of a woman in love, the radiance of one whose love begins to see hope of a love returned. She had seen the mare as a courtship gift, a prelude to an honorable offer of marriage—which he was not prepared to give her.

He was Sir Miles Raven, trusted intimate of the king, merely a knight now, but with Henry's continued favor, who knew how high he might reach? And to do that, he would need the right wife, one who could advance him by marriage and who would be in accord with his need to climb higher. So he would have to forget Gillian Mallory, daughter of the fallen Plantagenet aristocracy, with her eyes as blue as speedwells and her hair the color of sun-ripened wheat—and the passion that had begun to grow between them.

His course was clear. So was his sudden sense of self-loathing. He had allowed an innocent, trusting girl, fresh from a convent and vulnerable from the recent upheaval in her life, to fall in love with him. He had begun to love her, too.

Until now. From this moment on, he vowed with savage intensity, he would lead Gillian away from the love she felt for him, away from the pain she would experience when she learned what sort of man he was. It was better for Gillian to stop loving him now before her heart was broken.

As for himself, he did not know how he would learn to live with his loss. But deal with it he would. He had done wrong to play with the dangerous flame of attraction between Gillian and himself, but no more. He would begin to snuff it out—today.

The easiest way to put an end to it would be to return to court immediately, Miles knew. Gillian would get over her unwise love for him more easily if he was far away, especially if he acted as if he despised the rustic north country and longed for more sophisticated surroundings.

But he misliked the idea of being so distant from Kyloe Priory while his home was being built. He didn't know Angus MacDougall well enough yet to know if he could be trusted not to cheat him if Miles was far away. And MacDougall might need materials to be purchased. Needless delays could occur while the Scot sent word to Miles in the south.

And what of his vow to protect Gillian, at least while she was learning to manage Mallory Hall's lands, from those who would take advantage of her too-trusting nature? Brunt, for example. And he had not liked the way Lang had stared at Gillian, either.

Gillian had flown up the stairs, oblivious of Mag's curious face, and hurled herself into her chamber, slamming the heavy oaken door behind her. Only then did she allow herself the luxury of bursting into tears of humiliation and anger.

Miles had called her naive. Aye, she was a gullible fool to have believed that such a polished courtier as Sir Miles Raven could find anything to admire, let alone love, in an unsophisticated maid newly out of the cloister. He had been ashamed that Sir Oliver Lang might think that he entertained serious feelings for a humble north-country knight's daughter. Her gentle birth would count as nothing with one used to dealing with royalty. His protestations that Lang was untrustworthy didn't fool her! Sir Miles Raven was ambitious of making an advantageous marriage—which he might not be able to do if Lang spread the word of his love for a former nun!

Gillian had been so happy with the gift of Sultana, and now her pleasure in the beautiful horse was spoiled. She would have to insist that Miles sell the mare, for the sight of her would always remind Gillian of her foolishness in reaching for the unattainable.

Months ago, she had wanted nothing of the world and had been content to serve her vocation by prayer and caring for the sick. Now that the serene life of a nun was no longer possible, she had opened herself up to the world's possibilities—and had experienced in full measure its pain.

She could not return to the convent, but she could listen to her common sense. Her heart had ignored the warning of her head that loving Sir Miles was unwise.

He had obviously not returned her feelings, though his motives in giving her the horse were unclear. She did not want to believe he still merely wanted to seduce her—but what other reason was there? Obviously he did not love her, or he would not have talked to her with such contempt in his voice or have been so anxious for Lang not to think he cared for her!

Gillian was just rising to rinse her tear-swollen eyes with the water in the ewer when she heard the peremptory knock at the door.

It could not be Mag. Her housekeeper's knock was usually as diffident as the woman herself. Brunt, she knew, was gone. No, such a demanding pounding could only indicate Miles was outside her door.

"Go away!"

"I must see you, mistress. We have unfinished business." His cold voice was as imperative as his knock.

Of course. She had slapped him. No matter how insulting his words had been, it did not excuse the fact that her behavior had been no better than that of a fishwife.

With leaden feet and pounding heart, Gillian crossed the room and opened the door, horrified that he should see her swollen eyes and know himself the cause of her tears.

"Sir Miles, I must apologize for my unseemly behavior in striking you," she said, her eyes on the rushes beneath her feet after one hasty glance into his unreadable pale eyes.

"Nay, mistress. 'Tis I who must regret my offensive words. I was rude beyond bearing. My only defense is that I was worried, Mistress Gillian. You do not realize, in your innocence, the damage a man like that can do."

"You make innocence sound like a disgusting disease."

"So I did, but 'tis not. It is all too rare in this world," he said with a sardonic quirk to his brow, "and I feared for your hurt, if you trusted too much."

Gillian was silent for a moment. "Why *did* you bring me the mare, Sir Miles?" she asked at last, her throat aching with unshed tears.

He looked away, unable to meet her eyes as he began the painful process of pruning the green, living thing that was their love.

"You needed a horse." He kept his tone deliberately cool.

"Oh...of course. Well, I think under the circumstances, you should sell her. Perhaps 'twould be wise to offer her to Sir Oliver. He seemed interested. In any case, we wouldn't want him to get the wrong idea about our relationship, would we?"

There was a sweet reasonableness in her voice, and yet its temperature matched his. He was surprised, for he had not heard Gillian address anyone so coldly, and he found himself longing to thaw her just a little.

"Mistress, be sensible. I merely do not want such a man to sully your good name. But I want you to keep Sultana. You need a horse, and she's the perfect one for you. Come, didn't you find her gaits smooth as silk, her dainty manners appealing? Does she not please your eye?"

Everything he said about the mare was too true. Gillian loved her already. She knew she should remain adamant, but she found herself saying, "Very well, Sir Miles, but I insist on repaying whatever you spent on her, as rapidly as the revenues from my sheep and rents will allow." Gillian was pleased that her voice did not tremble nor her eyes waver as she faced him.

How badly he wanted to refuse, to boldly declare that the mare was a gift of love and would remain so; but he knew that to do so would destroy his resolve to quench the love smoldering between them before it got out of hand. He must let her keep her pride as he dampened the flame that would have warmed them both.

"Perhaps that would be best. I am sure you are wise to keep matters on a businesslike footing between us, mistress. I am, after all, but your temporary tenant."

Chapter Eight

Gillian saw little of Miles for the next week, for he left for the Kyloe manor site at dawn and returned late in the evening, frequently after she had supped and retired.

If he was avoiding her, Gillian told herself she was relieved, for surely it was easier to rid herself of her deep feelings for the Sussex knight in his absence. Her days were full with the many duties involved in restoring Mallory Hall to its former prosperity, and she took on many tasks that could properly have been left to her steward and his wife. And if she dreaded the nights, when she lay tossing restlessly in the big, lonely bed, no one need know but herself.

Her chief pleasure during these days was saddling Sultana and riding her over the hills, politely declining Brunt's offer to go along for her safety.

She thanked him, but an attendant was unnecessary, she said. Border reivers hadn't struck the area for years, and she seldom rode beyond the boundaries of Mallory Hall's tenant farms. Having company, especially the taciturn Brunt, would somehow spoil the exhilarating sense of ownership she experienced on her rides. *This is mine,* her heart sang as she rode across the apron of mud flats at low tide and over the gentle, humpbacked hills, *just as it was my*

*father's, and his father's before that—and one day it will
thrive again.*

Gillian was enchanted, riding among the remaining
flock, by the sight of the new lambs gamboling about near
their mothers, bleating playfully as they chased butterflies
and each other. Each ewe and lamb, she had learned, was
called a couple, while a ewe with twin lambs was a double.

One day, spying Jock the shepherd outside when she
passed the home farm, she rode down to greet him. She left
there carrying a bleating orphan lamb on her saddle.

"Perhaps one of the other ewes..." she had begun protesting when Jock had suggested slaughtering it for her and
sending the meat up for her supper.

"Nay, mistress, I've tried, and none will have him, poor
wight. They've all got their own lambs, and some of them
twins, and I've even checked the other farms for ewes that
have lost lambs. Nay, we'd better put the wee bugger
down—he'll starve t'death soon. Wouldn't ye fancy a supper of tender spring lamb?"

Gillian had looked, horrified, at the spindly-legged lamb
who had retreated, bleating piteously, to a corner of the
pen.

"Could he not be raised with a bottle, Jock? We frequently had a cade lamb at the priory."

The shepherd shrugged. "I've no time for such, mistress. There's the dagging to be done, and the dog and I
must hunt for the wolf that killed his dam if no other sheep
are t'be lost, and shearing time's soon."

"Nay, I meant I should take it home. I had Brunt purchase a cow in Ross, and she's producing enough milk to
spare. Young Ned would be delighted to help me, I'm sure.
Would the lamb survive, think you?"

Jock stared at the lamb, who was once again attempting
to nurse from the unwilling ewe, then back at Gillian.

"Ye've a tender heart, mistress. Aye, it might work, if ye'll see him fed at least four and better six times a day. He's a determined one, might make a fine ram someday if ye're successful."

Back at the Hall, she found Ned mucking out stalls in the barn. As Gillian had predicted, he was quite willing to assist her with raising the lamb and ran off excitedly to the house, saying he thought they had a nipple that could be attached to an empty wine bottle, for they had once raised an orphan calf.

He returned while Gillian was still unsaddling Sultana. "Mam's heating up th' milk we got from th' cow this mornin'," he announced, going to the stall in which the lamb was pacing, still bleating in confusion. "I'll feed him when she brings it out, mistress—Mam said t'tell ye that ye had a visitor waitin' fer ye in th' hall, and perhaps ye'd better go on in."

"Of course," murmured Gillian, her brow wrinkled in puzzlement as to the identity of the visitor.

"Oh, and mistress..." Ned called after her retreating figure, "could I name the lamb?"

She gave distracted permission. There was only one who had said anything about visiting. Her stomach gave an uneasy lurch at the thought.

Sir Oliver Lang rose from his comfortable position on the settle as she entered the hall, bowing as she self-consciously smoothed her dusty, mud-spattered skirts.

"Sir Oliver! What a surprise! I fear I smell of horse and sheep—I was not expecting a caller, you see!" Briefly she explained about the orphaned lamb.

"Mistress Gillian, I see you have a soft heart for helpless creatures," he said, unknowingly mimicking Jock's earlier words. "But I do not see why you should be surprised at my coming. I told you I would like to take you riding, and so here I am."

"Alas, I have taken my ride already." Gillian was relieved that she had the perfect excuse for not going, though she strove to put disappointment into her voice.

"So I found when I arrived, and I was devastated," he said lightly, with such a comic grimace that she was forced to smile. "Now that I have waited for so long, the least you can do is have a cup of wine with me. Your housekeeper has already offered me refreshment, but I said I would wait for your arrival."

In spite of her first impression of Sir Oliver, she began to relax in his presence as he talked pleasantly of this and that. He seemed harmless enough.

She summoned Mag and asked her to bring wine. After it had been set in front of them, Sir Oliver took up the reins of conversation again.

"My friend Sir Miles is at the site of his new manor?" His face remained smooth and bland.

Gillian nodded, allowing Sir Oliver's calling Miles "friend" to pass unchallenged. "I believe 'tis progressing well. His master builder is a very industrious Scot. He has some excellent ideas about making the convent over into a comfortable manor house."

But Sir Oliver did not want to discuss architecture. "One hears that you used to be a nun. I'm curious, mistress—what would you have done if Raven had not come along to rescue you from certain destitution?"

So the story of Miles finding her had gotten around, probably thanks to Brunt, who had doubtless embroidered it beyond recognition.

"It's true that our convent priest had stolen the pension moneys," she admitted, "and Miles found me when I was weak from fatigue and hunger. He convinced me that there was no use in seeking another convent, that I must find a place in the world. But 'twas I that found the papers certifying Mallory Hall was mine,'' she added, not without a flash of pride.

He ignored her last words. "You must naturally regard Sir Miles as a hero straight out of chivalry," Sir Oliver said lightly, but his dark eyes bored into her, missing nothing.

Several days ago, in the first flush of love, she would have agreed enthusiastically. Now, she contented herself by saying, "Sir Miles was merely being kind. He could not tolerate an unjust situation."

"Mistress, you are too modest! Are you sure he did not help you with the secret desire of winning your admiration and gratitude?"

"Certainly not," she said. "Any gentleman would have done the same." Gillian was aware he was watching her reaction very closely, and fought to control the heat that threatened to rise above the neckline of her riding dress. Her feeling of relaxation with this man vanished.

"How very praiseworthy of him, then. But he is such a handsome devil with that black hair and those cold blue eyes, do you not think? All the highborn ladies at court are smitten with him, I can tell you."

"No doubt he has to fight them off," Gillian said as if it mattered less than nothing to her.

"But you do not join their ranks?"

She shook her head, forcing herself to look into Sir Oliver's black eyes.

"Good for you! You are a sensible lady, Mistress Gillian. Dare I hope, therefore, that there is room in your heart for another, vastly different suitor?" His rounded face was all appealing earnestness—yet the appeal struck no answering chord in her heart. She knew she must discourage him, but how was she to do so without hurting his manly pride?

She managed to produce a heavy sigh and a regretful look, knowing she must save his pride. "I was meant to be a nun, Sir Oliver. The king's unfortunate decree makes that life no longer possible in England, but, nevertheless, some women were not meant to marry. I am very content as I am."

Sir Oliver looked distressed. "Mistress Gillian, surely you speak without knowing the ways of the world! A lady, especially one of property, is not safe alone! She is prey to those who would defraud her or dishonor her. When the novelty of your situation wears off, I am sure you will reconsider. I have much to offer a lady, mistress. Belford already had a sumptuous abbot's house, so there was little to do to make it comfortable. In addition, I have vast lands in Kent, *and* a secure place in His Majesty's favor."

Just then Ned ran in, excitedly calling for her. "Mistress Gillian! The lamb's taken the whole bottle! I've named him Tag because he follows me everywhere, see?" Ned stepped aside, and the aptly named lamb bleated as if proud of his progress.

"So I see, Ned, but lambs belong outside—and that is why..." she began, wincing as the lamb proceeded to relieve itself on the rushes, and the pungent smell filled her nose. "Take him back to the barn, Ned, and then return and clean out those rushes."

"Yes, Mistress. But the name—"

"Is *fine,* Ned. Tag it is. Now remove him immediately."

Gillian rolled her eyes in apology for the interruption, but secretly she was relieved, for the diversion had given her time to choose her words carefully.

"Perhaps you are right, Sir Oliver, but in truth I am but a simple woman. I thank you for the honor you offer me, but I fear I am not suited to being your lady. The prospect of going to court, as I am sure you must do periodically, would only terrify me. Nay, I am best left among my hills and my sheep, sir."

He shrugged. "I will not give up hope, but perhaps you need time to realize what difficulties you undertake. I will leave you now to your many duties."

Miles returned in time for supper that evening, and though their greetings were courteously warm, each could feel the other watching warily, seeking some clue as to the other's thoughts. Their attempts at conversation were stilted.

Gillian chose not to bring up the subject of Sir Oliver's visit, knowing it would provoke scowls or worse. Now more than ever, she wished she knew the secret of the enmity between the two men.

Instead, she stuck to safe topics, such as the story of Tag the lamb. After first describing how she had happened to bring it home, she told Miles Ned was now so enthusiastic about his new charge that he had begged his mother to be allowed to sleep in the barn next to it.

They were just finishing a satisfying meal when they heard the sound of a carriage coming into the yard.

"I am not expecting anyone...are you?" asked Gillian in surprise.

"Nay."

A serious of knocks summoned Gillian to the door, with Miles following closely behind her. It was dusk, not a time that visitors came calling in the Cheviots.

A tall, imposingly dressed older woman stood in the doorway, her fur-trimmed cloak open at the neck, showing an expensive brocade gown. Though the light shed on her by the lamp in the entranceway was dim, there was something about her features that was familiar.

"Good even, I am seeking Sir Miles Raven," she said in carefully modulated tones.

Gillian's "He is here" was lost in the woman's joyous cry as she spied Miles over Gillian's shoulder.

"Miles! There you are! I'm so glad!"

Gillian drew back in surprise as the woman rushed forward without another glance at her. Then she noticed that there was another female standing in the yard by the carriage driver, as if uncertain whether to follow the first one in. She, too, was richly dressed, in a gown the skirts of which were pinned back to display a petticoat embroidered with English blackwork. A black velvet French hood framed a heart-shaped face of classic beauty.

Miles was saying, "Mother! Whatever are you doing here in Northumberland? I thought you were at Ravenwood, awaiting your first grandchild!"

The woman laughed merrily. "And so I was, until 'twas born—and now you're an uncle of a fine, lusty boy, my son! But seeing Lyssa safely delivered and the wee babe doing well, I found myself free to worry about you, Miles!"

Miles chuckled in a half-embarrassed fashion and drew Gillian forward from the shadows. "I assure you, there was no need. Lady Kathryn Raven, may I present my hostess, Mistress Gillian Mallory."

The woman studied Gillian quickly, and though her gaze was thoroughly assessing, it was not unkind.

"So this is Mistress Gillian," the woman murmured in her Sussex accent. She sounded pleasantly surprised. "Please pardon us for appearing unbidden on your threshold, mistress, but—"

At that moment Miles noted the figure still standing in the yard. "And you've brought Linnet!" he exclaimed, dashing outside.

Gillian's throat constricted suddenly as she watched the man she loved embrace the young woman who stood in the yard. *So this is why he could not let himself love me,* she thought. *He has a sweetheart, and his mother has brought her to him.* If she could have bid the floor open up and swallow her at that moment, she would have done so.

But after directing the carriage driver to the barn and telling him to come into the kitchen after he had put away the horses, Miles turned to her with no trace of discomfort on his face as he led the other woman forward. "Mistress Gillian, I would also present Linnet, my sister."

His sister! Of course. As Gillian began to breathe again and the girl was brought into the flickering circle of lamplight, Gillian could see that Linnet had the same pale eyes as Miles, though hers were more truly gray than blue, and the hair peeking out from her hood was as ebony-hued as that of her brother.

Linnet smiled sweetly and extended her hand. "I am pleased to meet you, Mistress Gillian. I, too, would apologize for our intrusion—though once our lady mother gets an idea into her head, she is heedless of formalities such as invitations!" She laughed as if it was a familiar joke.

"You are both very welcome, of course," murmured Gillian, still dazed by their appearance, which was so sudden that it almost seemed magical.

"Wonderful," said Lady Kathryn, and stepped toward the table without the least hesitation. "I vow my belly is writhing in hunger. We've barely eaten since dawn, and spent our midday at the bottom of a hill while the driver sought to unstick the carriage from a muddy rut. I have been shaken to death, I tell you! I'm too old for such jaunts!''

"You'll never be too old, Mother," Miles said fondly, as the two women were shown to seats at the table. "You are a force of nature." It was clear he was fond of his mother, and for a moment Gillian envied him the relationship. How she wished her own mother were here to advise her.

Miles and Gillian helped Lady Kathryn and Linnet to fill their plates and cups.

"Have you heard the grim news from court, brother?" Linnet asked after taking a few bites.

"Nay, I fear we are rather isolated here in the north, though when I left it appeared Queen Anne was about to fall. As selfish as Henry is, surely the queen must realize she bears some blame for her arrogance and grasping."

"I never liked the creature," Lady Kathryn confessed, "but we fear she faces worse than being put aside as poor Queen Catherine was."

"Worse?" Miles put down the goblet of wine that had been halfway to his lips.

Linnet nodded. "Just as we were passing through London, the news on everyone's lips was that two of the gentlemen of the queen's household had been arrested. There was a tournament at Greenwich, which King Henry had left in the middle, acting as if he was offended with Queen Anne. 'Tis said Sir Henry Norris had picked up the queen's dropped handkerchief, which angered the king."

Miles frowned. "It seems the king is about to accuse Anne Boleyn of adultery," he said musingly, as if the fact was ironic.

"But for a queen 'tis treason," Linnet said.

"For which the penalty is death," Miles finished for her.

Gillian gasped. "Would the king actually kill her? The mother of his daughter?"

"'Tis to be hoped not, of course," Lady Kathryn put in. "But 'tis an open secret that the king lusts after Lady Jane Seymour, one of the queen's attendants, and he still lacks a male heir."

"Then poor little Princess Elizabeth will doubtless be declared bastard, just as her half-sister Mary was."

Gillian shook her head in disbelief. "How very awful that all these things could happen at the whim of one self-centered man." Then, realizing what she had said in front of one of Henry Tudor's own courtiers, she looked up to find Miles Raven's eyes on her. "I'm sorry. I fear bluntness is a fault the convent did not entirely erase."

"You may certainly speak freely so far from court, Mistress Gillian. None here would tattle on you. But in front of others, such as your new neighbor, Sir Oliver Lang, 'tis wise to guard your tongue."

As Miles explained to his mother about Lang's purchase of the nearby abbey, Gillian noted that he gave no indication of what *he* thought of his sovereign's actions. Doubtless, prudent speech was an engrained habit among Henry's courtiers, she thought cynically.

As if to change the subject from the dangerous topic, Miles turned to Lady Kathryn. "Why *are* you here, Mother?"

The older woman took a long draft of wine before answering. "Oh, my, this is embarrassing in front of you, my dear," she said, and Gillian was surprised to see she was addressing her. "But as all has turned out so well—" she indicated her surroundings "—I must confess that I was worried about my son."

"Worried, Mother? Whatever do you mean?" Miles asked.

Lady Kathryn had the grace to blush. "Silly of me, but when your sister and I received the letter about how you were lodging at a house owned by a former nun, I became concerned." She swallowed as if having trouble clearing her throat.

Everyone at the table waited expectantly for the woman to finish. Gillian, glancing away from the self-conscious Lady Kathryn, caught Linnet's eyes across the table. They were dancing with amusement.

"What our lady mother means, Miles," Linnet said at last when the woman seemed unable to continue, "is that she was worried that you were living in a rough stone cottage with some common woman eager to practice her wiles on you—"

"Linnet! What have I told you about being so blunt!" remonstrated Lady Kathryn. Then she said apologetically, "Obviously, such is not the case."

"Obviously," echoed Miles dryly. "What an ill-bred family Mistress Gillian must think us."

"Oh, my dear, I *do* beg your pardon," Lady Kathryn said to Gillian. "I must appear a dreadful meddler! Your house is lovely, my dear, as are you."

"Thank you," Gillian managed. She was a bit overwhelmed by the other woman's torrent of words, but not offended. She couldn't help but like Lady Kathryn and her plainspoken daughter, and realized how the situation must have sounded to the Ravens in Sussex. She was certainly glad, however, that they had repaired and refurbished so much about the hall in such a short time! Only yesterday she had helped Mag apply whitewash to the walls.

"The house is not what it once was, of course, but in time I hope to see it restored."

"I am sure you will," the older woman said with an approving nod. "Mistress Gillian, would it be possible for you to put us up for the night? I promise we will not trespass further on your hospitality—"

"But of course you must stay as long as you wish!" Gillian assured Miles' mother. "I'll warrant Sir Miles will wish to show you his house in progress, and you must not come so far only to turn back! There is only one spare chamber suitable for you, but if you do not mind sharing it . . ."

"That would be perfect, my dear! My son, she is charming!"

Helplessly Gillian looked away from the beaming Lady Kathryn and into Miles Raven's sapphire eyes. Clearly, his mother was reading more into the relationship between Miles and Gillian than that of a tenant and his hostess. But Miles said nothing. 'Twas merely that he was too polite or gallant, Gillian told herself, to tell Lady Kathryn she was mistaken in front of her.

Excusing herself, Gillian summoned Mag and went to set the guest chamber to rights. She hoped that while she was gone, Miles would explain the true situation between himself and her to his mother.

Chapter Nine

When Gillian returned, the three were warming themselves in front of the fire. She had heard Miles's voice raised—in anger?—as she had come down the stairs, but she had been too far away to hear his words. When she came over to the trio on the settle, she noted that Miles's fists were clenched in his lap. His brow was furrowed. She could feel the tension emanating from him.

Lady Kathryn appeared mildly distressed, yet determined, while the expression on the face of Miles's sister could only be described as cheerfully defiant. Why? Gillian wondered what could have been said in her absence that could have produced such varying emotions. Surely Miles had only to explain to them that they had mistaken the situation? What else was there to be said?

Then she noticed the bolts of cloth piled by the settle. Brunt and the carriage driver were in the midst of unloading the ladies' belongings from the carriage; the bolts of cloth must have come in with the various trunks brought by the ladies.

There were at least eight lengths of cloth in varying colors from sky blue to scarlet, and in differing fabrics from deep-piled velvet to luxurious silk. A box stood next to them, filled with laces, buttons and other trimmings.

"These are lovely," said Gillian to the ladies, running an appreciative hand over the soft velvet. "Did you find a cloth merchant somewhere along the journey?"

Linnet grinned knowingly as her mother spoke. "I brought them from Ravenwood. They are for you, my dear. My son mentioned in his letter that being newly out of the convent, you had little clothing save what you could use of your late mother's, and he asked me to bring a selection of fabrics for new gowns. Linnet will be delighted to help you in the making, as she is quite an accomplished seamstress," she added proudly.

"We'll have such fun, Mistress Gillian!" put in Linnet, eyes shining in anticipation, while Gillian was still struggling to find her voice. "I know all the latest styles from court, and I can sketch them for you, to see what you like!"

Miles groaned inwardly. He should have known when he had first written his mother to give her his location, shortly after he had come to stay at Mallory Hall, that she would do something like this. An obedient and docile wife to his late father, Lady Kathryn had positively blossomed during her brief widowhood. Miles had begun to wonder if she had been secretly unhappy with her somewhat authoritarian spouse, the merchant-turned-gentleman Thomas Raven. Formerly content to stay by her own hearth and see to her husband's needs, she now loved to travel.

Knowing her appreciation of interesting detail, Miles had only meant to give his mother some background about his hostess when he described Gillian's history and the resultant paucity of her wardrobe. Perhaps he would have done better to describe Mallory Hall in more detail, however, so that his mother would not have feared he was living in a hovel with a man-hungry schemer! Perhaps then Lady Kathryn would not have come hotfooting it up to Northumberland to check on him.

He had just spent the last few minutes of Gillian's absence listening to them praising Gillian. Linnet had been impressed with Gillian's beauty and her fine blue eyes, while his mother had spoken of her lovely manners and shy friendliness.

"She has good breeding," Lady Kathryn had said, summing up her opinions. "And anyone could see she has feelings for you, my son."

He had been allowing them to rattle on, but Lady Kathryn's smug expression as she had made her last remark was too much.

"You have us half wed already," he growled. "Yes, Mistress Mallory is a comely, winsome lady, but you must forget any such ideas. She is my hostess, nothing more."

"Nonsense, Miles!" his mother said with an airy wave of her hand. "I've seen the way you look at her."

He had to convince her. "My lady mother, please. We would not suit."

Lady Kathryn looked troubled. "There…there's no one else, is there? No one like that spoilt, selfish Celia Pettingham? Oh, please tell me you are not considering her again!" she cried, wringing a fold of her gown.

"Nay," he said with a wry twist of his mouth, "though the lady *did* seem to have a reawakened interest in me once she heard of my new property and King Henry's recent favor. 'Tis just that I am not good enough for Mistress Gillian Mallory."

Lady Kathryn bristled. "Did she say that? She—"

Miles held up his hand. "Nay. But I know myself, Mother. What am I? A courtier! I love the pageantry of court life, while she would despise it for its hypocrisy, and me with it. She's as uncomplicated as these northern hills. And as incorruptible. I need a woman like me, Mother, a woman who understands what I want, who will bring me powerful connections and mayhap more wealth.'' The last sentence was spoken almost defiantly.

Lady Kathryn sighed. ''Miles, your father achieved much in his life, but I think we were happiest when he was just a wine merchant in London. And you cannot make your mother think you're just an ambitious courtier. I'm more apt to believe what you said first, my son. So you think you're not good enough for Gillian Mallory, eh? A man should always feel that way about his beloved.''

Linnet grinned in agreement.

Before he could argue further, however, Gillian had reappeared. Lady Kathryn and Linnet found it prudent to retreat soon after, pleading travel weariness, and Gillian had shown them to their rooms, leaving him alone with his thoughts.

Miles was still sitting there, scowling, when Gillian returned with her cloak over her shoulders.

''Where are you going at this hour?'' he inquired, a harsh edge to his voice.

''To feed my new pet.'' She was determined to ignore Miles's brusque tone. Whatever had Lady Kathryn told him to make him even more moody than he had been lately? ''Young Ned offered to do it, but he saw to the suppertime feeding and promised to get up during the night, as well. I can't let him have *all* the fun.'' She smiled gaily, and was successful in coaxing the ghost of a smile from him.

Much to her surprise, Miles followed her to the kitchen, watching in silence as she warmed up some of the milk left in a pitcher from the afternoon milking and poured it into the nursing bottle. She was even more surprised when he followed her out to the barn.

Beyond the circle of light spread by the candle she carried, they were enveloped in darkness. Somewhere in the spring night, an owl hooted to its mate. Within the barn, all was quiet, except for the stamping of Miles's stallion as he scented his master. After receiving a quick pat and a scratch behind the ear, Cloud went back to munching leftover hay in his manger. Gillian looked in on Sultana, too, and the mare nickered a greeting. Already there was a strong bond of affection between the mare and her mistress.

Tag, the lamb, came trotting up to the stall entrance to see them, bleating his eagerness as he smelled the milk.

"Ah, look," Gillian said as the lamb began to suck on the bottle, his woolly tail wagging as he took in the warmed milk. The candlelight revealed the recumbent form of Ned, who had apparently fallen asleep with his charge.

Miles left her side for a moment, returning with a saddle blanket, which he silently placed over the boy to protect him from the cold.

She thought Miles had followed her out to say something, perhaps to reveal why he had looked so disturbed after she had left him alone with his mother and sister. It seemed obvious from the care he took not to touch her or even to stand too close that he had no intention of using the cover of darkness to act in a way that could be interpreted as affectionate.

At last she broke the silence. "Your lady mother and sister are delightful, Sir Miles. Were you very surprised to see them?"

"Completely."

She tried again. "Your sister Linnet is lovely. She's going to break hearts before long."

"She already has, the minx. Lovesick swains lay siege to Ravenwood whenever she is there, mostly country lads she's grown up with. She'll go off to court as one of the queen's ladies soon, so that she may make a suitable marriage."

Gillian could hear the affection in his voice for his sister, but once the topic was exhausted, both fell silent again.

"I was astounded by the gift of the cloth, Sir Miles. 'Twas very generous."

"It was *nothing,* mistress." He sounded almost annoyed. "They have a whole storeroom of such fabric, just waiting to supply their slightest whims. My family is wealthy, as you know. Enjoy it, please, with an easy conscience."

Gillian came close to retorting that her conscience had no need to feel uneasy, but that his apparently did. She decided against goading him, however, and said only, "I will. 'Twill be fun to design clothing with the benefit of Linnet's knowledge of the current mode."

The bottle empty, she gave the lamb a last pat and indicated with a gesture that they should return to the house.

The moon had come out from behind a cloud while they had been in the barn; it now bathed the yard in a beneficent, silver-blue light. Moonlight was the last thing Miles, fighting his impulses, needed.

"I hope meeting me has reassured your mother," Gillian said beside him. "That the Raven name was still quite safe, I mean."

"Oh, she's quite reassured, believe me," he ground out, "and would be more so if she could see *this.*"

Goaded beyond bearing by the silvery play of moonlight in Gillian's eyes and her musical voice, he pulled her roughly into his arms, kissing her with irritable thoroughness before she had time to ask him what he was doing. A moment later, as her astonishment had melted into the heat of response, she relaxed, her arms stealing around his neck as she returned his kiss—just as if they had not discussed, only days before, the importance of keeping their relationship on a businesslike footing.

Then, as suddenly as he had seized her, Miles thrust her from him, staring at her upturned face in the pale light as if trying to discern how to blame her for his actions. Finding only her puzzled reaction to his abrupt, unexpected behavior, he let her go. With a smothered oath, he walked into the house, not waiting to see if she followed or not.

Above him in the manor house, the shutters that shielded the guest chamber from the cool night air were quietly put back in place.

Miles had apparently told his mother that the work at the building site required his presence on the morrow, for Lady Kathryn and Linnet seemed undisturbed the next morning when they arose and found him gone. Gillian privately wondered if he had repented of his impulsive moonlit embrace and was avoiding her.

Resolutely putting the question aside as unanswerable in his absence, however, she devoted herself to making sure her guests were comfortable and to getting to know them better.

Lady Kathryn was an active woman who seemed to have no intention of sitting idle and allowing herself to be waited upon. Shortly after she had broken her fast, she was busy in the kitchen, her long sleeves rolled up about the elbows, showing Mag how to do a favorite dish of Miles's that featured rabbit in a peppery cream sauce.

Linnet followed Gillian to the barn, pronouncing herself enchanted by the lamb and entreating her hostess to let her hold the bottle for the hungry Tag. She was equally impressed by Sultana. The mare had poked her aristocratic head curiously out of her stall as the girls passed, and had enjoyed the younger girl's cooing admiration as Linnet stroked her ebony nose.

"You say Miles bought her for you?" Linnet asked, her gray eyes sparkling. "Oh, Gillian! How thrilled you must have been!"

"Her price is only a loan," Gillian insisted, her hands up as if to calm the girl's excitement. "I will be repaying your brother as soon as I can. 'Twas merely that I needed a horse."

Linnet appeared unconvinced. Fearing that she was jumping to an unwarranted conclusion, Gillian would have liked to say more, but realized there was nothing she could say that would not lead Linnet to think Gillian was being too modest.

After Tag had been fed, nothing would satisfy Linnet but that they begin cutting out the material for the first of Gillian's new gowns. Gillian selected a soft periwinkle blue wool as being practical as well as pretty, and after measurements had been taken, the bolt was spread out on the table to be cut out.

"I would suggest a low, square neckline with pleated linen to fill it in partially," Linnet said, confident in her expertise. "We'll slash the sleeves and tie them with gold cord, and part the skirt so as to show your underskirt beneath."

Gillian felt a little overwhelmed. The sketch that Linnet had made showed a bodice that appeared indecently low to Gillian's convent-bred eyes, but Miles's sister assured her that even middle-aged matrons wore them thus.

"Besides, this stiffened buckram that lines the bodice flattens one so that it doesn't look as if one has much bosom anyway," Linnet confided with a girlish trill of laughter. "And you can use my French hood with the pearls on the upper and lower billiments to complete your attire. It will be *so* stylish, you'll see!"

Gillian wondered what good such modishness would do among these northern hills where she was surrounded by sheep and humble folk such as the Brunts, but she didn't want to dampen the girl's enthusiasm.

She was enjoying herself, too, she realized. All those years spent in the same monotonous black serge and starched white linen seemed a millennium away as she surrendered to the delight of the sumptuous fabric.

Linnet was like the sister she had never had. Gillian had been discouraged from making close friends with the other young novices. A nun should love all her sisters in religion equally, the novice mistress had taught, and in any case Gillian had had little in common with the other girls who loved to giggle about lads they had known and to sigh over opportunities that had seemed then to be forever lost to them.

Almost before she knew it, the afternoon had passed, and while Linnet stitched the bodice and Lady Kathryn began the embroidered petticoat, Gillian went to offer Mag help with supper preparations.

Miles returned in late afternoon, and though he did not seek to speak to her privately, Gillian thought he did not seem unhappy to see her. She felt his eyes upon her whenever she was not looking at him, and when their gazes met it was as if Miles could not bear to look away. He seemed less angry than he had been recently, and though she did not understand the reason for the change, she resolved to let him come to her when and if he would.

Miles had been regaling them with descriptions of how his new house would look, what had been done that day and what Angus MacDougall planned to have accomplished by week's end when Lady Kathryn interrupted.

"When do you plan to show us this wondrous place, my son?"

"Yes, when, brother?" chorused Linnet. "What about tomorrow? It promises to be fair."

Miles smiled at his sister's eagerness. "I suppose we could make an expedition to Kyloe tomorrow. 'Tis only about an hour away. You could go in the carriage, Mother, with Linnet, while Mistress Gillian and I ride."

Linnet pouted at the thought of riding in the lurching carriage, but as she had no palfrey with her, she could hardly do otherwise. She was not in bad spirits for long, however.

"Let us make it a picnic," she suggested to Gillian. " 'Twould be such fun! Oh, say that we may!"

Gillian glanced at Miles to see if he minded, but at his nod murmured, "I don't see why not. It does sound enjoyable. I shall speak to Mag about the food."

"Psst, Gillian! Let me in! I have something for you!" came the whisper at the door the next morning when Gillian was barely awake.

Gillian opened the door to find Linnet, already dressed for the day's outing, carrying a garment over her arm.

"I've brought you a riding dress—wouldn't you like to wear it today?" Miles's sister asked, extending the garment.

Blinking sleepily, Gillian gestured her inside. " 'Tis very kind of you, Linnet, but I have a riding dress."

"As fine as this one?" Linnet flung open the shutters and held up the dress for Gillian's inspection.

The riding dress was made of violet velvet and made Gillian think of spring, of shy wildflowers growing in profusion at the edge of mountain burns. It had gold frogging to close the fitted bodice, an upstanding Medici collar and sleeves that were puffed at the shoulders, then fitted closely

to the wrists, with one long slash from elbow to wrist to
show the kirtle beneath.

Gillian sighed, a sound of pure feminine delight.
"Ah...'tis gorgeous. But why don't you wear it?"

"I'm not riding today," Linnet pointed out, "and anyway, 'tis a trifle large through here—" she indicated the
bodice "—but 'twill fit *you* to perfection." Linnet's figure
had not fully bloomed as yet, though her girlish bust gave
promise of a future lushness. "Besides, this color suits me
better, don't you think?" She gestured toward her own
gown, which was made of a bright burgundy that did, in
fact, complement her ivory fairness better than the violet
would have. "Go ahead, try it on."

Gillian could not resist, though she wondered why Linnet was so eager to have her appear at her best.

It was breathtakingly perfect. Gillian knew it by the way
Linnet's mouth dropped open, to be covered by her hand a
second later as she looked at her in frank astonishment. She
could not stop herself from looking in the silvered glass,
though she knew it was vain.

The riding dress fit as if it had been made for her, lovingly emphasizing her womanly curves. The color darkened her blue eyes.

"Oh, Linnet, thank you!" was all Gillian could say.

"But wait—I have forgotten the best part!" She returned moments later, carrying something behind her back.
With a flourish, she brought it forward.

It was a halo-brimmed hat of matching violet, with am-
ethysts set in the brim. A drooping ostrich feather added a
dashing touch to the side.

"You wear it tilted so," Linnet explained, setting it on
Gillian's head to demonstrate the proper angle, "with your
hair tucked up beneath in this little undercap."

Gillian saw in the mirror a sophisticated lady worthy of any royal court.

"Won't I be . . . overdressed?" she breathed, trying to force herself to look away from the enchanting vision in the glass. " 'Tis just a ride and a picnic, after all."

"Wear it," ordered Linnet, as if she was not two years younger than her hostess. "You want to, don't you, and besides, 'twould give me pleasure to see you in it."

Gillian would not have been truly female if she did not appreciate the lovely picture she made in the glass and secretly long to wear such a flattering garment in front of Miles.

"You are too kind," she said at last, hugging the girl.

Having pinned up the honey-blond curls that had grown longer in the past few weeks, and setting the hat at the proper jaunty tilt, she descended the stairs.

The look on Sir Miles Raven's face was all the proof she needed that she had been right to accept Linnet's offer.

Chapter Ten

Miles himself looked mightily splendid in a doublet and breeches of royal blue, both slashed to show a scarlet lining beneath. On his head he wore a matching hat in a style similar to hers. His boots were of soft Spanish leather with the top folded down, revealing several inches of powerfully muscled legs clad in white hose. His sword swung from a belt riding low at his waist. The total effect was one of lusty, potent masculinity, and Gillian felt her heart skip a beat. She was unaware that she hesitated a moment, her eyes widening at the sight of him, but Lady Kathryn saw it.

He did not allow the tribute in his eyes to reach his lips, but his expression was enough for Gillian.

Northumbria was on its best Maytime behavior that day, with scarcely a cloud high over the Cheviots. Lady Kathryn and Linnet were just commenting on the natural beauty of the gently rolling hills when the group was hailed by a horseman coming from the northwest.

"Damn, the only human being we see would have to be Lang," muttered Miles, but so quietly that his voice did not carry to Lady Kathryn and Linnet in the carriage. "I wonder what possible excuse he has to be so far from Belford. I'll warrant he's gone to spy on Kyloe, curse his black soul!"

Gillian said nothing, but watched as he cantered toward them, his hand raised in greeting.

"Good day, Sir Oliver!" she called out politely, which earned her a glare from Miles. She ignored it, and added, "Have you come from Kyloe Priory? 'Tis just where we are going! Tell me, is it progressing as well as Sir Miles claims?" Her artless questions sounded completely innocent, but she was rewarded by the sight of a guilty look rapidly flashing over Lang's bland, broad features.

"Why, no, 'twas such a fine day, I came up on the moor to see if I could scare up some grouse," he said, pointing to the bow and quiver tied to his saddlebow. "Good day to you, sir," he added to Miles, who had nodded as his only acknowledgment of the other knight's presence. "And who are these beauteous ladies? I vow, sir, since you have come north, I find you surrounded by pulchritude at every turn!"

Gillian had to stifle a giggle at the fulsome compliment.

"Mother, Linnet, may I present Sir Oliver Lang, late of court and most recently of Belford Abbey? Sir Oliver, Lady Kathryn Raven, my mother, and Linnet, my *sister*."

Sir Oliver glanced at Miles' tight-set jaw and at the ice-cold eyes that stared at him from beneath dark brows.

"Lady Kathryn, Mistress Linnet, I am *charmed* to make your acquaintance! I had heard your sister was a beauty, Raven, but I must say—"

"Nonsense, Linnet is scarce out of the nursery," growled Miles, cutting him off.

Miles would have said more, Gillian sensed, and it would not have been polite, but Lady Kathryn spoke up, smoothly interposing courtesy. "Sir Oliver, how pleasant to meet you. Miles has told us so much about you."

Gillian was interested to see that Sir Oliver turned a trifle pale at the older lady's words and wondered why, but there was nothing in Lady Kathryn's face that revealed whether she knew why her son so heartily disliked the other man.

Linnet merely inclined her head and gave him a smile, gracefully acknowledging Sir Oliver's compliment without blushing or appearing embarrassed. Gillian marveled at the younger girl's poise until she remembered that Linnet had been exposed to the ways of the polite world while she, Gillian, had been isolated in a convent, studying old manuscripts in the company of women.

"We must not keep you from your hunt," Miles said pointedly.

"Oh, but I would *love* to come along to see your new manor. And it looks as if I would be doing you a favor, Raven, by serving as an additional escort. Why, one never knows when the murdering Scots may pour over the border again!"

He seemed impervious to Miles' basilisk stare, as was Linnet.

"But of course you must come along, Sir Oliver," she said, fluttering sooty lashes at him. "We have a picnic meal packed that would surely feed ten, let alone five. You must come, or we will eat more than is good for us!"

Sir Oliver shrugged cheerfully at Miles. "The ladies command, and I must obey. But hold a moment, and I will tie my mount at the back of your conveyance and join your delightful company, ladies."

As he did so, Gillian stole another glance at Miles. His face was hard and set, a carefully controlled mask of leashed anger. "Pray do not worry," Gillian whispered to him while the others were occupied with settling Sir Oliver between them. "I have a feeling your sister has a great deal more discernment of character than you give her credit for."

"Ah, how reassuring that you think so, *Dame Ancilla,*" he gibed. Then, seeing her wince, he softened his tone. "Pardon me, Gillian. I would not bite at you, but Linnet is dear to me, and I had preferred that she and such a blackguard never meet. But at least here I may keep my eyes upon him."

As they rode the rest of the way, Gillian could hear Lady Kathryn telling Sir Oliver, in response to his question, that they had come to visit her son and see his new home, and how relieved she had been to find him living pleasantly at Mallory Hall during the long process of remodeling Kyloe Abbey.

"Yes, Mistress Mallory is a wonderful hostess, is she not?" He smirked as he said it.

"Quite," Lady Kathryn agreed innocently. "She has provided us every comfort and encouraged us to stay as long as we would."

"Excellent, excellent! Then you will find me a frequent visitor at the Hall, and you must come to dine at Belford. My new manor is quite close to Mallory Hall, you know."

"We would be pleased," Lady Kathryn said, oblivious to her son's stormy countenance.

Then they climbed the winding track that led up into the Kyloe Hills, and suddenly Kyloe Priory—or what was left of it—was before them.

Already Gillian could see that Miles' builders had made a difference. The priory had been laid out in a rectangle, with the chapel forming the back one of the two long sides, the chapter house with the nun's dorter on the above floor being one of the wings and the frater, where the nuns had eaten, the other. In the convent's heyday the lay sisters' dorter had enclosed the rectangle as the other of the long sides, but it was now demolished, and the cloister garth was filled with piles of stone from it and the wall that had enclosed the convent. A man pushing a wheelbarrow load of stone from one of the piles looked up at the approaching riders and the carriage and called out a greeting.

"Hullo, Wat, is your brother-by-marriage about?" Miles called. "I've brought visitors to view your handiwork!"

"Aye, Angus is in th' chapel," the workman said with a grin. "He'll be pleased t'see ye, sir. He has much t'show ye."

The "chapel" now little resembled the house of prayer where the Benedictines had come to chant the office several times a day. The choir stalls where the nuns had sat to sing and pray had been removed, as had the stained glass depictions of the Annunciation, the flight from Egypt and the sorrowing Mother of God standing before the crucified Christ.

Gillian stood still for a moment as she entered, taking in the changes, remembering that there, where the floor was raised, had been the altar where she had prayed over the dying prioress, Mother Benigna—had it only been scant weeks ago? She found Miles regarding her then, and it seemed he was remembering, too.

In front of one of the now glassless windows a man stood at a workbench, his shirt sleeves rolled up to the elbows, poring over a rolled-out scroll. At their approach he looked up.

"Ah, Sir Miles! I was hoping ye'd stop by today, sir! And ye've brought visitors, I see. Welcome, ladies and gentlemen."

Miles swiftly introduced his mother, his sister and Gillian, and finally, as if he begrudged the necessity, Sir Oliver Lang.

Angus had ignored the latter while greeting Lady Kathryn and Mistress Linnet, then had turned his direct gaze to Gillian. "So ye waur one o' the good sisters in religion who inhabited this place? A shame, that it could no' go on sarving God as it had sae well, mistress. Tell me, is it hard t'see it so?" His hand swept around the vast room, meaning the convent as a whole.

"It makes me sad to see piles of rubble where buildings and walls once stood," she told him honestly, "but Sir Miles has said much of your talent, and I trust you will make beauty out of what now looks like chaos and ruin."

Her words pleased him, she could tell by the way his already ruddy complexion flushed a deeper red. Flustered, MacDougall turned to his employer. "Sir Miles, I wonder if ye waud hae a look at this, sir. 'Tis a drawing of the parget work that nephew o' mine in Dalkeith envisioned for the front o' yer hall. Magnificent, is it not?" He held out the scroll so that all could see.

On the parchment was a charcoal drawing of the family emblem, a fierce-looking raven with a twig of some plant in its mouth. Its wings were outspread, its claws extended, as if it was just preparing to land. Around the edges were decorative borders of ivy and flowers, with the motto "I keep what is mine" at the bottom. Though the drawing was crude, it had been carefully done, and both the bird and the vegetation looked lifelike even though they lacked color.

"He can translate this to plaster, as a raised design?" Miles asked.

At the Scot's nod, Linnet exclaimed, "But this is wonderful! It looks so real, I expect to hear it caw, do not you, Mother?"

Lady Kathryn nodded, while Gillian pictured the plasterwork design adorning the front of what had been the chapel and would now be Sir Miles Raven's great hall. The pargeting would be a handsome effect on the house of a gentleman.

"I plan to have the high table there, on what was the altar," Miles told them, "though most often I expect I will dine in the great chamber upstairs, which can be reached via that staircase, there," he added, pointing.

"That used to be the night stairs, by which we would descend to the chapel to sing the offices of Matins, Laud and Prime," Gillian told them.

"I can't imagine getting up and down all night like that," Linnet said. "It makes me yawn just to think of it!"

"It *was* the most difficult thing for me about convent life, but the novice mistress had a long birch rod especially for poking sleepy novices awake—rather ungently," Gillian admitted with a rueful smile. "I soon learned not to fall asleep during the night offices."

"Come upstairs," Miles bid them, and they all ascended the stone staircase worn smooth over the decades by nuns' feet as they had come to worship from the adjoining wing. "As Mistress Gillian can tell you, this was the prioress' chamber," he said when they all stood in the long room. "I intend to make it into my great chamber, with an anteroom leading into my bedchamber."

"And where will the other chambers be, my son?" Lady Kathryn asked.

"I intend to place them in both other wings, where the nuns' dorter was and over the nuns' frater, and add another staircase at the other end of the hall."

"You will enjoy great privacy that way," Sir Oliver commented in his sly way. Miles continued to ignore him.

Gillian groaned inwardly as an enticing image came to her of Miles and herself, savoring solitude in the luxurious chamber that would be here, isolated from the rest of the household in delicious intimacy. Fool! She would never see the interior of Sir Miles Raven's bedchamber at Kyloe Manor, and it was folly to torture herself imagining it on a winter's night, with a fire crackling in the fireplace, shedding its reflected heat and light on lovers in bed....

"And where do you intend to place the kitchen, Miles?" Lady Kathryn inquired, not missing the way Gillian had suddenly looked away and was clenching and unclenching her hands.

"I will place it just in back of the high table, with a roofed passageway leading into the great hall."

"Very wise," Miles' mother approved. "I greatly mislike the way food cools when it is brought to table from faraway kitchens."

"And now, why don't you all seek out a good place to enjoy our picnic, while I consult for a few moments with my builder?" suggested Miles, noticing Angus MacDougall waiting respectfully at the entrance.

As Lang escorted the ladies down the stairs, Miles watched them leave, then turned to his master builder.

"Was there a problem, MacDougall?"

"Nay, Sir Miles. All seems tae be progressin' well. The weather has been good and the lads hae been warkin' steady. I just wondered if ye knew, sar, that yon knave's been seen skulkin' in these hills, spyin' on us?"

"You mean Lang? I suspected as much, when we met him just coming from this direction, though he wouldn't admit it."

"I don't trust the man. There's somethin' verra cagey aboot him, sar."

"He and I are enemies at court, MacDougall," Miles said, and explained how his mother and sister had invited him to accompany them, not knowing of the depth of his dislike of Lang. "Keep me informed if you see him around here again."

"Aye, sar, that I will."

"Was there something else, Angus?" Miles asked, noticing the Scot's hesitation.

"No, sar, not really. 'Tis just... Weel, I see what a bonny lass Mistress Mallory is, if ye don't mind my sayin' so. Is she your intended, Sir Miles?"

"No," Miles said, wary, for the Scot rarely became personal. He could see that Angus was startled at his abrupt tone, when Miles added, in a tone less curt, "But you have a good eye, Angus. In truth, Mistress Mallory is very... bonny."

He turned on his heel and descended the stairs, aware that Angus MacDougall was still watching him curiously. He suddenly wished he had not acquiesced in this outing, or had just brought his mother and sister, if there had been a way to do so without being churlish to Gillian. Having her here, so breathtakingly lovely in the violet riding dress that accentuated her beauty, he could not help but picture Gillian as the lady of the manor he was building. And now he must go out to the others and tolerate that sly scoundrel Lang. Somehow he had to pretend to ignore the way the man was alternately ogling his sister and Gillian.

He suspected the other knight leered at Linnet merely because he knew it annoyed Miles. Lang usually went for riper blooms, not young maidens barely grown to womanhood. But he had seen the way Lang looked at Gillian, and it enraged Miles all the more because he had no right to object if Lang offered Gillian an honorable wooing.

They had the food all spread out on a blanket on the garth, the square of green that had once been enclosed on all four sides by the cloisters.

"Come, sit down, brother, we've been waiting for you," invited Linnet, patting a spot on the grass, which would put him between herself and Gillian. Was his sister trying to throw them together? Then he saw that Lang had stationed himself on the other side of Gillian, and thought no more about Linnet's possible hidden motives.

"Mag seems to have thought of everything," Gillian commented, handing him a cold leg of chicken and a thick hunk of wheaten bread. There were also freshly baked tarts, a wheel of cheese, a salad of onions, leeks and dandelions, and comfit cakes. "Some wine, Sir Miles?"

The food was delicious, and for a few minutes, what little conversation there was concerned its tastiness. Then, as if noticing how pensive Miles had been, Lady Kathryn turned to him.

"I meant to tell you when we arrived, Miles, your man of affairs sends good reports of your shipping. The *Ravens' Pride* brought in a wonderful cargo of Bordeaux—how you manage to deal with the French so well I'll never understand."

"Good intermediaries," he mumbled.

Lady Kathryn tried another tack. "Have you had any time to work on plans for your stud? I know you said the king was interested in a colt from Cloud."

He wished she wouldn't discuss his business matters in front of Lang, but didn't know how to signal as much to her. "I've been too occupied with the building to do much, and I've yet to obtain the right mares to breed to Cloud. Gillian's mare was an unexpected good find, but of course a palfrey like Sultana is too small. I believe the present barn will do for my brood mares, at least until I can build something bigger."

His mother seemed satisfied. Then she turned to Sir Oliver. "I suppose, sir, that you have heard of the shameful happenings at court?"

Lang looked distinctly uneasy, Miles noted. "I have been gone from court for a time, my lady," he answered, "but matters were...unsettled...between the king and the queen when I left.''

"Matters were becoming *settled* quite rapidly as we left the south, if that is the proper term." She repeated what she had told Miles and Gillian. "Why, Sir Oliver, you look unwell. Could it be the wine? I did not notice you were consuming overmuch."

Miles had never told his mother the story of finding Lang with Anne Boleyn, and now he watched with secret amusement as Lang's complexion rapidly went from livid to green.

"And the queen herself?"

" 'Tis likely she will not escape unscathed, after what Henry did to Catherine of Aragon! 'Tis a pity she miscarried that son this winter!"

"God save the queen's grace," said Lang weakly, darting a nervous glance at Miles, who said nothing.

"I think it all sounds horrid!" Linnet declared. "Let's not talk of foolish people at court, when 'tis so far away! Miles, tell me where you're going to put the gardens. Shall you have a maze?"

"Would it be *amazing* if I did not?" Miles inquired with a wry grin. He was glad Linnet had changed the subject.

"Oh! I hate puns!" cried Linnet, throwing handfuls of grass at her brother. "But of course you must have a maze! 'Tis practically a requirement of a fashionable estate! You should put it at the back of the house, and put a comfortable bench in the middle, where you can sit with your true love of an evening!" Innocently she glanced at Gillian and back at Miles again.

"And you, Mistress Gillian," Miles said, suddenly turning eyes of silver blue on her. "What say you? What shall I plant in my garden?"

"Only Tudor roses, I should think," she retorted, her eyes locked with his as if the others were not there.

"Oh, I think a white rose or two would not look out of place," he could not resist saying. And then he added, as if to himself, "And perhaps I shall dig a pond, and on it place a white swan."

Lang, sitting there, decided that he would like to write of what was going on in the north to a certain party at court.

Chapter Eleven

That evening Gillian left the supper table while the others were still lingering over their wine. She thought to combine two errands, that of thanking Mag for her extra effort in making the picnic food and obtaining a warm bottle of milk for Tag. She felt guilty about leaving the orphaned lamb too much in Ned's care, for he had other chores assigned by his father.

She found Jack, Ned and little Harry in the kitchen, but not Mag. Ned told her that his "da" had wanted to talk to his mother. Gillian hoped they were upstairs and Brunt was encouraging his wife to rest, but she doubted it. Making a mental note to seek Mag out on the morrow, she went to the barn with the warmed bottle.

Gillian was already in the stall and in the midst of feeding the hungry lamb when she heard a soft, thudding sound from a nearby stall, as if one of the animals was lunging against the side of the stall again and again. A series of grunts, interspersed with a soft whimper, told her that the makers of the noises were human. She felt her face flame as she realized what Brunt and his wife were doing. It was too late to leave without risking being heard herself, so Gillian decided to remain silent and hope that they would leave without knowing she had been there.

A few moments of silence followed, and then Gillian heard Brunt speak.

"Now get my supper, woman, and see that it's better than the slop ye gave me for my noon victuals, whilst ye gave the gentry chicken and cakes!"

Satisfying his lust did not seem to have put the man into a cheerful frame of mind. Gillian froze as Brunt's voice, which had been surly, became an angry ranting. "Ye give me horse bread and cheese! I'll teach you to short yer lord, woman! I get peasant's fare, and they get tarts and salad, to eat as they sit there in their velvet and silk?" There was the sound of a ringing slap in the dimness, and a woman's muffled sob.

"But, George, that's what ye alwus ate! And the mistress buys the food, and we are in their employ!"

"Bah! It wasn't always so, until the damned king turned loose those parasites in the convents!"

"But that isn't Mistress Gillian's fault, George! 'Tis her rightful place, and yet she's been very kind t'us! We have more t'eat now than we did, an' she could ha' put us out on the road, ye know!"

"All I know is ye didn't used t'talk back t'me, when I was master o' the hall!" There was the sound of several thudding blows in rapid succession, and a woman's moans of pain.

Gillian's resolve to stay hidden was forgotten as she lunged from the stall, intent on stopping Brunt before he inflicted any further hurt on his wife.

"Stop it! Cease this instant, or I *will* put you out on the road, but by yourself, Brunt! Your poor wife doesn't deserve this treatment, especially in her state, a state you've put her in, you know!"

Brunt had been caught literally with his breeches down and still dangling around his skinny knees, and was therefore somewhat handicapped when faced with the blond, avenging angel that was Gillian Mallory. The fact that he was not sure if the mistress had heard him tupping his wife in the darkened stall before he began to hit Mag slowed his reaction further still. Nevertheless, his blood was up and he resented Gillian's intrusion.

"'Tis my right t'do with my woman as I wish, Mistress Mallory," he blustered. "'Tis none o' yer affair—nor does it become ye t'be spyin' on folk enjoyin' a little privacy!" A wave of stale ale fumes wafted from the belligerent man.

"I came out here to feed my lamb!" she flared. "I had no intention of overhearing you taking your pleasure in the barn, like a rutting boar! And I very much doubt Mag would call it *enjoyable,* as far gone as she is with child!" She glanced at the shamefaced Mag. "If there's any repetition of your hitting your wife, Brunt, you shall find yourself dismissed, and I will give her and the children the choice of staying with me!"

"Please, mistress, 'tis not necessary!" cried Mag, tearfully throwing herself at Gillian's feet. "Brunt's in his cups, 'tis all. I'm used to it, really, mistress."

Gillian was not convinced. There was a bruise already discoloring her housekeeper's face, but she saw that her spirited defense could potentially make things worse when she was not around to help Mag. "All right, Mag. Brunt, consider yourself warned. And have a little care for your wife. Remember, 'tis your babe she carries!"

Brunt just stood there eyeing her, a sullen glint in his small eyes. "Yes, Mistress Mallory," he said at last. As Gillian left the barn, he thought about how often he had imagined taking Gillian Mallory as he had just taken his wife.

Gillian walked to the house on shaky legs, still trembling from the adrenaline that had coursed through her

system after her confrontation with Brunt. She was furious, and frustrated, too, that Mag could be so passive, apparently feeling it was her duty to tolerate whatever
treatment Brunt gave her.

Miles had been right about Brunt. Gillian now heartily
regretted her generous impulse to keep the man on as her
steward, yet if she had not, Mag and her sons might even
now be wandering the roads with George Brunt, slowly
starving. How could she have helped them without keeping Brunt?

Were the higher folk any better off? The queen herself
stood in grave danger, if the tales from court were to be
believed. Gentlewomen seemed no more immune to any
violence their lords chose to offer them than a common
woman was.

I'll be no man's chattel, Gillian vowed. *I'll learn to be
self-sufficient, and run Mallory Hall as well as any man.*

Mag came to Gillian in the hall the next morning as she
sat alone, breaking her fast before her guests had arisen.
"I'm grateful t'ye, mistress, truly I am, fer what ye did last
even. 'Twas very brave o'ye."

"Nonsense, Mag! I couldn't let him beat you. I'm not
afraid of him, and I won't let him hurt you!"

Mag's eyes were downcast. "Thank ye, mistress," she
mumbled. "I pray for ye every night."

Gillian was touched, and a bit shamed, for now that she
had been away from the sound of the convent bells calling
her to regular prayer, her own prayers were frequently said
in haste as she arose in the morning. All too often, when she
lay in the great bed at night, her thoughts turned to more
worldly matters, such as the running of Mallory Hall—or
the man whose chamber adjoined hers.

* * *

The shearing party was held a week later. There was great anticipation among Gillian's tenants, who remembered how Sir William had always provided a feast at the home farm after the shearing was done. During the years after Sir William's death, the close-fisted Brunt had not held the party, and each tenant had had to take care of the necessary spring task alone.

Gillian had pleasant memories of past shearing parties, of the delicious meat pasties, cakes and pies made by the farmers' wives, and the singing by ale-flushed farmers as all savored the celebration in the midst of their otherwise simple lives. It was easier to get the shearing done with many hands to share the work, and Gillian was determined to make this event as enjoyable as any she could remember.

At the home farm there was a large enclosure, and all the tenants had driven their flocks to it early in the morning. Each sheep had a distinctive dab of color marking its rump, which indicated which flock it belonged to—blue for the home farm, yellow for Tom Small's, red for Will Rowe's and so forth, so that each farmer could regain his sheep when they were done. When Gillian arrived at midmorning, this pen was a cacophony of bleating sheep, each indicating just how unhappy it was to be subjected to this harrowing procedure.

At one end of the pen there was a long shed, open on one side, which gave shade to several shearers as they skillfully shifted each protesting sheep about to clip the heavy fleece. Others waited to catch the sheep just outside of the shelter to daub them with tar to keep the flies away from any nicks on the newly bare hides.

The farmers' wives were kept busy supplying their men with cool drafts of water between sheep; a couple of them were even shearing the sheep themselves with dexterous ease.

"How is it going, Jock?" called Gillian, dismounting from Sultana and tying her reins to the enclosure rail.

"Well, mistress. Yer tenants are goin' at th' sheep with a right good will. They know the sooner all are sheared, the sooner they may enjoy themselves."

"And our flock—will we have enough fleece to make a good profit in Ross, think you?"

Jock scratched his chin before replying. "Not as good as in years past. I think ye know the size of our flock is much diminished," he said, casting a meaningful glance at George Brunt, who was downing a cup of ale while "supervising" the shearers, "but we'll keep the wolf from th'door, right enough. And we'll need to keep more rams from this year's lambing, for once yer flock is larger, the two old rams ye have won't be enough to tup more than the hunnerd or so ye have now."

Gillian blushed at the earthy term Jock had unthinkingly used to refer to the rams' servicing of the ewes, but Jock had gone back to his work.

Her eyes, wandering to the shearers as they worked among the struggling sheep, caught sight of a figure she had not seen before. Sir Miles Raven was shearing sheep right along with her tenants!

He wore an old pair of breeches and a white shirt, which was open at the neck, and he was laughing at some jest the farmer next to him had made. His face was ruddy and gleamed from his exertion. He had not yet seen her.

Gillian felt her heart lurch within her at the sight of this courtier of King Henry's, dressed like a peasant and engaged in the dirty, smelly task of sheepshearing. She had been busy in the kitchen helping to prepare the food for the feast when he left, and she had assumed he would be going to Kyloe as he usually did during the day. There had been no need for him to lower himself to such a task, and she was touched that he had chosen to take part. It was obvious her tenants were impressed, also, for as she watched they traded jests with the Sussex knight, and a red-cheeked farm wife brought him a cup of cold ale.

Just then he finished the black-faced ewe he had been shearing. The sheep bleated as he raised her to her feet and gave her a pat, which sent her careening off in search of her lamb. Catching sight of Gillian as she entered the enclosure and strode toward him, he waved and straightened.

"Well! Can this be Sir Miles Raven, courtier of Greenwich and confidant of the king?" she teased. "Have you decided shearing sheep is more to your taste than dressing in velvet and silk and mingling with royalty?"

Actually, he had been thoroughly enjoying himself, Miles realized, though one old ewe had landed a kick on his thigh that was already aching. Once they had seen he was not afraid of a little hard work, Mallory Hall's tenants had shown him unfeigned hearty friendliness. Their unsophisticated good natures seemed a lot more genuine than all the artificial courtesy and compliments that were bandied about between courtiers and court ladies.

And now Gillian was here, clad in a serviceable old brown dress that nonetheless managed to complement her coloring and trim figure. He watched as she returned the greetings of her tenants and their families. She was sincerely interested in each of them. It was apparent she had not just come to assure herself the work was getting done, for after watching for a few minutes, she rolled up her sleeves and began to shear sheep right alongside him.

It was a long, dusty afternoon, for with the flocks combined, there were at least three hundred sheep to be sheared.

It passed quickly, though, for Miles, achingly aware of the woman working steadily beside him, humming as she clipped the wool from each sheep and tossed the fleece into the pile behind her.

He stole glances at her, loving the sight of her flushed face and blond ringlets slipping from beneath the plain linen cap, entranced by the sight of her breasts straining at the bodice of the brown dress as she struggled to hold a sheep still.

He realized suddenly that he had never been as happy as he was at this moment, far from the intrigues and maneuverings at court, with its scented, expensively dressed men and women so busy jockeying for favor with the king that they did not have time to be with their spouses.

He would not remain happy away from this woman, who threw herself fully into everything she did, who had faced such great changes in her life and met them head-on.

He wanted to be happy. He had assumed he would be, married to a highborn, wealthy lady who was well-suited to adorn his arm at court functions. If such a lady was adept at warming his bed, so much the better. All at once, however, life without Gillian Mallory seemed meaningless and empty.

Miles had been heavyhearted for the past fortnight, convinced he must end his growing feeling for the woman beside him. But he was weary of forcing himself to smother a love that was demanding to exist. Now he loathed the idea of marrying a lady who would probably never be content here in the north, but would be continually clamoring to return to court.

In the midst of shearing a particularly recalcitrant old ram, Miles knew what he had to do. Perhaps he would never rise any higher in the world; he might even sink into obscurity as a north-country rustic, but it no longer mattered. He wanted to marry Gillian. He had loved her, he now realized, ever since she had defiantly informed him that he would have to help her bury the prioress.

Miles' decision made, he turned to face Gillian, only to find that she was studying him as if aware of the struggle within. Her speedwell-blue eyes locked with his, and in the midst of the bleating noise and stink of sheep, it was as if they were the only two people that existed. He could see the pulse beating in the blue vein at the side of her neck. Unconscious that she did it, she licked her lower lip as she gazed at him, and his mouth went dry. He felt a tightening in his loins. It was all he could do not to seize her then and there and kiss her until she parted her lips and let his tongue mate with that little pink tongue of hers.

Miles saw the hectic flush rising in her cheeks and wondered if she could read his mind. He opened his mouth, unsure of what to say, but just then they were interrupted by the arrival of his mother, Linnet and Mag, who had come in the carriage, bringing Mallory Hall's contribution to the feast.

The shearing done, the shearers and their helpers left the pen to the sheep and went to the trestle tables that had been set up next to Jock's cottage. The farm wives had brought their finest meat pies and pastries, just as Gillian remembered, and had been roasting several pigs over spits all day long. Mallory Hall had provided a large barrel of Mag's home-brewed ale, roast venison, comfit cakes and great crusty loaves of bread and fresh-churned butter.

Her tenants feasted as enthusiastically as they had sheared. Their bellies soon filled, children ran gaily around their families, who sat in the grass, eating and drinking.

Talk was merry as each tenant tried to outboast the other in the amount of fleeces he had sheared.

"I can't think when I've had a better time," Lady Kathryn commented, accepting a refill of her ale from a passing farm wife with a pitcher. She, too, had mingled with the crowd as if she had grown up among them, and it was obvious they appreciated her lack of pretence.

The men became ruddy-faced from the toasts they made to "Mistress Gillian Mallory, the beauteous lady of Mallory Hall," and as each was more florid in his praises than the last, Gillian became rather rosy-faced herself from pleased embarrassment.

Someone had brought out a carved flute, and Linnet had brought her lute, and before long couples were singing to the tunes they improvised between them.

Then Linnet strummed an introductory measure and said, "I believe you know this one, brother."

Miles nodded and stood. "This is a composition of King Henry's," he said, then sang.

"Alas, my love, you do me wrong
To cast me off discourteously
For I have loved you so long,
Delighting in your company.
Greensleeves was all my joy,
Greensleeves was my delight.
Greensleeves was my heart of gold,
And who but my lady Greensleeves?"

He seemed to be singing only to her. The rough velvet of his voice had lifted her above her humble surroundings to an enchanted plain of joy and wondering. Did he mean the words he sang? Was she "all his joy, his delight"? Did he mean that he loved her in all truth, or was Miles just singing prettily arranged words?

Chapter Twelve

It was an eternity before she could find out the truth. Her tenants, having discovered a troubador in their midst, were not about to let him sit down again so easily. Miles was kept singing by the farmers and their wives, who called out names of songs, and he obliged them whenever he knew the words. Linnet joined in on some of them, adding her girlish soprano to his manly voice. She had told Gillian of their singing duets at Ravenwood at Yuletide.

When the tenants ran out of titles, they nevertheless clapped and stomped until Miles sang court favorites these northern Englishmen and women had never heard.

Clearly, Miles was savoring the regard of the tenants after their initially cool reception of him. At one point, however, while stopping to quaff a cup of ale to soothe his throat, he cast a rueful glance at Gillian, which clearly communicated his desire to be elsewhere with her.

Sitting on the blanket, her belly full of good food, feeling the faint glow from the ale she had drunk, Gillian saw Miles Raven's pale eyes upon her. She felt a premonitory tingle at the base of her spine. What would happen later, she wondered, now that he had made love to her with those blue-silver eyes? Had he mesmerized the ladies at court in just this fashion, ensorcelling them with his gaze and the magic of his voice?

And what of her resolve to be no man's chattel? Somehow, with the love she felt for this man singing through her veins, leaving behind her goal of self-sufficiency seemed no longer loss but gain. Miles would not enslave her, he would *join* her in love. Together they would be stronger than either could be alone.

Then, as she watched, he raised his cup to her, first toasting her silently, then adding: "Good men and women, I give you the lady of Mallory Hall, Mistress Gillian Mallory." There was wild, enthusiastic applause, but all she noticed was the tribute in his eyes.

Blushing, she stood and curtsied to her tenants, but before she could resume her seat, Lady Kathryn called out, "Would you sing to us, Mistress Gillian? You have been used to spending a great amount of time singing in the convent. I'll warrant you have a pretty voice."

"I . . . I fear I know only songs of the church," she faltered. "We were not allowed to sing else."

"That's as it should be," roared a hearty farmer sitting toward the back. "Go ahead and sing them, for 'tis not your fault you are not still in your convent, though we're lucky to have ye as our mistress!"

She sang "Angelus ad Virginem" without music, her lips shaping the words hesitatingly at first, then allowing the perfect clarity of her voice to come through. Then Linnet's lute joined her as she sang, "I Sing of a Maiden That is Matchless," and she sat down to resounding cheers.

"An angel, 'tis our mistress! An angel!" she heard one tipsy farmer say, before his ruddy-faced wife shushed him.

"Speech, speech!" arose the cry.

She looked to Miles, Linnet and Lady Kathryn, but they would not rescue her. At last she stood, saying, "I thank you all for coming and helping with the shearing, for many hands indeed make light work. I wish you the best of luck as you sell your fleeces at market, and thank you for being such good tenants. I shall strive always to be a good mistress of Mallory Hall, as my parents were before me. If you need aught, if 'tis in my power, I will give it to you. And now, it grows late. Have a safe journey back to your homes."

Gillian had to be patient then as each of her tenants felt it necessary to come up to thank her personally for the party and to wish her well. Then, their flocks having been driven home earlier, they packed up their belongings, leftover food and dozing children and went their ways.

By unspoken consent, Miles and Gillian lingered until the farmers had all departed before they mounted their horses. They wanted to ride to the Hall alone together, to explore the feelings that had been voiced with their eyes all evening.

As if she sensed their wishes, Lady Kathryn professed fatigue and a wish to hurry home. Linnet and Mag left with her.

Now, with Jock having retired into his cottage, they were alone as they rode away from the home farm. A sliver of moonlight shone high above the gently rolling Cheviots.

"'Twas a very enjoyable day," Miles said at last, turning to her as they rode. The moonlight made his pale blue eyes gleam silver.

She pretended mocking disbelief. "You *enjoyed* that hot, fatiguing task? Come, sir, you shall have to do better than that to fool this simple maid."

"It had its less than enjoyable moments," Miles admitted ruefully, rubbing his aching thigh where the sheep had kicked him. "But yes, laugh as you will, dear Gillian, I did enjoy myself today, both during the shearing and at the party afterward. Your tenants are good people.''

She nodded wordlessly, drowning in the deep pools of his eyes.

''When my brother gave me this land,'' he continued, ''I hated the fact that it was in the north, so far from Ravenwood and the attractions of court. Sussex is a softer land, as you often remind me,'' he added with a grin, then grew serious. ''But I've come to see that I could be happy here, Gillian.''

''Oh, Miles, I'm so glad.'' He had come to appreciate this wild, hard land as she did! ''Then you plan to use Kyloe Manor as more than an occasional refuge from court?''

''Yes, though if King Henry calls upon my service in war, I shall have to go. But life in the king's circle no longer seems so fascinating to me,'' he said, shrugging to indicate his struggle to put his feelings into words. He took a deep breath. ''I could be happy here, Gillian—but only with you.''

She stared at him, reining in her horse, but her heart galloped at a runaway pace. ''What . . . what are you saying?''

He jumped off Cloud and seized her hands as they lay trembling on the saddle pommel. ''That I love you, Mistress Gillian Mallory, and I want you. I know when I met you you had been just about to take eternal vows to serve God. Do you still long to be a nun, Gillian?''

''I have learned our Lord has other ways to serve Him, Miles,'' she admitted.

''Then marry me, my lovely former nun, and be my lady, and bear my babes.''

She slid from the saddle into his waiting arms. ''Yes, Miles! Oh, yes!''

It was fortunate that their mounts were both well-trained, for as Miles began kissing her as if he might never stop, each dropped the reins. The mare and stallion drifted only a few feet away, and sensing that their owners were going to be busy for a while, stopped to graze.

He loved her, he wanted her, he would wed her. Her heart sang, as she surrendered to the delirious joy of response to his fervent lovemaking. Before, in the bothy, he had talked only of wanting, and his caresses had sent her to the brink of surrender. When he had kissed her outside the stable in the moonlight, he hadn't talked at all, but had thrust her from him as if his attraction to her had been unwilling. But now, whatever had held him back from fully committing his heart to her no longer existed, and she need not fear to give her own heart into his keeping. The realization that he was hers was as potent as any aphrodisiac.

"Oh, Miles, I love you," she breathed, when his mouth left hers to trail fiery kisses down her neck. "And I must confess, sir," she said, her breath coming a little raggedly as his hand began to caress her breast, "that I want you, too!"

Minutes went by, minutes filled with kisses and touches, stroking and caressing, while their pulses raced with each other. Gillian was conscious of a raging thirst, a thirst that could only be slaked by Miles.

She heard him groan. He, too, was in torment. "Miles, must we wait until we are wed?" she asked at last, her voice thick with longing.

He chuckled at the eagerness that matched his own. "Ah, sweetheart," he said, looking regretfully around at the stark countryside revealed by the sliver of moon. "I would not take you like some country shepherdess, love, on the cold, hard ground! And besides, sweetheart," he teased, chucking her under the chin, "you smell of sheep!"

"So do *you*, sir," she returned tartly, but she smiled as she said it.

Apparently he wished to wait, and though she ached to tell him it did not matter to her if they first coupled on the heather-covered hills, some maidenly shyness held her back. What would he think of her if she told him that?

Mag had used the time until her mistress arrived at Mallory Hall to excellent purpose, for when Gillian reached her chamber, Mag and Jack were emptying steaming buckets of hot water into the oaken tub.

No sight could have been more welcome than that. Gillian had been anxious to cleanse herself of the stench of sheep, and had assumed that she would have to use the cold water in the ewer, for surely Mag would be abed. After all, she had put in an exhausting day, too, though heavy with child, and had not the invigorating benefit of new love.

"You are indeed the best servants in England." She sighed, gazing at the welcoming tub of hot water and then at Mag, who had lingered though Jack had departed.

"Go to bed," she bid her. "I think I can manage not to fall asleep in the tub and drown," Gillian added, faking a yawn that was not entirely convincing, for she had never felt less sleepy and more alive. She was certain Mag had seen her kiss-swollen lips before she left.

In spite of her tingling excitement, Gillian *did* doze as the soothing heat of the water soaked away the fatigue from her muscles. After washing her hair, she lay back in the tub, stretching luxuriously and closing her eyes.

She awoke with a start, though Miles had shut the door quietly enough.

He wore a shirt under a dressing gown, but his hair was damp and he smelled of soap. For a moment, he seemed to be a figure out of her dreams, and she blinked sleepily at him, smiling. He grinned, his eyes gleaming in the light of the pair of candles she had left lit on a nearby table.

"Gillian, love..."

The sound of his voice woke her from her trance, and she realized that she was quite naked in the oaken tub, and that the level of water did not quite cover her breasts from his interested gaze. Gillian gave an involuntary squeak as she grabbed for the towel that Mag had left within easy reach.

She did not dare to look at him again until she was standing outside the tub, dripping, swathed in the folds of the towel. "How did you... I mean, I wasn't expecting..." Her voice trailed off as her eyes met his, and she saw the love and desire smoldering in the quicksilver blue depths.

"Did you forget the door between our chambers, sweetheart? It wasn't locked, so I thought... Gillian, am I not welcome?"

There was no arrogant overconfidence in his voice, just an appealing huskiness that wrapped itself in warm tendrils around her heart and sent fire coursing, swift and sweet, through her veins. The same desire that had claimed her only an hour ago under the Northumbrian night skies claimed her now, and she met his inquiring gaze. She had never felt surer of anything in her life, though there was a tremor in her voice as she said, "Yes, Miles, you are welcome, indeed."

"We must dry you off, or you will get cold," he murmured, indicating the gooseflesh on her shoulders above the towel she still clutched around her. "Nay, love, don't be ashamed of your body before me, for 'tis perfection...." Gently he loosed the towel from her hold and patted her dry all over, lingering around her tingling breasts and belly. Then, pulling off his dressing gown and putting it around her trembling shoulders, he indicated she was to sit before the framed silvered glass upon the dressing table, and he toweled her hair dry, then combed through the damp ringlets.

Gillian stared at his reflection in the wavy glass as he smoothed the tangles from her curls. It took only a few moments, for as yet her hair had only grown to graze her jawline, and then he whispered, "Come, love..."

She turned on the bench and he bent to her, scooping up her slender form. She could feel his heart beating rapidly as he carried her to the curtained bed in the corner of the room. His dressing gown came open as he gently deposited her there, baring one breast, but she no longer strove to cover it.

With one swift, impatient motion he pulled off the open-necked shirt over his head and dropped it negligently by the bed. Then, his eyes locked with hers, he bent to untie the strings of his last garment, the full short pants called slops, and they slithered off his lean hips.

Now he stood naked to her gaze, his manhood standing proudly out from his body. To her innocent eyes, he looked enormous, and suddenly the haze of desire that had clouded her brain parted enough for her to feel fear. If all men were built thus, then the act of love could only be an act of brutality. Had her gentle mother truly received her father thus?

He saw her eyes widen and the way she shrank back and reached for the covers, and mentally cursed his thoughtlessness. This was no experienced woman of the world, used to the ways of passion. Gillian was an innocent maiden, newly released from the cloister, who came to him with nothing more than her love for him to armor her against the pain of losing her virginity. And because he loved her, he vowed that her initiation into physical love would be as wonderful and free of fear as he could make it.

"Gillian, don't be afraid." He kept his voice low and soothing, as one would speak to a fractious horse, and kept his movements smooth and unhurried. He lay down beside her on the bed, gathering her up comfortingly in his arms but allowing the sheet to remain between their bodies.

"Gillian, I promise we will do nothing that you don't want to do. You have but to say the word, and I will stop, sweetheart, do you understand?"

He felt her rigid body relax slightly, and she nodded at him, but her eyes remained wide and wary. "I just didn't know, Miles, I didn't know...."

"No, of course you didn't," he said reassuringly. "But you don't know how wonderfully your body is made, love. It can take me, all of me, if we go about this in the right way. I won't rush you, my darling. We have all night, and all the rest of our lives. Let me show you how wonderful you can feel."

Gillian lay back trustingly on the pillows, comforted that he did not mean to fall on her like some ravening wolf, knowing that she could stop him if she wanted to. But something in his eyes dared her to go on, to let him guide her to the paradise that awaited. Surely she would be the poorer if she let fear govern her now.

"Kiss me, Gillian."

It was easy enough to obey that command, for she had kissed him before. For long moments it was all they did. He kissed her gently, then lingeringly, his tongue doing wonderful things to the inside of her mouth, things that stoked the fire inside her until her arms stole around him. He pushed the sheet down far enough that only her breasts were bared and then went back to kissing her, letting her experience the tantalizing sensation of her breast pressed up against his chest and the rasp of the hair that curled on his chest against her bare skin as he moved against her. Then his hand closed on her breast, stroking it, cupping it, circling the nipple until she gasped with delight.

"You are so beautiful, Gillian, my treasure... so beautiful...."

He could have been speaking Greek to her at that moment and she would have understood, so in tune was she with the universe then, for the universe was this chamber, this bed and the velvet sensations that he was setting loose within her. Her breasts tingled and felt heavy.

Miles's mouth left her lips, kissing her jawline and caressing her slender neck, and then it closed around one nipple as his hand reached for the other.

Her back arched into him as he suckled, and she felt mindless with joy. The sheet still between their lower bodies, she felt him pull her closer, felt his manhood rubbing against her thigh through the linen. It felt like a burning brand, yet it did not scorch her. She was dimly aware of a moisture between her legs that seemed somehow connected to the enticing way he was moving against her.

There was more, there had to be. The path lay in front of them, yet blocked by the barrier of the linen between them. The fire that had flickered before was a conflagration now.

Hardly knowing what she did, she pushed the sheet aside, sucking in a deep breath as she felt him accept the silent invitation. Suddenly there was nothing between them, and the full length of their bodies touched.

Wary of frightening her again, Miles lay still, allowing Gillian to feel him wanting her, yet not moving to take her. He waited for her signal, and it came in the form of a soft moan and a slight movement of her hips. Then, gently, he inserted a knee between her legs, letting her feel the pressure of it, then letting his fingers stray downward.

He touched her and was pleased with the moisture he felt there and the ragged sound of her breathing that revealed the depth of her arousal. She was wonderful. All those years in a convent had not spoiled this woman who was made for rapture, who had been created to love him.

It was becoming harder for him to control the raging need this wondrous creature had engendered in him, but control it he would. It had never mattered so much before, but it was everything now. He would not give rein to his passion before he had taken her through the pain and on to joy.

He began to stroke her now, gently, tantalizingly probing the entrance to her womanhood just a little way, but lingering on the outside to massage the little flower there, until he felt her nails digging into his back, urging him on. She was ready, though she did not know what she was ready for, and the small, inarticulate sounds that escaped from her throat confirmed it.

"Gillian, listen to me, love. I must hurt you for a moment, only a moment, once and never again. And then there will be pleasure, sweetheart—"

Miles didn't give her time to be afraid, but entered her in one swift, smooth stroke, swallowing her brief cry of pain with his kiss. Then he began to move within her, slowly at first, then as her hips began to rotate with his, faster and faster, pushing her until she fell over the edge, and then he allowed himself to fall with her, and they collapsed together.

Chapter Thirteen

Afterward, he held her close and told her how much he loved her, and they made delicious plans in the guttering candlelight.

"We'll be married as soon as possible," he told her, basking in the radiant sense of well-being they shared. "Then we'll live here until Kyloe Manor is built."

"And we'll alternate between residences," she insisted firmly. "I love this place, Miles, though your new, grand manor house will be home to me, too."

He kissed her, nodding in agreement. "And while we stay at Kyloe, we can refurbish Mallory Hall until 'tis every bit as grand," he promised her. "You will make a splendid knight's wife, sweetheart."

"Lady Gillian Raven, of Kyloe Manor and Mallory Hall," she said, savoring the name on her tongue. "Sir Miles and Lady Gillian—ah, Miles! I still can't believe it! I love you so!"

"And I, you," he said, then: "Wait a moment. I shall return immediately."

Curiously she watched as he donned his dressing gown and disappeared through the door that communicated between their two chambers. She smiled, remembering how she had vowed to always lock that door on the day he had brought her here—and realizing she had forgotten for several days to check that it remained locked.

After a couple of moments he was back, bearing a skin of wine and a single cup.

"I was thirsty," he announced cheerfully, "aren't you? We shall have to share the cup, since I might be heard were I to go down to the kitchen at this hour, but that's no hardship, is it, love?"

She shook her head, watching in appreciative silence the play of candlelight on the planes of his angular face as he poured the wine, then handed the cup to her before doffing his gown and climbing into bed with her.

"You don't suppose we were heard while we . . . ?" Lady Kathryn seemed to like her, but she might feel very different toward her if she knew her son had been welcomed into Gillian's bed before the sacrament of marriage had been celebrated.

"Nay, don't worry," he assured her, "and she would think no less of you if she had. My mother adores you. She's going to be delighted to hear I have finally come to my senses and asked for your hand."

"Oh, Miles, are you sure?" she asked, doubt tingeing her voice. "After all, you're a knight from a prosperous family who fought for the Tudors, and high in Henry's favor. You could look much higher than an impoverished former novice whose family were Plantagenet supporters. Wouldn't she want you to marry someone who could further your potential for advancement? Someone whose family stands secure in Tudor favor also?"

"No, my little worrier," he said, pulling her close against his furred chest with one hand while taking a long draft of wine from the cup in his other hand. "In point of fact my mother knew long before I realized it that that sort of woman was all wrong for me. Ah, Gillian, I've been lost for so long! But you'll see, she'll jump for joy—as will Linnet. Would you mind if the wedding were at the parish church near Ravenwood? I think she would like that, for that way all the family could meet you, and Mother could busy herself with the details."

She'd been handed the moon... dare she ask for a star, too? But she had to be true to herself. Miles must love all she was or not at all.

"I do not mind *where* we marry, Miles, but the priest there... is he one of Henry's?" She meant, did he acknowledge Henry as supreme head of the Church of England, as the king demanded ever since he had broken with Rome?

Miles rubbed his hand thoughtfully through his beard and mustache. "It won't be a valid marriage to you if the priest has taken the oath, will it?"

She shook her head, afraid to speak.

"I'm afraid he has. Father Ambrose is a pragmatic soul, though a good man. What are we to do, darling? I'll have the Pope himself marry us if you like!"

"There is a priest at Ross—only a few know where to find him—and Mag says he holds to the old ways. Could he marry us first, secretly? Then we could wed again with your priest."

"We can marry a hundred times if you like," he told her, smiling fondly at her earnestness.

"Miles, you are the best of men!" she cried softly, throwing her arms about him.

"Nay... I would have you know I have been as venal and selfish as any at court," he said, serious now. "But no more, my little nun. I... I don't deserve you, Gillian Mallory... but I shall always love you." They kissed, long and deeply, as they sank back into the nest of pillows.

"Miles, I...I do not look to wed a saint," she said, propping herself up on one elbow and teasing him by allowing her golden curls to tickle his nipple.

He quivered at the sensation, feeling the heat settle in his groin and his shaft harden. "Saucy wench! Surely you did not learn these tricks in the convent! Is every daughter of Eve born knowing how to entice a man?"

Gillian grinned, obviously pleased at the effect on him. "An old woman told me I had a mouth made for kissing once, but I didn't believe her at the time." At his raised eyebrow, she told him of Elizabeth Easington's words.

"Well, see that you keep that passionate mouth just for me," he growled in mock-threatening tones.

"I am yours, *only* yours, my Miles," she told him, pulling him into her arms. "Let me show you again how thoroughly I am yours...."

The week that followed was the happiest period Gillian had ever known in her life. When Miles informed his mother and sister, with a blushing Gillian present, of their plans to wed, Lady Kathryn and Linnet were even more thrilled than Miles had predicted. Immediately they set about making plans for the wedding at Ravenwood.

She was surprised when Miles also told them of her wish to be married secretly by the Ross priest who had not signed the oath of allegiance to Henry VIII, and more surprised when Lady Kathryn made no objection.

"Whatever makes you feel as if you and my son are truly one is what you must do, my dear," Lady Kathryn said, with such a twinkle in her eye that Gillian wondered if she had, in fact, realized where her son had slept last night. What a remarkable woman!

Gillian was warmed and reassured by their total acceptance of her as Miles' future wife, and her face reflected her inner radiance. Sure of herself now that she was sure of Miles Raven's love, her step was buoyant, her laughter sparkling, her humor contagious. The joy that lit her face from within gave her an almost unearthly beauty that shone through the limpid blue eyes whenever she looked at her beloved, or thought of him. Gillian Mallory in the full bloom of love, was so infinitely desirable that Miles ached to touch her any time she was near.

Miles, who no longer needed to avoid Gillian or take refuge in businesslike formality to deny his love for her, was once again the man she had fallen in love with when she had first faced him in the convent. Even the arrival of Sir Oliver Lang's promised invitation to dine at Belford Abbey failed to make a dent in his good spirits.

Gillian was aware that he despised the man, though she did not know why, and half expected Miles to refuse to accompany the ladies. Miles, however, seeing how his mother and sister were looking forward to seeing Lang's home, insisted it would be churlish of him to refuse.

"It will be a celebration of your betrothal," Linnet said, clapping her hands. "How surprised Sir Oliver will be! I rather think he fancied our Gillian for himself, do not you, brother?"

Miles nodded, but only Gillian saw that his eyes were grim.

The dinner went well enough, with Sir Oliver playing the genial, urbane host, congratulating his "excellent friend" on his good fortune in winning Gillian. Of the three women, though, only Gillian was aware of the coldness in Miles' eyes and the tightening of his lips when he looked at Lang as they dined in the splendor of Belford Abbey.

The days were joy-filled and full of purpose, but they lived for the nights. When everyone had retired to their respective chambers, and all was quiet, Miles would come through the door that communicated between their chambers.

Gillian began to look on that door as magic, for when it opened and she saw her lover standing before her, what followed were hours of enchantment in which they experienced all the delights of passion. Miles was an imaginative lover, pleasuring her in ways she had never dreamed were possible and teaching her ways of making love that made her blush just to think of later. He could bring her to the point of climax, then delay it, teasing her by partially withdrawing, then thrusting partway into her so that her desire built in waves of ecstasy and she was about to scream when he finally ended her sweet agony.

Then, as they lay back on the pillows, spent, they would talk, sometimes for hours, telling each other stories of their childhoods, of their dreams, of their plans for the future.

Always he left her before the dawn, not wanting to cause Gillian embarrassment before his mother and her servants. He wouldn't have been at all surprised if his mother knew about his nocturnal visits to Gillian's chamber, but if that shrewd woman noted the violet shadows beneath his love's beautiful blue eyes, she said nothing, and continued to speak of how pleased she was that Gillian would soon be a Raven.

Gillian suspected Mag had guessed that Miles had become her lover. On the morning after their first night together, Gillian had not noticed the spot of blood staining the sheet until her servant remarked on it as she whisked the linen off for laundering. Gillian, aware that she was blushing, mumbled something about her flux coming early, but she imagined the sharp-eyed woman wasn't fooled, especially when she asked Mag to request a meeting with the priest hiding in Ross.

But what would she do if her monthly flux stopped, if Miles got her with child? She knew the possibility of such a thing happening increased every time he loosed his seed within her, but it didn't worry her very much. They were going to wed very soon, at least by the priest in Ross. If the babe's birth date set old women to counting on fingers back to the date of the official wedding, so what? Gillian would not have given up these nights of heaven for fear of gossip.

Elizabeth Easington had been right. She, Gillian, had a very sensual nature. Now that Miles had introduced her to the delights of physical love, she hungered for his touch, and revelled in the power of the attraction between them.

It was evening, and Miles would soon be home. He had ridden into Ross to see the priest, Father Bertimus, who had requested a meeting with Miles before he wed them on the morrow. She sat toying with her food, hoping Miles would arrive in time for dinner, for she had expected to see him by now.

None of the three women said much, for they didn't want Brunt, who had no knowledge of the priest his wife periodically slipped off to see, to overhear, but their eyes danced with secret joy.

"More wine, Lady Kathryn?"

"No thank you, my dear." Her voice changed to a whisper, though they had not seen the taciturn steward since the meal began. "I really do think 'tis not too soon to call me mother, or perhaps you would prefer the lovely French *belle-mère?*"

Gillian grinned. "I'm just a plain north-country girl—Mother."

"You're a darling, and my Miles is a lucky man," the older woman said, laying a hand affectionately on Gillian's, "but tomorrow is a big day and I think 'twould be wise for me to retire early. I imagine Miles will be along any time now, but don't stay up too late, dear. The bride shouldn't have shadows under her eyes!''

"I think I shall go up, too. I need to put just a few finishing touches on Gillian's dress," Linnet said, and departed with her mother.

Gillian was dozing on the settle before the fire an hour later when the pounding on the door startled her awake.

Who could that be? Miles wouldn't knock. "Mag?" she called, but George Brunt had already come from upstairs to answer the door.

A cool draft of air made the fire flicker even as Gillian was filled with a sense of dread. Was Miles hurt? Had he fallen from his horse or been set upon by brigands?

She heard Brunt's voice, and then the higher-pitched voice of a woman answering him. A moment later her steward showed the woman into the great hall.

"Lady Celia Pettingham," Brunt announced.

She was dressed in black velvet, and her hair, which had been shaken loose from its confinement underneath the French hood she carried, was a sable cloud that hung to her waist. A curl or two had been brought forward to dangle enticingly over the low décolletage of her gown, and its dark hue served to set off starkly the contrasting ivory fairness of the woman's complexion and the uniqueness of her lavender, almond-shaped eyes.

Gillian stood uncertainly, wondering who she was but knowing instinctively that the woman had come to destroy her.

"May I help you?"

Lady Celia Pettingham stared down her long, aristocratic nose as if from a great height, though Gillian was actually the taller woman. She studied Gillian for the space of several heartbeats, while Gillian felt herself flushing under the scrutiny.

"Yes, I certainly hope so," the woman said, casting her eyes around her as if she had just awoken in a pigsty and had no idea how she had gotten there. "I am looking for Sir Miles Raven."

"He...he isn't here at the moment, though I expect him soon," Gillian answered slowly. "May I...ask your business with him?"

Lady Celia looked amused and gave a little tinkling laugh.

"You must be Gillian Mallory, the, ah, *mistress* of the manor," she said, looking Gillian up and down. "Not here to meet me? Why, the naughty boy!" Again that tinkling laugh that made Gillian want to clench her fists. "My business with my betrothed? Why, I fear 'tis personal, Mistress Mallory, though I mean no offence."

Chapter Fourteen

"Betrothed?" Gillian heard herself say over the roaring in her ears. "Sir Miles did not m-mention that he was betrothed." *Blessed Mother, let it be a dream, and let me wake up now!*

"Ah, he is a rascal, is he not?" Lady Celia said confidingly. She plucked at a ruby pendant on a string of pearls, which was all that filled in a perilously low cut, square neckline. "But I must confess he had a reason, and I fear 'tis my fault." She rolled her eyes in a self-deprecating fashion. "We had...words...shortly before he left London. I wanted to be married sooner, so that I could be at his side to...support him in the wilds of the north, and he, the dear boy, wouldn't hear of exposing me to such hardship. He pampers me so."

Celia had come north immediately after receiving Lang's letter. In it, Lang had waxed eloquent about the toothsome former nun in whose home Miles was cozily ensconced. Ever since overhearing the conversation that told her not only of Miles's new estate, but that Miles stood high in King Henry's esteem, Celia had thought she would lure him back to her side some day—when it was convenient. Now, when life at court had become a dangerous game, it was time to come north and retake what was hers.

Gillian Mallory was nothing like the scheming, simple country wench Celia had expected, however. Celia looked more closely at the blue-eyed woman with the short blond hair who stood staring at her as if she were a ghost.

Celia had not survived court intrigue as long as she had without being perceptive. She sensed that Miles and this woman were lovers. No wonder Sir Oliver had urged her to come north, bless his crafty soul.

"There must be some mistake—"

"Yes, and I know it was mine," Lady Celia interrupted. "I should never have left things thus, but pride, you know."

Inwardly Gillian seethed with rage. 'Twas obvious that this noblewoman was one of Miles's former bedmates! How dare she pursue him here? She cut in in a voice as composed as Lady Celia's. "My lady, are you saying that you and Sir Miles are *formally* betrothed? 'Tis hardly possible, for he has asked me to marry him. We . . . we are to wed t—soon."

The court beauty standing before her was not even perturbed. Again, that tinkling laugh that set Gillian's teeth on edge. "I'm sorry, I know it truly isn't droll to you, Mistress Mallory, but I've seen this happen before. Miles is apt to say anything when he sees something—or someone—he wants. He is a courtier, you know. The end justifies the means to King Henry's new men, don't you know."

"And it doesn't bother you, this habit you claim he has?" Gillian asked. *The woman was lying. She had to be.*

Lady Celia crossed the floor to Gillian and placed a beringed hand comfortingly about her shoulder.

"Nay, for he's a man, and a man must be a man, must he not? His strayings have naught to do with the marriage we will make, a marriage based on similar family backgrounds and similar goals. I understand these things. I merely regret that he's toyed with your... affections, my dear.''

Gillian brushed the cool hand off her shoulder, causing the woman's incredible amethyst eyes to widen in surprise. She opened her mouth to tell Lady Celia Pettingham exactly what she thought of her. ''I'm not—''

''What is the meaning of this? Celia, what in the devil's name are you doing here?'' said a voice from behind Gillian.

Neither of them had heard Miles come in. He had entered via the kitchen after putting Cloud in the stable.

With a glad cry, Lady Celia hurled herself into Miles Raven's arms. ''Oh, Miles! At last!''

''Celia...'' Miles found his voice as with difficulty he disengaged the clinging woman who had buried her face against his neck. ''Why are you here? You should not have come.'' He held her at arm's length, painfully aware of Gillian staring at them, her face stricken.

''I know,'' Celia said with a sigh, ''I should have let you know I was coming. It was a dreadful journey, so do not rebuke me, dear love, for I've been fully repaid for my sins.'' She turned her back to Gillian and already seemed to have forgotten her presence. ''But I had to get away from court, darling! It's all been so horrible, with the queen being executed, and all those young men—''

''Anne Boleyn—*executed?*'' Lady Kathryn, who had suddenly appeared on the landing, said.

''Yes, Lady Kathryn. Oh, 'tis good to see you, too, madam, and you, Linnet!'' she added effusively to the girl who stood next to her mother, her night rail covered by a shawl. Then Lady Celia allowed her face to regain a somber, almost tragic expression. ''The queen was beheaded on Tower Green on May nineteenth, the day after five men accused of adultery with her were put to death—including her own brother!''

"Dear God!" gasped Lady Kathryn.

"And the king has already married Lady Jane Seymour!" added Celia. Then, starting to cry, she said, "I tell you, it's been awful, Miles, just awful! I was so frightened! Anyone who had been the queen's friend was in fear of his or her life! So you see, I had to come!"

Darling. My dear love. Gillian had not missed the endearments Celia sprinkled in the midst of her dreadful news. And Miles, his face a pale, unreadable mask, had said nothing beyond, "You should not have come."

Lady Kathryn was wringing her hands, apparently too distracted by the astonishing news from court to have noticed the pet names. Linnet, clearly ill at ease, seemed frozen in place.

Gillian felt as if her stomach had dropped to her toes. What did she care what happened to a queen in faraway London? Miles had never been free to love her, and now the woman who had a prior claim to his heart had appeared. Did she expect that Gillian would meekly surrender her bedchamber with its connecting door along with the man she loved?

"Lady Celia, I regret to say I have no guest chamber fit to accommodate you," Gillian said, and was gratified at the way the woman's head jerked around as if she had forgotten Gillian's presence.

Lady Celia's nostrils flared, and the amethyst eyes narrowed. "You would put me out on the moors at night, Mistress Mallory, with naught but my two lackeys? So much for Christian charity! Miles?" She turned to appeal to the man still standing behind Gillian.

"Mistress Mallory is right, Celia. But you need go no farther than Belford. I'm certain your old friend Sir Oliver Lang will be quite willing to take you in."

The sable-haired Celia's mouth tightened, and suddenly she was quite unlovely. She glared at Gillian, then Miles, as if contemplating what she dared say. "Very well, Miles. But I'm not certain those louts can find Belford, and I do not wish to be benighted in the hills. Please, Miles, would you be so kind as to escort us?"

"I believe the steward could—" Miles began, then stopped. He was furious with Celia for having come here and upset Gillian like this on the eve of their wedding. The gall of the woman, after the way she had once treated him! He decided it would be best to speak to Celia privately and make it crystal clear that he wanted nothing to do with her ever again.

"Never mind. I will do it," he ground out. "Just give me a few minutes to ready my horse." He would tie Cloud to the back of the conveyance and ride inside it so that he could speak to Celia, then ride back after he had rid himself of the troublesome lady at Belford.

He was aware of his mother and Linnet going up to their chamber. He turned to Gillian, speaking in low tones. "I'm sorry, love. I—I'll be late. Go on to bed, and I'll see you in the morning." He gave her a wink, trying to remind her wordlessly of how special tomorrow was, but she avoided his eyes, and when he would have raised her chin with tender fingers, she flinched away from him.

"I will see to Lady Kathryn," she said tonelessly. "She's still upset about the queen. Perhaps a hot posset..." Gillian strode away, her posture rigid.

Miles clenched his fists, now wishing he had refused and summoned the surly Brunt to escort Celia, leaving him free to be with Gillian. He needed to hold her and kiss that look of betrayal away. But it was too late now. He was aware that Celia was waiting, watching the scene avidly. She wouldn't be smiling that cat's smile when he was done talking to her.

"My dear, you must not think… I mean, you must trust Miles. I'm certain he has no feelings left for that devious baggage." Lady Kathryn said, her eyes full of dismay when Gillian came to her room with the steaming posset.

"I'm sure you're right, Lady Kathryn," Gillian murmured, not wanting to give vent to her anger. This woman, kind as she had been, must have known about the betrothal. Betrothals were nearly as binding as marriage in the church's eyes—even Henry's church, were they not? How could Lady Kathryn and Linnet have allowed her to go on believing she had a future with Miles, even if he was willing to deceive her? Her voice was brittle as thin ice. "I find I have the headache. I believe I will retire, just as Miles suggested."

Linnet, who had been sitting by the bedside, looked uneasily at her mother. "She's quite upset. Perhaps I should talk to her."

"Nay, I'm certain she needs to be alone, perhaps have a good cry. Poor girl! A bride is nervous enough even if all goes well the night before her wedding," Lady Kathryn asserted. "Let's blow out the candle, Linnet, dear. I make no doubt all will be set right in the morning."

Remembering the gliding, noiseless walk she had been taught as a Benedictine, Gillian fought the urge to run to her chamber. Once there, however, she shot the bolt, then strode to the other side of the room to lock the door that communicated with Miles's chamber.

What a fool she had been this last week, imagining that such a well-favored, powerful gentleman as Sir Miles Raven could actually love her and want to marry her! Lady Celia Pettingham was the sort of woman men like Sir Miles *married,* not an inconsequential former nun with no living family who owned a shabby little northern sheep farm. She had given herself to this darkly handsome liar, who was no doubt laughing to himself even as he stole her virginity, and was already promised to another woman!

Miles' evident distress at Celia's arrival did not sway her in her bitter judgment. Certainly Miles Raven was dismayed, the blackguard! He had planned to have her as a bed partner for a while yet. Perhaps he would have even gone through with the secret wedding, knowing he could always have it set aside by the king's powerful clerics. All the while he would keep his betrothed in the south, as ignorant of his duplicity as she, Gillian, was! A bitter laugh escaped her. Almost, she could find it in her heart to feel sorry for Lady Celia Pettingham, who must face the fact her future husband had been unfaithful to her while she was no doubt planning their nuptials!

Her face burned with anger as she thought of Lady Kathryn and Linnet witnessing her shame. They must have known that Miles was affianced! How could they smile and seem to approve his wooing her? How they must be laughing at her now, the ignorant little Northumbrian girl who had allowed herself to be seduced by their handsome son and brother with no more than vows of love and promises of marriage. How many other women had sold themselves so cheaply because of Miles Raven's honeyed tongue?

She had been so proud of her improvements at Mallory Hall, so pleased that under her care and Sir Miles's guidance, the manor was beginning to prosper and her tenants were as happy as they had been in her parents' time. Her dreams rose up to mock her now—her glorious plans to continue the running of her manor while living part of the time at Kyloe Manor as Lady Raven, with occasional trips south to visit Ravenwood and the court in the company of her husband, Sir Miles Raven!

Eyes blinded by tears, Gillian thought of what it would be like to continue to live here once Miles had married his Lady Celia. For he would marry her, she could see that. He *should* marry her. They were birds of the same feather. Miles would see it, too, once he had had the chance to be alone with Celia again.

She could imagine the pitying looks her tenants would give her once they heard the news, for she had no doubt that they had sensed her feelings for Sir Miles. She could see the disdainful sneer on Lady Celia's face if they should ever chance to meet. And Sir Miles Raven, damn his black soul to everlasting hell, would no doubt find reasons to come over to Mallory Hall, sensing that despite her anger at his duplicity, she could not so easily stop loving him!

No, she would not stay here to struggle gamely on alone, easy prey to such as Sir Miles, unless some gap-toothed genteel widower took pity on her and offered her honorable wedlock in exchange for sharing her estate! Suddenly the ownership of Mallory Hall seemed more of a burden than a privilege, and it was a burden she no longer wanted.

The Benedictine Rule had been correct when it taught that possessions corrupt the soul, and it was better in God's sight to own nothing. And the saints had been wise when they preached that the best state was the celibate one, for only grief followed when a woman allowed herself to love an earthly man. She had not known how happy she was when she had worn the Benedictine habit and had owned nothing and loved no one but God and her sisters in the religious community.

Well, she could not reenter the convent, but she did not have to remain here to be the recipient of pity and disdain.

Staring into the gathering gloom in her chamber, she decided what to do.

Gillian's chamber door remained closed that morning as Lady Kathryn and Linnet broke their fast in the great hall.

"Let your mistress sleep, Mag," Miles' mother told the housekeeper with a concerned nod of her head toward Gillian's bedchamber. "She had an upsetting evening, as I'm sure you know, and possibly did not fall asleep until late. She probably needs her rest, poor lamb."

Mag nodded, and a smile of understanding was exchanged between the two women. Lady Kathryn was a gentlewoman, but she spoke to one as if one were a human with feelings and intelligence. Mag saw where Sir Miles had gotten a great deal of his charm. Pray God it was not too late for that charm to save the love between the knight and her mistress.

Miles sat at the table, his breakfast untouched, his gaze unfocused as he rubbed his chin. It had been the middle of the night before he had arrived at Mallory Hall, emotionally drained after leaving Celia at Belford. Celia's snide, shrewish remarks had left no lasting sting, nor had the sight of her running into Sir Oliver Lang's arms crying of Miles' ill-treatment. Lang's smirking countenance had made him want to give the other knight a sound drubbing, but he had forgotten it as soon as he departed the abbey.

All the way home, he had looked forward to stepping through the door into Gillian's chamber. If she slept, he would not waken her; but if she lay wakeful, perhaps he could begin to ease her troubled heart. He just wanted to assure himself that the woman he loved was all right. But the door had been locked.

The sun was high in the sky when Mag, knowing that her mistress rarely remained abed past dawn, finally dared to check her chamber. The door swung easily inward, having been unbolted hours ago when Gillian had left the room.

Chapter Fifteen

''*Marry* her? Surely you've gone mad, Miles dear,' I told him, 'with no one to keep you company here but sheep and dull northern rustics! Sow your last wild oats if you must, have an *affaire* if you're besotted with the wench, but you can't have lost your wits enough to be serious about marrying her!' But there's no talking to him, Oliver! He's determined to go ahead and wed that little nothing, no matter that it will ruin his position with the king!''

Celia laughed mirthlessly as she spoke to Sir Oliver Lang in the luxuriously furnished parlor of the former abbot's house of Belford Hall. "He claims he *loves* her, can you believe it? 'My dear Miles,' I told him, 'the word is *lust*. 'Tis lust you feel for her, and why not? She has those huge blue eyes, those golden curls, that ripe little body—of course you lusted after her, the more so because I foolishly spurned you for a time. I have realized my foolishness, and 'tis still not too late for us to recapture the passion we feel for one another.'" She frowned, remembering how she had leaned over toward him in the swaying carriage, pulling off her French hood, loosing clouds of scented, midnight-black tresses around her shoulders.

"I confess my sins, sweetheart," she had purred as she took hold of his forearms, putting just enough pressure against his doublet that he felt her ten long nails digging in. "Forgive my earlier mistakes, love. I should have known no man could satisfy me as you do. I want you back in my bed, love, but not only that—I want to be your wife." She leaned against him, letting him feel her voluptuous breast against his arm, and raised her lips expectantly. "Kiss me, Miles," she whispered huskily. "Then take me. Right here and now. I cannot wait to be yours again."

Miles had remained motionless, staring at her with those cold, silver-blue eyes. In desperation, Celia had reached down and placed his hand on her breast. Her face burned with angry shame as she thought of how he had stiffened and withdrawn his hand.

"Don't, Celia," Miles had said firmly, and backed away until their bodies were no longer touching. "Don't do this. It will not alter matters. 'Tis not that you are not a very attractive woman, Celia. You know you are very beautiful, and you would be...an adornment to any man. We just don't suit, you and I."

"Not suit? I'm the daughter of the Marquis of Brockworth, one of the premier nobles of the realm! My lineage is impeccable, and a connection with my family could not but be advantageous to any gentleman in King Henry's court! I could have chosen considerably higher than a mere knight, you know! I could aspire to being a duchess without looking too high!"

"And mayhap you still should, Celia," Miles had answered impassively.

"It must be Gillian Mallory's helpless air that has ensnared him," Celia told her listener. "I can just hear her. 'Oh, please sir, will you help a poor, cloistered girl to learn the ways of the world?'" she mimicked in falsetto tones. "I'll vow he was most happy to show her!" All at once she realized that her voice had risen to a screech. She gave a very creditable imitation of a lady bereft of her love, and crumpled, her face bathed in tears.

"There, there, my love, do not grieve so," soothed Lang, coming to her side. He smoothed Celia's hair and offered her a lace-trimmed, perfumed handkerchief. "Have I not told you oft enough, sweetheart, how I love you, and would count it all honor to receive the smallest smile from you? Forget him, Lady Celia. Say instead that you will wed me!"

Celia felt appeased by his offer, but Lang *was* still a mere knight. She was more determined than ever to do better than that, but she leaned against Lang and sobbed the louder. "Oh, Sir Oliver! You are so good to me! Miles is such a beast!"

Miles stood looking at the empty chamber.

"Her mare is gone from the stables!" called Linnet, who had dashed outside when the discovery had been made.

"She's probably just gone to visit some of her tenants," Miles said. "Gillian was rather distressed last night."

"She had every reason to be," Lady Kathryn returned tartly. "The audacity of that Celia! Yes, that's probably what Gillian did. Never one to sit idle and stew, that girl," his mother said approvingly.

Miles sighed deeply. "I'd better go find her, and see if there's still to be a wedding today." He pictured Gillian sulking on the hills somewhere, and hoped he could be the one to make her smile again.

Mag had come up to join them. "Sir Miles, she didn't tell me or Brunt she was going anywhur t'day—'tis very unlike her." She moved into the chamber and stared at the open wardrobe. "Some of her clothes be missing! I think she's left, Sir Miles!"

"Nonsense!" he insisted. "I know she was upset, but she has a manor to run! It's more probable that she would insist that *I* leave, blackguard that I must be to her!'' He forgot he was speaking to a servant. "Likely she's just gone into Ross for the day, though I told her she should never go so far alone. She's probably venting her spleen buying supplies, rehearsing how she'll tell me what a scoundrel I am!'' He couldn't stop the cold icicles of doubt that pierced his heart, however.

She had not taken much. The fashionable gowns that Linnet had helped her make still hung there in all their velvet, silk and brocade glory, but what was missing, he saw, were the practical everyday gowns that she wore when working around the manor—the gowns that she would naturally take if she had chosen to flee.

When he got to the barn Ned was staring at the empty stall at the other end of the barn from Cloud's stall. The boy said he had found the black mare's stall empty when he had come to feed Tag just after dawn. He had assumed his mistress had gone for an early ride.

Miles was in the saddle five minutes later, galloping in the direction of the shepherd's bothy in the hills. Fortunately the weather was bright and sunny, not at all like the last time he had hurried to that spot, he thought sardonically. Perhaps she had gone to that isolated shelter to be alone, hoping she could lick her wounds and weep in uninterrupted solitude. He was comforted by the picture of himself flinging open the door, startling her in the midst of her tears, and dashing over to sweep her into his arms. He would kiss her tears away, by God!

The bothy, however, was empty, so empty he could hardly believe he and Gillian had shared a moment of such intense passion there.

She would be in Ross, buying provisions or perhaps some frippery to soothe her injured feelings, he told himself fiercely. He would come upon her on the narrow high street of the village, her arms loaded with bundles, and he would jump down from his stallion, carrying her off by force, if it was necessary, to make her listen to him. The image kept him calm enough while Cloud galloped the mile into the Northumbrian village.

The proprietors of the few establishments along the high street knew Mistress Mallory well, and liked her, for she always dealt fairly with them and paid her bills, but they had not seen her today, they told him.

Truly alarmed now, he galloped his stallion back to Mallory Hall, taking the time to stop at each of the tenant farms and the home farm, but the answer was always the same. No one had seen Gillian Mallory today.

George Brunt was crossing the yard between the barn and the kitchen entrance to the house when Miles jumped off his lathered stallion.

"Has Mistress Mallory returned?" he demanded, praying the steward would reply in the affirmative.

Brunt shook his head. "No, Sir Miles."

"Do you know anything of where she has gone?"

Lowering his head as if in regret, Brunt tried unsuccessfully to hide a smirk of triumph. "No, Sir Miles, that I don't."

"God help you if I ever find you've lied," Miles retorted coldly, raising a hand to cut off the steward's whining protestation of innocence. "Come take Cloud—see that he's walked to cool him and then rubbed down and fed. I may have to go out yet again."

Brunt glared resentfully at the tall knight's back as Raven went into the house. He was glad he had not volunteered the fact that he had awakened to the soft sound of Gillian Mallory's footsteps on the stairs just before dawn. He had heard her make her way to the kitchen, and then he had watched out the window, a few minutes later, as she rode the black mare away from the Hall, heading south.

She had been carrying a wrapped bundle that Brunt guessed consisted of clothes and the food she had just obtained, and at that point the steward had realized she was running away. The silly fool, to let a quarrel with that arrogant bastard Sir Miles cause her to leave behind her property and home! It would be too bad if he never has the chance to humble that haughty bitch in the way a man does best, but if it meant he'd once again be master of Mallory Hall, let her go, and good riddance!

Gillian reined in her mare on a sandy dune below the coastal town of Lynemouth. It should have been a magnificent sight, for the waves here crashed in unfettered by sheltering islands and bays, but she felt curiously numb.

How could she feel the beauty of the sea when her heart was dying? At least, that was how it felt to her. Surely an ache so deep and sustained meant that death was near.

It was not until this morning, when she was well away from Mallory Hall and its tenant farms, that she had given vent to the full extent of her grief. The rising sun had glistened on her flowing crystal tears. As Sultana had galloped along, she had flicked her ears at her mistress's keening wail, but the sound was soon swallowed by the wind which whistled among the heather-covered hills.

She would not need a heart, or tears, for the rest of her existence. Gillian had no idea what she meant to do. She only knew she could not stay at Mallory Hall and smile and go on with her life, pretending to be content with her sheep and with her struggle to restore the manor, while a few miles away, Lady Celia perched victoriously with her knight husband at the new Kyloe Manor.

Perhaps Miles had even fooled himself along with her. Perhaps, until Celia's coming, he had been convinced that he would turn his back on the advantageous marriage that beckoned to him with its siren song of added wealth and court advancement.

But Gillian had no doubt that by dawn's light Miles had realized he had nearly been a great fool to whistle all that down the wind for marriage to the likes of her. She was sure that on the journey over to Belford Abbey, the elegant Lady Celia of the sinuous catlike grace and incredible lavender eyes had won him back. Perhaps, comprehending that she had nearly lost him, Celia had even seduced him into making love, and Gillian was sure that her own innocent passion could not compete with Lady Celia's wiles.

She had no heart left for the struggle to make Mallory Hall prosperous again, for dealing with the surly and untrustworthy Brunt, for pretending to her tenants she was capable of being a good mistress of the manor. Though she felt a pang at leaving the dependable Mag so near her time, and the two engaging boys, not to mention Tag the lamb, she knew they would cope well enough without her. They had gotten by before she left the convent; they would doubtless continue on with their lives, no better or worse than most folk.

The fishing boat that had been coming in had been beached on the sand, and a man was clambering out, followed by a pair of dark-headed children, a boy and a girl who scampered along the edge of the water looking for treasures washed up by the tide. The fisherman, evidently their father, took a moment to watch them with an indulgent smile upon his face before turning his attention to his nets.

Gillian's heart knew a new ache as she stared at them, realizing that here was another joy she would never know—that of bearing children. She had cherished a picture in her heart of the several children she and Miles would create together—black-haired like their father, most of them, with maybe one daughter as blond as herself. She had dreamed of them all playing around her knee, one or two perhaps sitting in her lap while she taught them their letters, putting to good use the education the nuns had given her.

Of what use would her education be now? she thought bitterly. She would never know the joy of motherhood. But need that mean she could not experience the joy of having children about her? Could she not pass on the gift of learning? Perhaps, if she could not give life, somewhere there would be children she could teach.

It was the first faint glimmer of a purpose in her continued existence, and though she did not know how she would bring it about, Gillian somehow felt better. She had an aim, a goal beyond just avoiding future pain.

She would find some place in which she could be lost to sight—some place where it would be unlikely that Sir Miles Raven could ever find her.

Fool, she called herself. *'Tis unlikely he will ever look. He'll count himself lucky to have the beauteous Celia, and remember me as just one of the foolish maidens he seduced.*

Somehow she would find honest work to do, work that would take up all her waking hours so that when she lay down to rest she would be too tired to think of eyes of silver-blue and midnight-hued hair and lips that had kissed her with such consummate expertise. . . .

I will never give a man the power to hurt me again, she vowed. Surely over time it would grow easier to do without the touch of a man's hand, and his kisses, and the fever in the blood he could produce with just a look....

This vow made, she turned Sultana toward Lynemouth, intent on finding a hostelry for the night.

Chapter Sixteen

When Gillian fled Mallory Hall, she had taken with her the few shillings of ready cash that remained of Raven's rent money. A fortnight later, as she arrived at Bootham Bar, the northern gate into the city of York, she only had a few precious pennies left, and she was becoming truly anxious.

She had thought to gain employment in Newcastle, for in this bustling town on the Tyne there were many wealthy shipbuilders and merchants who had made their fortune in shipbuilding and sea coal. None of them seemed inclined to hire the slender, fair young woman who sought work managing a household or caring for their children, though several offered her less honorable positions, one even going so far as to offer to set her up in her own establishment—under his "protection," of course! She had fled the town when he seemed inclined to ignore her refusal.

She had stuck to the rural manor houses after that, but it seemed the owners of these estates also had no need of hiring yet another wandering, solitary female; many of them had already taken in displaced nuns, as well as homeless monks, and had no need for another charity case. Several eyed her beautiful black mare askance, wondering what a woman asking for employment was doing with an obviously costly piece of horseflesh. One Northumbrian squire even accused her of stealing Sultana. She had seen the covetous gleam in his eye, however, and sensing he would have no compunction about setting his mastiffs on her and stealing the mare, Gillian jumped on Sultana and galloped away.

She hated the thought, but as she traveled over the Yorkshire dales between the forbidding moors, she realized that unless she could find honest work soon, she would be forced to sell her horse just to live.

Surely somewhere in the large cathedral town of York she would find employment! Though it was not what she had had in mind, perhaps a priest serving at the minster would need a housekeeper. Then she realized it was all too likely they, too, would turn her away; clerics would not hire a young woman who was not ill-featured—unless, of course, they were not strictly celibate.

It was late afternoon when she entered the city. The guards at Bootham Bar had been kind enough to direct her to an inexpensive hostelry not far from the northern gate, where she could stable Sultana for an extra penny.

Gillian wanted to ask the innkeeper about the best place to seek employment, but after seeing the suspicious way in which his rotund wife stared at her, she did not dare. If that worthy woman knew she had but a few pennies—and a valuable horse—standing between herself and destitution, she might evict her out of fear that she would steal away without paying for her lodging.

Supper of roast capon, served in the inn's common room and washed down with watered wine, consumed another of her dwindling supply of coins. It was too late in the day to start knocking on doors looking for work, but it was a warm summer evening and she did not feel at all inclined to seek her bed yet. Her chamber was tiny and boasted only a small window; even opening that seemed to do little to dispel the close, musty atmosphere. It was likely she would be sharing her bed with another female or two, for she had not been able to afford a private chamber.

Feeling restless and ill-at-ease about her uncertain future, Gillian went for a walk.

The hostelry was but five minutes' walk from York-minster. Gillian was disappointed to discover that Vespers had just ended as she reached the magnificent cathedral, for she would have liked to attend the service. At least she could have a look now, she decided, and make it a point to come back for early Mass in the morning before her search for employment began.

Afterward, her footsteps took her farther into the ancient walled city, down St. Leonard's Street and onto the Lendal Bridge over the Ouse, the larger of the two rivers that flowed through York. She stood there, staring at the murky greenish-brown, sluggishly flowing water, wondering what the morrow would bring, when suddenly, from beyond the bridge, a screech rent the air.

On the other side of the bridge an old woman dressed in threadbare wool garments was attempting to fend off two lads who were taunting her. It seemed incredible that the poorly dressed elderly woman could have anything worth taking, but as Gillian watched she saw that they were after a small pouch she wore on a belt at her waist. The old woman was obviously determined not to give in easily, for her loud cries had alerted Gillian and she was swinging a cane with abandon, but she could not fight both of them for long. Even as Gillian watched, one of the boys seized the cane, wrenching the old woman off her feet while the second dashed in, fist clenched, to subdue the screaming old woman before seizing the pouch.

There had been something familiar about the bent posture and the woman's voice, but Gillian did not pause to analyze that. The youthful bandits would not scruple at physically harming the woman, and she could not possibly hold out alone until the watch would be summoned. The cane that the beldam had wielded lay forgotten a few feet away from where the boys now had her cornered.

Indignant that the youths would so terrorize such a poor old woman, Gillian snatched up the cane, then dashed into the fray, laying about her with the carved wooden stick and screaming louder than the old woman had.

The cane found its mark time and time again, eliciting groans and curses. Recognizing that their quarry was no longer helpless and that the combined noise was drawing onlookers, they decided to seek easier prey and fled down one of the side streets.

Gillian leaned over the crumpled figure of the old woman, reaching out her hand. The elderly lady took it with gnarled fingers, struggling to her feet.

"Are you all right, madam? Did those rascals hurt you?"

"Nay," the woman said, turning a wrinkled face toward Gillian and smiling grimly, "though I'll doubtless be sore on the morrow, at least they didn't get what they were after. Thank you for your aid, mistress. But wait . . . don't I know you, young woman?"

It was the same old lady who had held the corody at Kyloe Priory, who had left with the other nuns who intended to find another convent! As she stood gaping in amazement at the coincidence of finding the old woman in York, Elizabeth Easington spoke again.

"I have it! I never forget a face!" the old woman crowed in triumph. "Dame Ancilla, isn't it?"

"Yes, though I have returned to my name in the world, Gillian Mallory." She was suddenly alight with hope. If Mistress Easington was here...

"Is...is the rest of the community with you? Have they settled down in York?"

"Ha! Those foolish hens are scattered to the four winds! I have no idea where they are, and 'tis just as well, for none of them were capable of seeing to the welfare of a flea, let alone a poor old lady in their midst!"

It was obvious that Mistress Easington had not mellowed since leaving the convent, Gillian thought, suppressing a smile.

"But what of Mother Benigna, the prioress?" the old woman demanded. "Did you run off and leave her, young woman?" Her tone was accusing, as if it had been she who had stayed to care for the ailing prioress rather than Gillian.

Charitably, Gillian did not remind her of that fact, saying only, "The prioress died before I left Kyloe, mistress."

"Oh." Elizabeth Easington crossed herself. "She was a good woman, and very kind to me, God rest her soul—unlike many others."

It was not clear whether Mistress Easington included Gillian in that number or not. "How do you come to be here, mistress?" Gillian asked her.

Elizabeth Easington gave an ungenteel snort. "You may well ask! When it became apparent that your sisters in religion were never going to agree about anything, even so much as which way to seek a new convent, and were going to starve to death in their wandering, I demanded that they take me here, to my older sister's."

"Ah, 'tis good that you had someone to go to, after all."

"Little good it did me. I found my sister ailing, and though as you know I am in frail health myself, it was necessary for me to nurse her. Then she died in her sleep about a fortnight later, leaving me once again bereft, an old woman, not in the first flush of youth herself. I inherited a large old house and inefficient, slovenly servants who would rob me blind if I let them—'tis why I carry my money and jewels with me, you see." She patted the pouch, and now Gillian understood why she had been targeted for robbery. "My sister's daughter lives there, too—"

"Then you're not alone, after all," Gillian put in.

The old woman made a dismissive swish of her hand through the air. "Oh, but Margaret is no help, more like a hindrance. It's not enough that she's a widow with a pack of brats—I suspect she's simpleminded, too! Her children run wild all day, like the unlettered heathens they are! I can get no rest. It's too much for an old person to be saddled with, I tell you!"

How typical of the cantankerous old woman not to recognize her blessings when there were so many folk displaced and poverty-stricken. Gillian wondered why she dressed so poorly, when she apparently had ample funds to see to her comfort. Elizabeth Easington had become the neighborhood eccentric, it seemed.

The mention of the niece's noisy children, however, had given Gillian an idea.

"Mistress Easington, I was...working on a sheep farm near the convent for a time, but...that didn't work out," Gillian began, carefully filtering the truth. She didn't want to tell the nosy old harridan that she had been the mistress of a manor, for Elizabeth Easington would never understand her reasons for leaving. "What I mean to say is, I came to York to seek work. Perhaps I could come and be a companion to you, and help you in the household?"

The old woman stared at her for a long time, then cackled. "Ha! I should make you my housekeeper! That would set Cook in her place, yes, indeed! My girl, I think you're the very thing I've needed to bring those lazy wretches in line! And you can sing the Offices for me—'twould be so comforting to hear them again!"

Gillian smiled inwardly, wondering if she remembered half the Latin words anymore. Her days of singing plainsong seemed like hundreds of years ago.

"And what's more," the old woman went on, warming to the idea, "you're educated, and you can read to me of an evening! M'sister had books, but with these old eyes I can read nothing any more."

"You . . . you said your niece had children?"

"Yes, but they know well to stay out of my sight and hearing, the little wretches! Bothersome things!"

"Perhaps . . . when I'm not busy around your house, I . . . I could teach them?"

"A lot of good reading and ciphering will do that lot! Still, if you won't shirk the duties I assign you, I suppose you could teach them sometimes. It would have to be out in the stable behind the house. You won't stick to it, once you see how impossible it is, but you can worry about that later. How soon can you start?"

Gillian explained that she had paid for a bed in a hostelry.

"Nonsense, why should you sleep on a lice-ridden mattress when you can have a chamber to yourself and a mattress filled with down?"

Nothing would satisfy the old woman but going immediately to the hostelry to fetch Gillian's possessions, and the two set off immediately to retrace Gillian's steps through York.

The old woman declined Gillian's offer to ride Sultana, so courtesy forced her to lead the mare, matching her stride to Mistress Easington's slower one.

"'Tis clear you've not told me everything, girl," said Elizabeth Easington, pointing at the mare. "How does a poor displaced nun obtain a blooded horse such as that? Don't think to hoodwink me, Gillian, or whatever your name is! I won't have a thief in my house!"

Gillian sighed. She would have to tell enough of the truth to satisfy the old woman, though she would bend the facts to avoid talking about Sir Miles Raven. Her heart ached to pour her troubles out to someone, but she did not want her relationship with the tall, dark knight to be chewed on like a bone.

"I'm not a thief, I swear on the rood, madam. Sultana is mine. I told you that I was working on a sheep farm—but I did not tell you that the farm was mine. After the prioress died, I . . . was going through some of her papers, and I found out I was the only living heir to my parents' land. I bought the horse to get around on my land. I suppose 'twas vanity to buy such a fine mount, but I fell in love with her." Gillian patted her horse's sleek neck, and Sultana curvetted as if knowing she was being talked about. Gillian hoped God would forgive her for altering the facts slightly.

They walked through the deepening twilight in silence for a few moments. In houses on both sides of them, shutters were being closed and bolts shot as York prepared for the night ahead. "What did you say your name was? Mallory? Yes . . . now I remember!" the old woman put in triumphantly. "Mallory Hall, of course! Well! 'Tis more than just a sheep farm, girl—as I remember, 'tis a fine manor house with several tenant farms! And you left all that behind? Why?" Elizabeth Easington asked, incredulous.

Gillian hoped her attempt to sound pious would be convincing enough to allay the nosy woman's suspicions. "I suppose I had been a nun too long, but I . . . wasn't comfortable with owning so much, with having my tenants paying me money. I left the land to my steward and decided to resume a more humble life and work for my living...." Her voice trailed off as she studied the old woman to see if Elizabeth Easington believed her.

"Hmph! As if being the mistress of a manor isn't hard work! And it didn't bother you to keep a costly horse!" Elizabeth Easington countered shrewdly.

Gillian kept her eyes to the cobbled street beneath her shoes. "Yes, I suppose that does seem contradictory... but I love Sultana."

The old woman snorted again. "Of course you do—she's a winsome thing, but the rest is pure poppycock, girl. There's a man in this somewhere, isn't there? Aha!" she cried as Gillian looked away, biting her lip and fighting for control.

"Please, I can't speak of it—maybe later, but not now. Don't ask me to, or I can't stay with you."

"Oh, all right, stop that puddling, girl! I can't stand weepy women! Tell me or not, as you please!" the old woman said in exasperated tones. "But I knew you would tangle with a man eventually. Didn't I tell you something of the sort when we lived in the convent? I'm never wrong about these things!"

Elizabeth Easington made no more inquiries about the man she was sure Gillian had fled, however, confining herself to remembrances about Gillian's parents and convent life. In another few minutes they had come to her home, a fine half-timbered, two-story house near Micklegate Bar.

Chapter Seventeen

Two months after a distraught Miles had galloped away from Mallory Hall in search of Gillian, he cantered up the lane toward the manor house, hoping desperately he would find she had returned in his absence.

He had spent a month searching Northumberland for her, seeking her in villages and cities, farmhouses and deserted abbeys. Everywhere he went, he asked if anyone had seen a beautiful woman with blond hair, possibly riding a black mare of Arab blood, but the replies he got were always in the negative. In the rural farmhouses, he received a more pleasant reception than Gillian had sometimes been given, for no one minded speaking to a richly dressed knight proffering coins for information. On two occasions, however, he had the feeling that the person to whom he was speaking was lying, but his most charming smile and an offer of a princely reward if Gillian Mallory was produced failed to meet with success. He wondered if Gillian was in fact hiding within those farmhouses; he had glanced quickly at the windows, hoping to catch her peering out at him, but if she was there, there had been no sign.

She obviously did not want to be found, he concluded bitterly, cursing himself for the thousandth time for the mistakes he had made that had caused her to flee him in pain and anger.

He had returned to Mallory Hall just long enough to collect Lady Kathryn and Linnet so he could escort them home to Ravenwood, and they continued to make inquiries as they journeyed southward. Miles had then ridden on to Greenwich and paid his respect to King Henry privately that night, though—a signal honor.

"We have hopes she is with child already," Henry confided over an excellent supper.

"I pray it is so, Your Majesty," Miles murmured, and then talk progressed to his progress in remodeling Kyloe Priory.

"Will it be ready for the grouse hunting next fall, think you, Miles?" Henry had boomed.

"I believe so, Your Majesty, if my Scots mason continues at his present rate," Miles replied. He couldn't imagine the increasingly obese monarch striding over the moors, but perhaps he meant to remain in the hall in comfort while his gentlemen brought down the birds.

"And is there a colt coming of your splendid stallion? You promised us one, you know."

Henry on horseback was another unlikely picture. "Nay, not as yet, sire. I . . . I have not found a fit mare for him in the north," Miles said, realizing he had hardly spared a thought for the king's request for a colt from Cloud since meeting Gillian. Certainly the matter had faded into insignificance since Gillian had left him.

Henry looked disappointed, then thoughtful. "You do not seem the same, my once-roguish Raven. What troubles you?"

Miles looked up, surprised at the king's perceptiveness. "Ah, 'tis naught, sire. Perhaps a visit to Smithfield in search of a mate for Cloud on the morrow will pick up my spirits. I beg Your Majesty's pardon."

"Nay, Miles, what you need is a wife! We would have all those dear to us enjoy the same, ah, domestic felicity we have discovered. Mayhap we shall try to find you the perfect woman to take to wife, eh?"

There could be no refusal of such an offer, but Miles could hope his monarch would forget. "Sire, you are too kind."

He did not go horse buying at Smithfield; his trip into the city took him to his shipping office, where his man of business informed him of the whereabouts of his half-dozen merchantmen. Then, giving in to the irresistible pull from the north, he set out on the road again.

And now he was drawing closer to the manor house, wishing with all his heart that Gillian would open the door and come running toward him, her arms outspread, ready to forgive him for the pain he had caused her.

It was the boy, Ned, who came out the door, however, with his little brother, Harry, as grimy as ever, clutching the older child's threadbare shirt.

"Good day, sir," the boy said in greeting, taking Cloud's reins as Miles jumped down. "Please, sir, did you find Mistress Gillian?" He kept staring at Cloud's back as if hoping he had merely overlooked her.

"Nay. She has not come back here, then?" His heart sank within him as the boy shook his head solemnly.

Miles was just about to ask to speak to George Brunt when a piercing scream rent the air, coming from somewhere upstairs.

"Me mam's havin' the baby today," Ned said, the worried expression that had already creased his brow at the mention of Gillian deepening. He paused to soothe little Harry, who had begun to whimper and pull at his brother's arm when he had heard the cry. "No, Harry, we can't go bother Mam now. She's givin' us our new baby brother." Then, turning back to Miles, he allowed his fear to show. "She's been hollerin' like that since afore dawn. She will be all right, won't she?"

Miles stooped down to the boy's height. "I expect so," he said gently. "Women have babes every day, and I'm told hollering is part of it." He hoped he was not giving false reassurance. Women also frequently died in giving birth or shortly thereafter, and when he had last seen Mag Brunt a month ago, she had looked haggard and sallow-faced, for even the help of Ned and simple Jack was not enough to spare her entirely from the unrelenting demands of the house and her selfish husband. When he had asked how she was feeling after seeing her rub her back, she had admitted that her back ached unceasingly and her feet were swollen past her ankles. She had given him a grateful smile and hid the coin he gave her in her bodice.

"May I speak to your father, or is he with your mother?" Miles asked the boy, who appeared encouraged by his reassurance. From above them another pain-filled wail filled their ears.

Ned looked at him as if Miles had suggested George Brunt was on the moon. "Nay, he's not with Mam, of course. Missus Small is helping her. My father says deliverin' brats is women's work."

Of course he would, Miles thought with disgust. The only work Brunt took on eagerly was getting his poor wife with child. The delivering of babies was usually left to experienced women, but Lady Kathryn had often boasted with pride of how her husband had visited with her in her travail to give her encouragement. Miles had pictured doing so when it came time for his son to be born, his and Gillian's....

He wrenched himself back from that thought with disgust. Gillian was gone, so there would be no babes of their blood.

"I'll just go in and see her, then," he told Ned. "Would you walk Cloud down until he's cool, then put him in his stall? There's a good boy."

In the hall he found Brunt, slumped in a drunken stupor over the trestle table with a half-filled flagon of ale at his elbow.

"Wake up, Brunt," he said, poking him none too gently. He received a groan in response, and then the man stared at him with bleary, red-rimmed eyes.

"Wha' izzit? Why ye botherin' me? Me wife's havin' m' babe, I need m' rest!"

"No doubt," Miles retorted, his eyes taking in the man's dirty, grease-spotted jerkin, his nose wrinkling at Brunt's acrid body odor. He thought briefly of upending the flagon over Brunt's head to see if the cold ale would help him sober up, but decided against it, for if the man had any information to impart, he would be less likely to give it if Miles made him angry.

"Have you seen Mistress Gillian at any time while I've been away, or heard any word of her? The truth now," he warned as Brunt's glazed eyes took on a crafty light. "I'll know if you're lying."

The screams began again, louder now. Mag Brunt was evidently nearing the end of her labor.

The quantity of ale Brunt had consumed on an empty stomach made him reckless. "Lookin' for yer whore, are ye, m' fine knight? I wouldn't want to give up the delights between those legs, either! Mebbe I set her up in a cottage in Ross as my doxy, and I go and have her whenever I feel the itch! Can't get any pleasure from my worthless wife right now—"

He said no more before Miles descended on him with fists clenched and beat him senseless, knocking out two of Brunt's few blackened teeth in the process. He should have known better than to expect any help from that dirty scoundrel. Hearing the boys returning from the barn, however, he took care to rearrange Brunt's limp form on the trestle bench, cradling the man's head in his arms so that his children would not see the bruises that would surely develop right away.

"Your father's sleeping right now, for he's had too much ale," he told them matter-of-factly when Ned and Harry entered the room. "Stay well clear of him when he wakens, won't you, for he'll have a headache and be in a foul mood."

Ned and Harry nodded solemnly.

Just then Mag wailed again, and the sound was followed by a more sustained, higher-pitched cry.

"I believe that's your new baby brother," Miles told the wide-eyed children.

Sure enough, five minutes later Mistress Small came down the stairs, holding a swaddled bundle.

"Yer daughter's born, and a wee bonny thing she— Oh!" she said, seeing Miles, then the unconscious Brunt collapsed on the table.

"I'm afraid the babe's father is a little too cup-shot to care right now," Miles told her, "but these boys would love to see their new sister, wouldn't you, lads?" Taking the blanket-wrapped, murmuring newborn carefully from the surprised woman, he sat down again, beckoning the boys forward with a nod of his head.

"There, now, isn't she pretty?" he asked Ned and Harry, who looked dubiously at the red-faced baby, who had begun to whimper and struggle within her swaddling.

"I dunno, we wuz promised a brother. Me da's goin' t'be angry. He said he needed more sons, now that he owned the manor again," Ned said worriedly, then put his hand over his mouth as if he realized he had said too much.

Miles said nothing. He could imagine how triumphant and overbearing Brunt had been, thinking he would again possess Mallory Hall without interference. "Let's not give up on Mistress Gillian yet," he said. "Perhaps she'll come back soon. But surely your father won't be disappointed about such a lovely, healthy girl babe," he went on, directing Ned's attention to the squalling baby. "She can be a help to your mother, you know. You've never had a sister before, have you? They're special, just as my sister Mistress Linnet is. Look at her tiny hands, and her perfect little fingernails," he invited, peeling back the worn blanket a bit.

Ned and Harry smiled in spite of their earlier misgivings as the baby began rooting at Miles' hand after it accidentally brushed her cheek.

"I think she's ready to suckle now, sir," the farm wife said, taking the baby from him. "You didn't find Mistress Gillian, did you? We've been so worried." Miles shook his head, and she said, "I figured ye hadn't, but I had t'ask. Wull ye come and see Mag before ye go?"

He waited until Mag had finished nursing her babe for the first time and was lying in happy exhaustion next to the slumbering infant. Her neighbor had changed the linens, and all signs of the long struggle to give birth had been removed.

"Sir Miles, Mistress Small said ye wuz belowstairs. Thanks for bein' with my boys, I knew they wuz scared."

"You have a lovely daughter, Mag. Congratulations," Miles said with a smile.

"She be right bonny, ain't she?" Mag's worn face softened as she turned her head to gaze lovingly at her child. "I'd love t'name her Gillian," she went on, not seeing Miles wince at the name, "but I'm sure Brunt wouldn't hear of't. He's going to be right peeved at me for havin' a girl child, but I'll tell ye, I've alwus wanted a daughter," she confided shyly.

"You must tell him how much help she will be to you in the kitchen, and how girl children always adore their fathers," Miles said with a wry wink, hoping it would work. "Besides, he helped make her," he pointed out reasonably.

"But George says girl children are the woman's fault."

He would, of course. "I imagine he takes full credit for his sons, though," Miles replied with a grin.

Mag gave him an answering wink, then turned serious. "I hear ye haven't found Mistress Gillian."

He shook his head. "I've looked everywhere, Mag. All over Northumberland and everywhere between here and Sussex. She may not want to be found, you know." Miles' shoulders slumped. He was suddenly weary from his journey, but he did not want to sleep at Mallory Hall, for Brunt would be nasty as a bee-stung bear when he awoke.

"Don't give up, though, will ye, Sir Miles?" the worn woman on the bed pleaded, impulsively seizing Miles's hand with her free one. "I just know ye waur meant t'be together, and ye'll find her, if ye keep lookin'!"

It was more than he knew. Now that he had not found her here, he could think of nowhere else to look.

He bid farewell to Mag after saying he would continue to look for Gillian. *God forgive me for the lie*, he thought as, an hour later, he cantered away toward Kyloe, where he intended to check on Angus MacDougall and the mason's helpers and spend the night at the site of his new home before heading back to court.

"Now, let's go over your lesson for today one more time, and then you may play," Gillian told the three girls who sat at the parlor table with their quill pens and scraps of parchment.

Summer was drawing to a close. It was already September, and it was growing dark earlier in the evenings. The girls had earned time to romp in the little garden behind the half-timbered house, and she wanted to see that they got it.

"Will you play with us, Mistress Gillian?" queried Grace, the youngest of the three girls, and the twins, eight-year-old Faith and Hope, chimed in in agreement.

Gillian's acceptance had not always been so easy. Elizabeth Easington had not exaggerated much when she had called the children brats who ran wild all day. Prior to Gillian's coming, they had had little discipline, for their mother, Margaret Nutting, while not feeble-minded, seemed still stunned by her sudden widowhood three years ago and went around the house in a perpetual daze. Their great-aunt was too selfish to do more than bribe them to play outside and leave her alone.

The twins, red-haired children tall for their age, acted as one, enjoyed their freedom before Gillian's coming, and they had turned their younger sister into a willing accomplice in their mischief. They resented any curb to their wildness, and Gillian had had to struggle with all the charm and firmness at her command to subdue them long enough to make them see how interesting and rewarding learning could be.

She had had their mother's support, weak as that was, for Margaret seemed to see in Gillian a hope of civilizing her children without rousing herself from the torpor into which she had sunk. Elizabeth Easington was slower in adding her backing, resenting the time Gillian took from her to win the children's friendship and then begin to teach them, until she noticed how much quieter the household was during Gillian's lessons. Then, gradually, her objections ceased, and Gillian began to make headway with the children in teaching them their letters and ciphering.

Her duties with the old woman were not onerous, for Elizabeth Easington required little more of her than being her companion for several hours of the day. Gillian read to her from the amply-stocked library, reveling in the books that had been Elizabeth Easington's sister's pride. Sometimes she sang to her. The old woman soon ceased asking for Gillian to recite portions of the Office to her, however, when she discovered how little the young woman remembered of the plainsong chants. Occasionally she would walk with her in the ancient walled city, knowing her employer felt safer now that Gillian was there to discourage the robbery attempts of neighborhood youths.

During the early afternoon hours, however, the old woman napped, and Gillian was free to use this time as she saw fit. When the weather was fair, she took Sultana from the stable down the street and rode out of the gates onto the low moors around the city. Sometimes, during these solitary hours, she wept, and wondered why her new life, as satisfying as it was, did not keep her from waking at night, longing for the touch of the dark knight who had broken her heart.

Chapter Eighteen

Miles' future home was not yet inhabitable, and there was no question of trying to continue to rent the master chamber at Mallory Hall. He had made an open enemy of Brunt, and he didn't trust the deceitful scoundrel not to attempt treachery. He did not fear Brunt, but neither did he want to spend his days guarding his back.

He didn't even want to go to the trouble of searching for other lodgings. Perhaps by the time his house was finished, he could be happy again among the rolling Northumbrian hills, but now he was haunted by memories of Gillian. If he remained here now, he would be looking for her on the other side of every gorse-covered hill.

There seemed little else to do but return to court. Perhaps it would be diverting to watch King Henry with his new wife, and Celia trying to ensnare a noble rich and powerful enough to suit her.

Miles went directly to Whitehall. Since he had not met the queen on his previous visit, he thought it wise to seek out an audience with the royal pair. Arraying himself in a sumptuous doublet of dark gray with slashed sleeves showing the scarlet shirt below, scarlet hose, and wearing on his head a gray halo-brimmed bonnet trimmed with garnets and a feather dangling at a jaunty angle, Miles felt once more a courtier. The plain linen shirts and buff jerkin he had worn while cantering over the hills of Mallory Hall had been placed at the bottom of his chest in his apartments at the palace; they were from another time, another life.

"Ah, Miles, my boy, 'tis good to see you again. Come and meet our queen," Henry boomed as Miles straightened from his graceful bow. "Sweetheart, may I present Sir Miles Raven, a rogue if ever there was one, but a charming rogue, withal."

It was not surprising that Miles had not seen her at first. Jane Seymour was small, with pale, placid features that blended into any background, and her eyes were so docile and uninteresting that he was reminded of a sheep. What a contrast to the elegant, striking Anne Boleyn with her snapping black eyes! Evidently it was a difference Henry was seeking, for he seemed well content.

"Sir Miles, we would bid you welcome to our court and hope that your stay will be long. My husband has often spoken of you," Queen Jane said in a bland, unremarkable voice.

"I am here to serve," he said, bowing again, after giving the queen a smile. He wanted to encourage her; Jane Seymour seemed like a shy little sparrow next to her husband.

Her thin lips curved upward slightly. "Just like myself, Sir Miles. The motto I have selected is 'Bound to obey and serve.'"

How apt, he thought, though he did not say so. He wished her luck.

"You're bearing your rejection well, Miles," Henry said. "We have heard Lady Celia is looking elsewhere for a spouse. We must admit we were surprised—you made a handsome couple."

"The lady and I discovered we would not suit, Your Majesty," Miles said.

"Very wise, very wise. Never trust a black-haired witch like that. Take a lesson from us."

Miles schooled his features not to react at Henry's tactless remark in front of Anne Boleyn's successor. "I have learned many things from you, Your Majesty," he said carefully.

Later that week a jubilant Celia Pettingham returned to court with her new husband-to-be in tow. He was the Marquis of Craningbourne, a full head shorter than Celia and already paunchy in the belly. What he lacked in looks, however, he evidently made up in deep pockets, for Celia was sporting a betrothal ring made up of diamonds and sapphires.

Gleefully she presented her betrothed to Miles at a ball. Miles wondered if she had told the unprepossessing marquis about him, but that balding noble was obviously too besotted with Celia to care about her former relationship to Miles or the fact that Celia was showing him off like a trophy. Miles wished them happy with easy grace, which caused Celia to glare at him, but after that she did not approach him.

By summer's end the court was at Windsor Castle. The king and his courtiers made merry with the ladies of the court, while the queen's brothers, Edward and Thomas Seymour, jockeyed with Cromwell for power. The king went to Jane's bed almost nightly, but whether he was successful in making a son was not yet apparent.

In the fall, events took place that caused the king to forget about more trivial pleasures.

At Hexham, in Northumberland, the king's commissioners for the suppression of the monasteries were refused entry to the abbey by its twenty monks and their tenantry. Three days later, in Lincolnshire, Cromwell's tax collectors were seized and murdered by the people. Within a few days, an angry but orderly army of thirty thousand commoners was marching on Lincoln with a list of grievances to lay before the king.

The town of York was all agog with the news of the spreading northern rebellion. Gillian and Elizabeth Easington heard of it as they were leaving Mass one October morning. A crowd had gathered in the minster yard and was listening to a local yeoman list the grievances that had been sent to the king in a petition from Lincoln, where the rising now centered.

A murmur was rising in the listening audience as each item was mentioned. Gillian was reminded of the singing of the wind as it wound its way between the hills at home. The murmur became louder as each new point was read, but by the time the new taxes were announced, it had accumulated the force of a storm.

"And most importantly, we ask that most of the monasteries that you have suppressed be allowed to reopen," the young farmer said, reading from a parchment copy of the petition.

"Gillian! You could return to your convent!" Elizabeth Easington said, gripping the young woman's elbow with excitement.

"My convent no longer exists," Gillian reminded her absently, more disturbed by other points in the petition. Did King Henry really plan to do all those things? Seize the plate, jewels and other expensive ornaments of local churches for his own use, and close local churches upon which the devout populace so depended? If so, he was practically asking for a rebellion. The traditionally conservative north, still staunchly Catholic, had swallowed the king's divorce and his becoming Supreme Head of the Church, but they would not stomach much more.

Gillian had rarely seen Elizabeth Easington so animated; the raddled old cheeks were flushed with color, and there was a spring in her step as they joined the throngs of people who were leaving to go home, all excitedly discussing the petition and the rumors of the king's plans.

Gillian said nothing, still disturbed by what she had heard. All around her merchants, farmers and goodwives were saying how they would resist if the king came to York and tried to take the goods belonging to the great minster or any of the smaller churches, or tried to levy those ridiculous taxes!

"But Gillian, dear, you took sacred vows! Have you become so worldly that you would not return if you could?"

Gillian's mouth twisted wryly at the irony of it. Elizabeth Easington, who had first remarked on her sensual features and encouraged her to wed, now urged her to return to the cloister. With the old woman in the throes of this new enthusiasm, though, it was futile to point out the inconsistency of her thinking.

But Gillian did not know if she would return to convent life, even if it was available to her. Even though the life she lived now was simple and circumscribed, she did not know if she could return to one in which her every moment, every thought, was part of a set routine.

"It's that man, isn't it? That one you won't talk about! You're still longing for him to return, aren't you?"

"Nay, Mistress Easington. That's over, and I no longer think of him," she lied. "'Tis merely that I am happy in your home."

"And I have been enjoying your company, my dear. You are very dear to me, child," Elizabeth Easington said, patting her hand as they left the church precincts. "However, I should feel it my duty to God to restore one of His brides to Him, should the convents reopen."

"But, mistress, you must consider—King Henry is very much his own man, from what I have heard. Just because the commons ask for something, he need not grant it. And he may be angry that the folk of Lincoln have dared to ask."

"Tush! He must consider the will of his people!" retorted the old woman, unconvinced. "When York and the other shires join Lincoln in the rising, he will see he has been wrong and must redress our grievances or lose his crown!"

From the buzzing of the townspeople all around them, it seemed that others, also, thought returning to the realities of yesterday were just that simple. All they had to do was assure the king of their loyalty, and what they asked for would be granted.

A king who would put his wife and her alleged lovers to death in such savage fashion did not seem the sort to allow himself to be dictated to. Gillian hoped with all her heart that the revolt would not spread to other shires, and that King Henry would answer the petition with restraint and tact. But it did not seem likely.

Fear always turned to fury in Henry Tudor, and seeing that he faced a serious threat to his authority, he was in a dangerous rage. He lost no time in writing a furious answer to the petition.

"Miles! I want you to attend the Duke of Suffolk when he goes to Lincoln to suppress this damned insurrection!"

"Yes, sire."

Just then the queen entered the chamber, sweeping a deep curtsy before speaking.

"What is it, sweetheart? You look disturbed," the king said, extending his hand.

Miles breathed a sigh of relief. Jane Seymour could not have arrived at a better time. She would soften King Henry's wrath as no man could.

"I am, dear husband," Jane Seymour said after nodding to Miles. She knelt again in front of the huge man who had made her a queen. "I have heard of the petition, and think some provisions of it good. I beg you to restore the religious houses, as they ask. Can't you see, this rebellion is a judgment against you?"

Miles sucked in his breath and waited for the human volcano to erupt. Henry's third queen could not have made a remark more calculated to enrage, not soothe. No one told Henry he was wrong—safely, at least. Henry went pale, then purple. "Haven't I told you not to stick your long, aristocratic nose where it doesn't belong? Get up, madam, and remember the fate of your predecessor!"

Jane scrambled ungracefully to her feet, and giving a moan of fear, ran from the room without a backward glance.

"Women! The most stupid creatures God ever invented! God should never have given them tongues!" Henry growled, turning to Miles. "Well, don't stand there gaping, lad! Get you to the duke, and show the commons I will not be defied by them any more than by a woman!"

The rebellion fizzled and died in Lincolnshire, for the groups of rebels had sought out their local squires to lead them. These worthies were, in general, not so naive about their chances, and it was these who got word to Henry and the Duke of Suffolk that they had been coerced and did not want to lead any rebellion. The Duke of Suffolk and his army reached Lincoln in a week, and on the thirteenth of October, the reluctant gentry leaders met with the duke to discuss terms of surrender.

Miles, riding near the head of the duke's delegation, breathed a sigh of relief as the Lincolnshire gentry began to surrender their arms. Thank God for the common sense of the gentry. Perhaps now King Henry would be merciful; Miles knew that Suffolk was going to recommend that the king grant a general pardon. Perhaps Miles could return to court, where he would stop looking for a glimpse of Gillian down every unfamiliar street in Lincoln.

The popular rising was not ended so easily, however. Word came that the rebellion that had flamed so briefly in Lincolnshire had spread across the Trent into York. The very class who had supported it so lukewarmly in Lincolnshire, the gentry, were the class who were its most ardent supporters in York. The army, which was already larger than the forces of the king while in Lincolnshire, was being called the Pilgrimage of Grace. Though it bore a religious name, Miles knew Henry would see it as a massively growing monster who must be ruthlessly dismembered.

Chapter Nineteen

"Christ crucified for thy wounds wide us commons guide which pilgrims be," chanted the army of the Pilgrimage of Grace as it wound through the streets of York.

The army was headed by Robert Aske, a Yorkshire lawyer who practiced in London. He had been visiting his home and was on the way to London when he crossed the Trent into Lincolnshire and became caught up in the pilgrimage. A well-educated, articulate man, he soon found himself the Great Captain of an army some said numbered sixty thousand and which was gaining more all the time. Its members were priests, monks, nuns and their sympathizers, merchants, farmers, lawyers, physicians, journeymen, even housewives, all of whom left their homes and places of business as if nothing was more important than marching under the banner of the Five Wounds.

"Gillian! I think they're coming this way!" cried Elizabeth Easington, standing on her doorstep and listening as the singing grew louder and louder.

"So it would seem. Perhaps you'll even catch a glimpse of the famous Aske," agreed Gillian, smiling at the old woman's earnestness. Though it was good to see her elderly mistress interested in something, she was worried about her, nevertheless. A fanatical light shone in Elizabeth Easington's eyes. She saw this commoners' army as the means of saving the old ways of life, and Gillian could foresee her giving every penny she owned to the cause, leaving her family and herself destitute in her enthusiasm.

Sure enough, the procession was coming down the narrow street that led past Elizabeth Easington's house. Gillian and the old woman could see the banner of the Five Wounds waving at the head of the procession, and then a man in a purple cape riding on a white horse.

Aske took off his feather-trimmed hat to wave it at the many citizens of York who leaned out of windows to throw kisses and coins. Young lads marched immediately behind the prancing white steed, she noted, gathering up the pennies and shillings so that none were lost.

Suddenly, as the banner was passing her house, the old woman dashed out past Gillian, shouting, "Master Aske! Great captain! Come in and have a cool glass of ale! Honor my poor house, sir!"

The lawyer turned army leader smiled beneficently at the old woman whose cap had gone askew with her exertions, glanced assessingly at the house, then back at his followers. "Why not? I've a thirst, to be sure, and if this good woman would quench it, who am I to say her nay? I am but a humble follower of Christ, after all."

Gillian noted he did not worry about the thirst of all those who followed him, but they did not seem to mind. "Good pilgrims, march on," he directed them, "and recruit those who would heed the call! Wait for me in the meadow outside Monk Bar, and I will join thee anon!"

The banner was picked up, and they marched on to do their captain's bidding as Gillian led the horse away to the stable.

When she returned, she saw that Robert Aske had been seated at the head of the table and was being served ale in her mistress's best mug by a flushed Margaret Nutting, while Elizabeth Easington looked on, beaming.

"Ah, here is the young woman of whom I have told you," said the old woman as Gillian entered the hall. "Master Aske, may I present Gillian Mallory, formerly Dame Ancilla, a displaced Benedictine of Kyloe Priory in Northumbria, another whom you will aid when the cause conquers King Henry's hard, sinful heart."

Robert Aske smiled at the old woman before turning to acknowledge Gillian. "Your faith is commendable, good dame, and shall be rewarded, I vow. We pilgrims shall restore the nuns to their convents, the monks to their monasteries and the True Faith to the realm with the prayers of good folk such as you. Mistress Mallory—Dame Ancilla, that is to say—I would call you to march beneath the banner of the Five Wounds. Will you heed the call, woman?"

Gillian swallowed as everyone in the room stared at her. "Master Aske," she said at last, "I am honored that you have asked me, but I must decline for now. I have taken on the responsibility of looking after my mistress and her household."

Everyone was silent for a moment. Gillian stared at her feet, wondering if Elizabeth Easington would be angry with her, but she guessed Margaret would be relieved. The young woman had made great strides in learning to care for her children and the house, but she still seemed afraid to deal with the old woman by herself.

"I can see that my selfishness has held you back from spiritual fulfillment, dear girl," the old woman said at last. "You cannot return to your destiny while you feel duty bound to care for an old woman. I release you from your responsibility, Gillian."

All eyes were upon her again.

"No, mistress, I'm sorry, but I cannot do it." *Please, Lord, let her leave it at that.*

"Then I see I have no choice. 'Tis what I wanted to do, anyway, but my fear did not let me see it till now. I will march with you, Great Captain," the old woman announced.

Gillian looked up, straight into the entreating eyes of Margaret. Her look said, *She can't go alone, she's too frail, she'll die on the march, do something!*

As a servant, Gillian was not in a position to tell the old woman her joining this march was too impractically ridiculous to consider, and Robert Aske obviously did not have enough sense to do so, either. Nor was Margaret going to be of any help.

Gillian had to try to reason with the old woman, to keep her from doing something clearly beyond her strength.

"Madam, if it means that you will stay here, I will go," Gillian said, praying Elizabeth Easington would agree, even though joining the pilgrimage was the last thing she really wanted to do. "Your niece and her daughters need your guidance and wisdom," she added hopefully, nodding toward the wide-eyed Margaret and the three girls huddling around her.

"Nay, let me not keep her from her duty to God," Margaret asserted, a pious twist to her mouth. "I feel I have learned much of household management of late, thanks to Mistress Mallory's help. I can manage while they are gone. And if Mistress Mallory were to accompany my aunt, I would certainly be less fearful for Aunt Elizabeth's safety."

Gillian darted a glance at Margaret in time to see a sly gleam come and go with lightning speed in the other woman's eyes, and she understood her at last. Perhaps Margaret had been a timid mouse before, but now she had seen a way to free herself of her aunt's yoke and the interference of a stranger!

"Thank you for your change of heart, Gillian," Elizabeth Easington said to her. "I feel Our Lord is calling me to join the pilgrims, but I, also, would feel better for your presence. How soon would you like us to report to the pilgrim camp, Master Aske?"

"Would an hour or two be sufficient to gather what clothing and food you would wish to bring? I urge you to bring nothing else, as we may be marching long distances to meet with His Majesty King Henry."

She could refuse outright to go along with this mad plan, Gillian knew. If she did, however, she would not be welcome to remain with Margaret Nutting and her daughters, however much Faith, Hope and Grace pleaded with their mother.

Glancing at Elizabeth Easington's frail build and fanatically earnest eyes, Gillian knew she could not abandon the old woman to her foolishness. However selfish and misguided she was, Mistress Easington had taken her in and given her food, shelter and even affection. Out of common decency, she must go along to watch out for her.

Who knew? Although he seemed to her to be too caught up in the flattery of his fellow pilgrims, perhaps Robert Aske *was* capable of bringing about the changes he and many of his fellow north countrymen thought necessary. Certainly God had used the simple and pure of heart to confound the mighty over the centuries. Why, in France a simple country girl had led an army and brought about a dauphin's crowning, even though she suffered martyrdom!

"We will be there, Master Aske," Elizabeth Easington said, without so much as another glance at the bemused Gillian.

* * *

Instead of being allowed to return home now that his part in suppressing the uprising in Lincolnshire was done, Sir Miles Raven was ordered to join the king's forces at Newark. This suited him well enough, though certainly not because he shared King Henry's fury against the rebels who would restore the monasteries and other institutions that Henry and his new men had abolished.

There was a restlessness within him that would not have allowed him to play the courtier at Whitehall and Greenwich, much less to visit his brother's estate in Sussex to dandle his new nephew on his knee.

He could not forget Gillian Mallory. The luxuriously dressed, beautiful daughters of the aristocracy, both those who frequented court and those known to him in the Sussex countryside, had renewed their efforts to catch his notice. Some had wanted him as a husband, others—with husbands already—had merely been willing to console him for Celia's well-publicized rejection of him, but none of them could coax more than a sardonic smile from that handsome face. It was a smile, moreover, which did not reach the cold, blue-silver eyes. His friends found they could not even lure him over to the Southwark stews for a night of roistering.

What could have happened to Gillian? Where had she gone? The more he wondered, the less he slept at night. He thought of all the qualities that he had loved about her, but that were most apt to lead her into trouble—stubbornness, loyalty, naïveté. Even though the latter characteristic had become tempered by a growing ability to be realistic, he was still not sure she could see clearly the evil that was often disguised by a veneer of goodness in some people. And once she had committed herself to a cause or a person, she often remained loyal too long out of stubbornness.

The more he thought about it, the surer Miles became that Gillian was somehow involved with the rebellion. Displaced monks and nuns, many of whom had been hungry vagabonds since the dissolution began, had been joining the movement by the hundreds, seeing in it a chance to return to the peace of the religious life. Why not Gillian, too? In her flight from him, she had probably seen the Pilgrimage of Grace as the perfect means to return to her former way of life.

But there wasn't going to be any perfect, easy remedy to the changes the king had brought about. Henry Tudor was not going to pat the rebels kindly on the head and bid them disperse to their homes and think upon the errors of their ways. When threatened, the Tudor king reacted like a cornered bull, and God help man, woman or child who got in his way. Miles feared for the idealistic common folk who had mistakenly thought they could bend the will of an opinionated, dangerous king.

Miles was determined to find Gillian, if it was humanly possible, while he attended the king's generals who had been sent to enforce the royal will, and save her from the consequences of her actions.

One evening, he lounged about the camp fire with other knights, discussing the rebellion.

"They say the Pilgrimage of Grace has some forty to sixty thousand men, and we have only seven thousand," Sir Nicholas Hampton said in concerned tones. "The rebellion is said to be spreading all over the North—Lancashire, Furness, Cumberland, Westmorland—all have risen against the king." It was plain that the thought of an actual battle frightened him.

Miles was about to say something that would reassure the young man when a new voice spoke up from behind him.

"They are but poorly armed monks and farmers and professional men, while we are trained in arms as knights and professional soldiers. We'll run them down like the traitorous dogs they are."

Miles looked up to see Sir Oliver Lang standing behind him. His boots and cloak were dusty and his face weary.

"Oh, hullo, Raven. How *good* to see you. I've just arrived from Northumberland, having brought a levy of men to serve with me. You'll remember George Brunt, I believe," he went on, gesturing at a man in the shadows behind him, who stepped forward with a smirk. "He's one of my right-hand men—can't wait to punish the Papist rebels who would deprive us of the lands we have been granted by the king's commissioners."

"No doubt," retorted Miles, quirking a brow at Lang and then at the grinning Brunt behind him. "How very commendable." He could not think of two men he was less pleased to see, but he was damned if he would let them provoke him.

"You seem to take this very lightly, for a man who stands to lose the property in which he has invested."

"I very much doubt the old nuns of Kyloe will regroup and seize the convent," Miles drawled.

His dry tones provoked laughter around the camp fire, which caused Lang to sputter, "Perhaps not, but it seems it would be perfectly all right with you if they did, or if the monks occupied my Belford again. Such an attitude may be called treason, you know."

Miles continued to study Lang, apparently unmoved. He did not fear that any of the other men around the fire were talebearers, but Lang was capable of any treachery.

"I would think that a man who wanted to remain in good standing with his king would take care not to be careless in his political position," Lang purred, glancing about the fire to study the faces of the other men. "After all, you had taken up with a former nun, hadn't you? They are known to be among His Majesty's most seditious subjects right now, aren't they? Perhaps you planned to give Kyloe to Gillian Mallory, once the rebellion was successful, and make her its new prioress."

Miles was on his feet and drawing his sword, all in the blink of an eye. The next thing Sir Oliver Lang knew, he had a pointed tip of cold steel uncomfortably pricking his throat, and behind the blade, the icy eyes of Sir Miles Raven.

"What do you know of Gillian Mallory? Have you seen her?" demanded Miles in a voice colder than his eyes.

"I? Why, no, I haven't seen her, but I'd wager she was part of this Pilgrimage of Grace, wouldn't you? She never did find the content in your bed that she found in her prayers, did she? I heard she had fled your, ah, attentions. Where else would the slut go?"

"Draw your sword, Lang. You are about to die, and I would not have it be said that you died unarmed."

The other knights had faded back, powerless to counter the bloodlust in both men's eyes, and the first clash of drawn swords had occurred when the Earl of Shrewsbury arrived to put an end to the duel.

"Cease this fighting, gentlemen, I demand it on the instant!" the earl barked, and at his gesture two of the knights went between the straining combatants. "What means this? The enemy, gentlemen, lies beyond the Trent! Who drew their blade first? Tell me, or I'll have you all whipped like common felons!"

Lang pointed at Miles.

"My lord, he impugned the honor of a lady, one who had been dear to me," grated Miles, still glaring at Lang.

"I'm so sorry, my lord, I did not know 'twas a *lady* of whom I spoke—I thought her merely Raven's trollop!"

Miles lunged at Lang again, but this time the earl held him back. "Gentlemen! We are not here to argue about women! I will not warn you again! Miles, come to my tent—have a flagon of wine with me and cool your hot temper."

Lang and Brunt soon left the circle of men at the camp fire, for it was clear the others blamed Lang for the quarrel with Raven. The two men walked off into the shadows where the perimeter of the camp overlooked the River Trent.

"Do you really think the Mallory wench is one of the pilgrims, Sir Oliver? Do you think we'll come across her?" Brunt asked the other man.

"Yes, I wouldn't be at all surprised. You'd like to see her humbled, wouldn't you, Brunt?"

"Aye, that I would," agreed George Brunt with relish, his small piggy eyes gleaming at the thought. "She put on such airs, takin' me rightful property from me and keepin' me from disciplinin' my woman proper, like she was so high and mighty—and then she became Raven's whore, just like any woman, a bitch in heat around the right man."

"You'd like to have her, Brunt, would you not?" asked Lang silkily. "Ah, I see you would. Well, I'll let you in on a little secret. So would I. The slut refused me, too, with false protestations of wanting to continue her nunly chastity! When we find the little rebel, we shall humble her all right—first I, as the gentleman—I can see you don't like that, my good Brunt, but never fear, there will be plenty of her sweet honey left. Once you have treated her as she deserves, we'll turn her over to the king's tender mercies. You need never worry about the ownership of Mallory Hall again!"

Chapter Twenty

The next day, the pilgrims marched south to Pontefract, then on to Doncaster. The autumn weather, fortunately, remained clement, dry and not overly cold.

Gillian, mounted on Sultana, was glad she had persuaded her mistress to ride an aging gelding that had shared the barn in York with her mare. Elizabeth Easington had at first been reluctant, protesting that for such a holy cause they should walk. Gillian suspected that the real reason was that the old woman disliked horses and always had, but Gillian realized that Mistress Easington was not capable of the marching that might well be ahead of them, and remained obdurate. She had even managed to enlist the aid of Margaret, who added her insistence that the two women could not be expected to keep up with the march while carrying all the supplies they would need for their well-being. And so, muttering discontentedly all the way, Elizabeth Easington had ridden out of York rather than walked.

More and more northern lords, knights and common folk joined the pilgrimage. They now boasted Lords Scrope, Latimer, Lumley and Darcy and Sir Robert Constable among their number of mounted gentlemen.

Everyone who joined the movement was required to swear the Pilgrim's Oath. Gillian had wondered if she was signing her death warrant with those words, recited while holding one hand on the Bible, the other on a piece of the True Cross.

The York pilgrims drafted a letter to the king much like the one from Lincolnshire, but also asking that the Lady Mary, Henry's daughter by Catherine of Aragon, be restored to legitimacy, and that the spiritual authority of the Pope be restored.

Now they could only wait for the royal response, and in Gillian's case, worry. Didn't these idealists realize that declaring Lady Mary legitimate again would imply that the marriage of her mother, Catherine of Aragon, to Henry had been valid after all, a fact the Tudor king had battled for years to overturn? Did they really think the headstrong king would meekly submit to the authority of the Pope again?

Elizabeth Easington's personality had undergone a radical change. Formerly a chronic complainer and a hypochondriac, she now no longer mentioned the aches and pains that she had claimed in the convent and at home in York. Little things, such as children running through the camp yelling in their play, seemed not to bother her. She went through the long, dull days with a beatific smile, content enough to spend them with her fellow dreamers, and urged Gillian to attach herself to one of the groups of displaced nuns in the pilgrimage.

"That way, you would have a convent to go to as soon as King Henry had seen the error of his ways," she pointed out with her new optimism.

Gillian resisted her suggestion. She did not feel like a nun any more, and she did not really believe the Pilgrimage of Grace had a chance of success. She was only here to protect the old woman, to see that she kept warm and got enough to eat—a difficult task, now that more and more recruits, many of them poor, poured into the camps.

Aske accepted anyone as a pilgrim without question, pleased at the swelling support. Many of the new recruits were as dedicated to the cause as the first pilgrims, but many more, Gillian suspected, saw the pilgrimage as a chance to escape their masters and enjoy a meal without having to work for it. They looked like they would steal anything that wasn't nailed down. Therefore, while Elizabeth Easington was off singing and praying, Gillian often spent her days guarding their food and their horses, the latter tied just outside the makeshift tent she had fashioned out of a few lengths of serge cloth. After several hours, the old woman would return, and Gillian would be free to mount Sultana and go in search of firewood and food.

She had set several snares in a tangle of hedge about a half hour's ride from the campsite, and had been successful in catching several rabbits this way. Though Mistress Easington complained of eating coney so frequently, Gillian varied the method of cooking them, roasting them over the fire one day, making a stew of them with wild herbs the next, and the old woman ate what she was given.

Gillian was returning with a pair of rabbits one evening when she saw a man sitting at the camp fire with the old woman. Not another hungry beggar for dinner, she thought with uncharitable annoyance. Many of the poorer pilgrims had found Elizabeth Easington to be an easy mark, and often tried to beg a meal rather than work for their own. The old woman seemed oblivious to the fact that her young servant was working as hard as she could to provide fresh meat just for the two of them!

The man stood as she dismounted from her mare, and accompanied by the old woman, walked up to her as Gillian tethered Sultana.

"Ah, look, my dear, I've found an old friend of yours from home," announced Elizabeth Easington. "I thought you'd enjoy a familiar face from your old home."

It was George Brunt who stood by the old woman's side, grinning at her obvious discomfiture. His eyes had lost none of the furtive gleam they had always held when he looked at her; his chin bore the usual ill-shaved stubble, and his forelock, as he pulled at it with mocking respect, was just as greasy as ever. The only thing that had changed were his clothes. Though still simple of cut and style, and spotted with grease as before, she could tell that the shirt, doublet and shoes were relatively new and clean. Brunt rarely spent money on clothing for himself and his family. She wondered briefly who had provided them.

"Hullo, Mistress Mallory, 'tis good t'see ye, I vow," he said, heartily, for Elizabeth Easington's benefit. "Ye shouldn't've worried us so by disappearin' like that. Me wife has fretted so, wonderin' if ye wuz all right—"

"Hello, Brunt," she said shortly, cutting off his false effusiveness. "I'm sorry that Mag worried, but I did what I felt I had to do. She must have been delivered of the babe by now. I hope all is well?"

"'Twas a girl," he muttered. "Named her Maria, we did, being the loyal Catholics we are—" he glanced at the old woman standing beside him "—but I insisted the wee lass's middle name be Gillian, in your honor, mistress."

"How nice, a new babe," cooed the old woman, as if she had always loved children. "I wonder you could bring yourself to leave her—"

"Yes, what *are* you doing here, Brunt?" Gillian interrupted, staring him down. "I'd have thought you one who had much to lose if the abbeys were restored—surely you can't want to be the tenant of the abbot again, now that I have left Mallory Hall in your hands.''

"I'm as devout a son of the church as ye'll find,'' Brunt protested in his whining voice.

"Gillian, I've invited Master Brunt to sup with us, thinking you'd want to hear about your old home,'' Elizabeth Easington said, looking anxiously at the young woman's grimly set features.

Gillian said nothing, just stared at her former steward. She could not be pleasant to him, even for the old woman's sake. She remembered too well the image of Brunt forcing himself on his wife in the barn.

"Nay, I wouldn't dream of robbin' ye two gallant women of yer food,'' Brunt said smoothly, surrendering at last in the face of Gillian's unyielding hostility. He'd found what he came to find. He needed to remain no longer. Lang would be pleased.

Gillian lay awake long after Elizabeth Easington began to snore, thinking about her encounter with Brunt. Why was he here? Only someone who didn't know him well would believe he adhered to the pilgrimage's ideals, "One Faith, One God, One King." Brunt's only god was himself. What did he hope to gain by marching with the pilgrims and exposing himself to the risks of rebellion?

Why did she feel his presence among the pilgrims had to do specifically with her? Now, in addition to the king's wrath, she had to worry about what Brunt was up to.

The Duke of Norfolk, still hale and hearty though he was over sixty years of age, had arrived to lead the royal forces.

Miles found it a curious choice on King Henry's part, for not only was he Anne Boleyn's uncle, but the duke made no secret of his staunch Catholicism and his disdain for

Cromwell. Miles would have been less surprised to find the duke leading the Pilgrimage of Grace, even though he had profited from the dissolution of the monasteries.

Yet perhaps Henry Tudor had made a wise choice, for the old duke had been a successful general at Flodden and many other campaigns. In addition, he had a brother in the Tower, because Thomas Howard had dared to become affianced to Henry's widowed sister. So the Duke of Norfolk would be perfect to negotiate with the rebels. With his loyalty suspect and his brother at Henry's mercy, he would be on his mettle to prove himself to his royal master above all.

"I have told His Majesty that we needs must negotiate with such a large force, for we haven't near as many men as the pilgrimage has," the Duke of Norfolk announced to the officers of the king's army, and many breathed a sigh of relief. They hadn't wanted to put fellow countrymen to the sword, and many of the pilgrimage's ideals were secretly shared by them.

Miles wasn't reassured.

The duke continued. "King Henry demands mass executions, but I believe I have persuaded him to keep it to a minimum."

"A minimum? What do you consider a minimum, Your Grace?" Miles found himself asking.

The old duke bent his unblinking, lizardlike gaze at Miles. "Ah, Raven, 'tis good to see you among this company. Whose lives must be forfeit? Well, certainly those scurvy abbots and monks who have dared to defy the king's commissioners. His Majesty is adamant about that. After that, well, we shall see, sir."

So Henry would hang religious men. Somehow, Miles could not believe the Tudor king would stop there.

"We will be meeting with the rebel leaders at Doncaster on the morrow," the duke went on. "My goal is to reach an agreement with them, so that they will disperse peaceably to their homes. But if we are to save the majority of them, I must stress to you the need for maintaining silence about what has been said here."

"Worried about your little nun, aren't you?" taunted a voice pitched low enough that only Miles heard.

He turned to face the smirking countenance of Sir Oliver Lang. As usual, the knight was shadowed by George Brunt.

"I can't imagine what concern it is of yours," he said, his voice as cold as the wind that whipped through the camp this late November morning.

"Fie, so unfriendly, sir! And yet I have knowledge that might interest you, Raven."

Miles waited silently, staring at Lang, ignoring Brunt. He was damned if he would beg secrets from these scoundrels.

Lang pretended great interest in the windfall apple he was peeling with his dagger. "Brunt has returned with the rest of the spies from the camp at Doncaster. Your little nun is there, right enough."

"Gillian, at Doncaster?" Relief at knowing where she was mingled with anxiety. If she was at Doncaster, she could be caught up in any trap King Henry might decide to spring.

"Aye, she's there, and wearing a badge of the Five Wounds just like all the other rebels. Be careful, Raven. Don't let your feelings for a mere woman cost you Henry's favor. Women are a shilling a dozen."

"Be careful to mind your own affairs," Miles said coolly, then left them. He would make sure that he was one of the escort tomorrow. He would find Gillian and see her to safety if he had to drag her all the way to Sussex.

Chapter Twenty-one

The Duke of Norfolk had another reason for desiring to negotiate with the Pilgrimage of Grace rather than come to an open confrontation with them, one he did not share with any of those serving with him. That reason was the realization that not only were the royal forces outnumbered, but that a sizable portion of the men at his command, gentlemen and commons alike, had so much sympathy for the rebels' cause that he could not trust the men he had in a situation of open combat.

He had not survived through all the vicissitudes of the Tudor reign without developing skill in judging men's hearts, even when they did not wear them on their sleeves. Sir Miles Raven, for example, had not betrayed by his tone or expression that he did not approve of the prospect of executing fellow Englishmen, yet Norfolk had seen his eyes.

There were several others, however, whose eyes had gleamed at the prospect of bloodshed and the opportunity for gain through the death of "traitors." Sir Oliver Lang had been one of those, Norfolk mused. He had never liked the man, though it had little to do with the fact that he had caught him staring lustfully at his niece, Anne Boleyn.

But he didn't need to like the man to use him. He suspected he would have need of men such as Lang when the negotiating was over and the trap was ready to be sprung.

On the sixth of December, great excitement swept over the pilgrims' camp as news spread that the Duke of Norfolk, as head of the royal army, had come to hear of the requests the pilgrims would lay before the king.

"We're going to win!" the pilgrims told one another. "His Majesty the king knows he has been wrong, and he is going to listen to us, the commons, who love him and only want England's good! Why else would he have sent the mighty Duke of Norfolk to treat with us?"

It had been raining steadily since dawn, and soon the well-traveled paths between the tents became quagmires, but even the bone-chilling wetness seemed not to dampen the spirits of the pilgrims. They flocked around the tent in which their petition was being laid in front of the duke and his escort by their leaders. Naturally, there was not room for all of them to be sheltered within, but no one seemed to mind. Each wanted to be among the first to hear the good news.

Elizabeth Easington, despite Gillian's pleading to consider the weather, had insisted on joining the throng outside the tent, scoffing at her servant.

"Tut, tut, girl, you do a great deal of worrying about my age and supposed frailty, but you're the one with a head cold, aren't you?" she cackled, though her look was sympathetic as she gazed at Gillian, with her reddened eyes and nose. "Stop fussing at me and drink your posset while I'm gone, so that you can start feeling better. You don't want to miss the victory celebration!"

Hours later, she was back, reporting that the duke had retired to consider their petition. The outcome looked promising, for Norfolk had smiled and waved at the crowd, who had knelt before him as a mark of their respect for him as the king's representative.

"And there was a gentleman in the mighty duke's train seeking *you*, my girl," the old woman added, and Gillian, who had been lying on her pallet, listening drowsily to Mistress Easington's hopeful enthusiasm, suddenly sat bolt upright.

"There . . . there was?" Wild hope coursed through her, ignoring her attempts to check its course by reminding her that her love for Sir Miles Raven was a bygone thing, killed by his duplicity.

"Aye, girl. And a handsome man he was indeed, with hair as black as the devil's heart and eyes like blue sapphires. He's the one, isn't he? The one you left behind in Northumberland?"

Gillian nodded, her eyes downcast, not wanting Elizabeth Easington to see the emotions that warred within her at this moment. From the old woman's description, it could be no other man.

"I was wrong to try to maneuver you into a nunnery again," Elizabeth Easington said in her decisive way. "You were meant for this man."

"You didn't tell him I was here, did you?"

"Nay, but only because he didn't ask me directly—it would be wrong of me to lie, you know," the old woman said with a pious twist to her mouth. "The ones he happened to ask didn't know you."

Her heart actually ached, but Gillian said in a flat, expressionless tone, "I don't want to see him."

Within three days the Pilgrimage of Grace had its answer. The king, as represented by the Duke of Norfolk, had assented to hold a parliament in the north so that he could personally consider their requests, and meanwhile had issued a general pardon for all acts of rebellion committed from Doncaster northward before the seventh of December, the Eve of the Nativity of the Virgin. Robert Aske had already torn his badge of the Five Wounds from his doublet and knelt for his pardon before Norfolk. In obedience to the king, he had ordered the army to disband.

"I cannot wait to be home, Gillian!" Elizabeth Easington said excitedly, as they began to pack their belongings into the saddlebags on their mounts. "I vow, I will even be glad to see those noisy brats, my niece's daughters!"

Gillian smiled at this evidence of the profound change that had taken place in her mistress's personality but wondered how Margaret Nutting would feel about having her bossy aunt back under the roof after being her own mistress for many weeks. She herself would be glad to sleep in a real bed at night, under a roof that didn't leak, and not have to worry that they would end up with the rest of the rebels, on the gallows, accused of treason!

In spite of all the rejoicing about the camp as the pilgrims prepared to disperse to their homes, though, Gillian still felt uneasy about the pardon. It had come too easily. She could not believe that Henry Tudor was going to let everyone escape without retribution. The old woman had told her that Aske had been invited to court, to personally lay his cause before the king and celebrate the holy season with him. In his place, she would not have gone.

She would be glad to be in her mistress's home in York for another reason, also. Ever since Elizabeth Easington had told her that Sir Miles Raven had been in the camp asking about her, she had felt exposed, vulnerable, as if she might encounter him at any moment. She had not slept well at night, and when she did sleep, it was only to dream of that lean, angular face, with the midnight-hued hair falling down over his brow and the eyes of blue silver. In her dreams, she found herself falling into his arms, though she told herself by day it was over, and she would never fall for such lies again.

"I believe all is ready. Let us go home then, Mistress Easington."

"I would have you go home with *me*, Gillian," a voice behind her said.

Gillian whirled, one hand still holding Sultana's reins. Catching a familiar scent, the black mare turned her head and nickered a greeting at the man who stood before them.

"How—how did you find me?" was all she could manage to say. She paled, then flushed as her heart began to pound.

Miles Raven looked magnificently handsome, she noticed absently. He was dressed in a doublet of dark blue velvet that darkened his eyes underneath the halo-brimmed cap that he wore. Doffing his cap, he swept her a bow so low that the jaunty drooping ostrich plume on the cap brushed the ground, then smiled at her, a smile so sweet it would melt the heart of an alabaster saint.

Which she was not. She was a real woman of flesh and blood, a woman—one of many, perhaps—whom the handsome scoundrel before her had carelessly seduced and played false.

"I've been scouring the camp ever since the negotiations began," he told her. "A few of the pilgrims knew you, but couldn't tell me where you were. So at last I just looked for the horse, hoping you'd still have Sultana. Hello, girl," he said, advancing and giving the mare a pat on her sleek black neck. "I knew my time was running short, as the pilgrimage was disbanding. I was desperate to find you, Gillian. Come home with me, love."

Miles reached out and caught her trembling hands, bending the full intensity of his silver-blue gaze on her.

She struggled to free her hands under the interested scrutiny of the old woman, but he wouldn't let them go, so she gave up and let them rest there while she fought against drowning in the compelling pools of his eyes.

"Nay, I can't. I won't, Miles. I won't let you hurt me again."

"I'd rather die than harm a hair on your head," he told her, his heart in his eyes.

"This, from the man who asked me to marry him in order to have me in his bed, while another in the south was betrothed to you?"

Miles was clearly taken aback, but then the light of understanding dawned in his eyes. "Celia told you we were betrothed, didn't she, the lying jade! Marry, it's not true, I swear to you by all we both hold holy, Gillian! I don't deny I was in love with her once, when I was newly come to court and dazzled by her dark beauty, but she soon jilted this mere knight!" he said with an ironic twist to his mouth. "'Twas not till she heard I had property, and stood high in the king's favor, that she became interested in me again! Can't you see, she lied to frighten you off?" he pleaded, taking her hands in his. "I would have told you all this, but you had already gone!

"I am *free*, Gillian, free to love you, to wed you, and I would do that right speedily," he amended hastily, glancing at the old crone nearby who was listening avidly to every word. "Gillian—could we talk somewhere, alone?" he asked, after a meaningful glance at their witness.

"There is no need," she countered stiffly, "for there is nothing I would say to you that I would not say in front of Mistress Easington, who is my employer. I am not going home with you, Sir Miles. My place is with my mistress, and I am going home with her."

"You are mistress of Mallory Hall, and it needs you, as I do," he said in the mellow, deep voice which had always wrapped itself so easily around her heart.

"Nay, it is no longer mine. I have given it back to...its former owner," she said. "I can't keep taking it away from the Brunts."

"If you let George Brunt rule it, it will soon become a wasteland," he told her with brutal honesty. "Brunt came here, didn't he?"

"Yes, he did," she admitted. "He...he made me uneasy, Miles. He's up to something, isn't he?"

"Aye, if only just spying for Lang," he agreed grimly. "Either one would sell his soul to the highest bidder."

At Gillian's surprised look, he added, "Those two devils had joined forces, you see, at least for awhile. Birds of a feather," he said, dismissing them with contempt.

Gillian watched him as he finished speaking. "I must bid you good day, Sir Miles," she insisted. "We have many miles to go before we will reach my mistress's home." Carefully she did not say where that was. "Goodbye," she added with a firmness she did not feel.

"Stubborn wench," he said, but there was more admiration than irritation in his tone. "You won't get rid of me that easily, after I have searched half the kingdom for you. I will escort you to your mistress's house, then."

"Really, there is no need. The roads will be filled with pilgrims returning home."

"And with thieves who might prey on them," he argued. "My mind is made up, Gillian."

"I think it would be quite pleasant to have Sir Miles' company on the journey," Elizabeth Easington announced, throwing her support to the tall handsome knight who so obviously adored her servant. What was wrong with Gillian, that she could not see the love shining in Miles Raven's eyes, if even an old woman could see it, Elizabeth Easington fretted. As for whatever sins he may have committed, surely she should forgive him now that he had come throwing his heart at her feet?

"It is decided, then," said Miles, grinning at Gillian's discomfiture. "You will have my company, will you, nil you, all the way to—madam, where do you live?" He hoped it was the farthest reaches of Northumberland, so that he would have as long as possible to win Gillian back.

"York, Sir Miles," the old woman informed him with a smile.

It was all too close, but now that he knew where she was, there was hope. Surely she wouldn't run away now that the coldest time of the year was upon them?

"See, Your Grace, I told you Raven had a sweetheart among the rebels. Secretly, he is one of them," Lang whispered from their vantage point behind a broad-trunked oak tree.

Norfolk peered around the bole of the tree and grunted. "Perhaps, but I am not yet convinced that his feelings for the gel make him a traitor. He didn't march with the pilgrimage, after all."

"Only because he feared to lose the rich property that came to him through the dissolution of the monasteries. He owns Kyloe Priory," Lang informed him.

Which you covet, Norfolk thought. "I will keep an eye on him, Sir Oliver," he said dismissively.

Chapter Twenty-two

By the time the old woman had made all her farewells and they were on the road to York, it was nearly midday. Elizabeth Easington's old bones could not tolerate a fast pace, and so they only made it halfway home that day, stopping at a hostelry in Snaith, where Miles bespoke them two rooms with a private parlor in between.

Miles Raven had exerted the full force of his charm during the afternoon as the miles went by under their horses' hoofs. He soon had Mistress Easington smiling and chuckling as he told tales of the court and its king. He had an especially droll voice, which he assumed when imitating Henry Tudor, and a way of puffing out his cheeks so that one could easily picture the rotund, blustering giant Henry VIII had become.

Gillian felt the potent force of his magnetism as he spoke, and was aware of the looks that were meant only for her. Being around him again, listening to his voice and looking into his eyes, was like being surrounded by a wave that threatened to pull her under to the treacherous current beneath. She was determined not to surrender, and held herself stiffly on Sultana, making monosyllabic comments when they were required of her.

Although she had been out of bed and felt much better than she had a few days ago, she was acutely self-conscious about her reddened nose and the sniffles and sneezes that caused her to reach frequently for her handkerchief. She hated for him to see her like this... and was annoyed at herself for thinking that way. It did not matter how she appeared to him. As soon as he had escorted them to York she would make it clear she never wanted to see him again.

"My dear Gillian, we must see that you have a hot fire and a heated brick between the bed linens tonight," Miles observed, interrupting his own story about Henry's new queen, after she had sneezed four times in rapid succession.

"I am not your dear Gillian," she retorted, but he just continued to grin at her as if she had spoken sweetly to him. She had to fight the warm feeling his caressing voice and his concerned gaze gave her! It was surely just that it was so nice to have someone caring about her comfort once again.

"Now, Gillian, is that any way to talk to dear Sir Miles?" reproved the old woman, clucking. "In faith, it will be lovely indeed to shelter under a roof, any roof, tonight! I shall not even notice if there are fleas in the linens, I shall sleep so sound!"

The old woman continued to champion Miles' cause, even pretending great fatigue after only a few bites of the roast capon and the eel and onion pie the proprietor had brought them for supper.

"I'm going to bed, Gillian. Nay, you needn't come yet," Elizabeth Easington said when Gillian would have arisen and left the private parlor with her. "Why not catch up on old times with dear Sir Miles? You two must have much to talk about, and you don't need an old woman listening!" She ignored her servant's dismayed face, and a moment later, Gillian was alone with Miles.

"Come over in front of the fire," Miles said, gesturing to a settle.

"Nay, I'm fatigued, as well. I think I'd really better be off to bed."

"Nonsense. The old woman's right, there is much left unsaid between us. Sit down over here, Gillian. I promise I won't bite you—or do anything you would not like," he added, with a reassuring smile as she continued to hesitate.

Gillian went as if she had no will of her own, and for a few moments, as he knelt to build up the fire in front of them, she gave in to the pleasure of just watching the powerful play of muscles beneath his doublet and hose.

"Mother and Linnet will be so relieved to hear that I've found you, and that you are well—ahem, or at least relatively so," he amended as she sneezed again.

Gillian did not know what to say. "I trust all is well with them, also," she said neutrally.

"Oh, indeed, Mother is busy dandling her grandson on her knee, and Linnet still collects the hearts of the local gentry's sons, when she is not planning wondrous gowns to wear at court someday."

Conversation died again.

The fire crackled, bathing their faces with reflected heat. A log, burned through in the middle, split and shifted, sending up a shower of sparks. Gillian was aware of his eyes on her, but she continued to stare into the orange and blue flames as if mesmerized.

"What will happen to the Pilgrimage of Grace, Miles? Surely Henry Tudor will not forgive them so easily."

He noticed she said *them*, and not *us*, as if she did not count herself truly a part of the popular movement. She had gone along to help the old woman. He had hoped that was so, for it would be easier to protect her if she was not a fanatic adherent to the cause. But how much dare he tell her without committing treason? He would die gladly if it meant she was saved, but he'd be damned if he'd lay his head on the block in a vain attempt to save others who would rather be martyrs to the cause!

"I'll tell you the little I know, but you must keep it to yourself, Gillian." His troubled eyes, palest blue-silver in the firelight, locked with hers until he saw her nod in agreement.

"The king is out for blood. This uprising has frightened him badly, you know, worse than any outside threat of invasion when he declared himself supreme head of the church, for 'tis his own people who have revolted and who have reminded him they have minds of their own."

"But Aske and all the others revere the king. 'Tis his evil ministers whom they would—"

"I know," he said, raising his hand to cut her short. "But 'tis not as King Henry sees it. I think he would turn the north into one big gallows if he thought enough of his nobles would go along with it."

A small moan of fear escaped her, and she put her hand to her mouth to stifle it. Her eyes were wide and frightened and glistened with unshed tears.

"Oh, blessed saints, I should have known better than to let her go and go along with her. But Elizabeth Easington is just an old woman, Miles! Surely they wouldn't harm an old woman? She's no threat to the realm!"

"I *believe* Norfolk and the others will cause Henry to moderate his ire, Gillian, but not without a few executions to make an example. Men like Aske, Darcy, Latimer and some of the abbots and monks who have gone back to suppressed monasteries. These men know the risks they took, Gillian—"

"Some of them, perhaps, but I don't believe Robert Aske really understood what he was risking. But surely King Henry won't harm him, Miles. He's gone to London at the king's invitation, under a safe conduct! King Henry's honor would be forfeit if he betrayed that pledge!"

Miles looked away from her earnest speedwell-blue eyes.

"I hope he has not put his head into the lion's mouth by doing it, Gillian. But meanwhile, I want you safe. You cannot tell Mistress Easington all that I have said, for 'twas said in confidence to the king's officers by the Duke of Norfolk. If the old woman spread what I have told you even to a few of the pilgrims, the rumors would cause a panic. It could lead to a real insurrection, and then there would be nothing to stop Henry from doing his worst. We could all die traitors' deaths."

Miles saw that she trembled. He forced himself not to pull her into his embrace to quiet her fears; she had to know the full extent of the danger.

"I believe you, and the old woman, as well, will be all right if you go back to leading quiet, undramatic lives. Elizabeth Easington must go back to living in York and go about her daily business just as if she had never left. None of her neighbors have any grudge against her, do they?"

Gillian shook her head. "Nay, in fact many of them went along on the pilgrimage."

"They'll all be busy keeping their own heads down, then."

"And I'll be there to watch over her," she added.

It was like a gauntlet thrown down between them, and he had to pick it up. "I had hoped you would not be living in York any more, sweetheart. I can keep you safe much more surely, Gillian. I want you to marry me."

He'd said it badly. He knew it as he saw her flinch.

"Marry you? Are you asking me just so you can give me the shelter of the Raven name? Just to be safe? I assure you, sir, you owe me no such favor!" she cried, turning away so that he could not see her tears. Saints, that he still had the power to hurt her so!

"Nay, sweetheart, don't turn away from me," he pleaded, seizing her hand. " 'Twas not at all how I meant to say it. Forgive me for an overset fool stumbling over his own tongue." She remained rigidly turned away from him, though she didn't yank her hand from his grasp. Emboldened by that small sign, he reached out and gently turned her chin so that she had to look at him. "The desire to protect you, my love, is but a small part of the love I feel for you, and will always feel for you, Gillian. I want you by my side always—as my wife. If God should bless me with children I want you to be their mother."

Sweet, beautiful words—like music to her ears! But she had listened to Miles Raven's facile tongue before, and look where it had led her—down the path of heartbreak! Now she jumped up from her place on the settle, striding as far away from him as the dimensions of the room would allow before leaning against the whitewashed wall and allowing the tears to flow.

Miles followed her an instant later. "Gillian, love, what is it?" Had she met someone on the Pilgrimage? Pain stabbed him as he thought of that possibility, but he had to know. "Is there . . . someone else?"

She laughed through her tears. "Nay, you big black-avised ox, of course there is not! But Miles, you hurt me so much before . . . I don't know whether I can ever trust so much again. I never want to hurt like that again, ever!"

He pulled her stiff body against him, smothering her sobs against his doublet. "Hush, now, sweetheart. What will Mistress Easington think if she wakes to hear you weep-ing? I could never love anyone else but you, particularly not someone as vain and selfish as Lady Celia. And I'll devote my life to showing you that your trust is well-placed, darling."

She gave a big shuddering sigh against him. "I—I don't know, Miles. I must think...."

"Then come back by the fire, love," he told her, the reflected flames dancing in his dark eyes, a devilish smile playing about those well-chiseled lips. "I will help you think." His lips descended on hers, drugging and persuasive with well-remembered sweetness. She felt her will weakening, rising to merge with his.

"Nay, Miles, we must not. I must have time. I don't know how long, but I will not run into your arms as I did before, foolish maid that I was."

He longed to banish the wary doubt in her eyes. He knew he could, if she would but let him love her. The fire had died down to embers, and doubtless Mistress Easington was deep in slumber by now. He would love to lay his cloak over the rushes and pull Gillian down with him, to drown her fears in his kisses!

But perhaps she must find her own way out of the morass of doubt and hurt into which she had fallen due to Celia's plotting and her pride. He wanted her to have faith in him, but she must find it in her own way. Firmly he smothered the rising heat in his loins.

"Very well, seek your bed then, love, and on the morrow I'll take you both back to York. Christmas is coming very soon. What if I give you a fortnight or so to think, and then I come to York sometime during the twelve days of Christmas for your answer?" He saw her considering what he had said, and pressed his advantage. "Then if your answer is yes, dearest Gillian, we can make plans to take you down to Ravenwood—in time to furnish your trousseau before the wedding, of course!''

She put her hands against his chest to keep him from kissing her again. If he did, she knew there was a good chance she would weaken and beg him to make love to her now and take her with him on the morrow. "Good night, Miles," she said firmly, her eyes gleaming in the shadowy light. "Sleep well until the morning."

Chapter Twenty-three

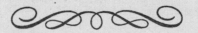

"Ladies, I must bid you farewell," Miles announced, after they had been at Elizabeth Easington's house in York for an hour.

"Why, Sir Miles, must you be off so soon? Your horse has barely had time to rest! Surely you will stay the night!"

"Nay, Mistress Easington, but I thank you for your kind invitation," he said, his eyes darting a quick glance at Gillian. She knew he would remain if she gave him the slightest encouragement, but she was determined to stick to the terms of the agreement. She could not think with him here, caressing her with his blue-silver eyes. "I think I will idle a while at court. But I will be back before Twelfth Night, Gillian."

Gillian could feel the old woman's eyes studying her speculatively, but she kept her voice steady. "Very well, Miles. Until Christmas."

"Mistress Nutting, it has been my pleasure to make your acquaintance, and that of your charming daughters," Miles said politely, bowing before he left.

Gillian saw the color quickly rise in Margaret's cheeks as she responded politely to the dark, handsome knight who had escorted her aunt and Gillian Mallory home. Gillian wondered what she thought of him; Elizabeth Easington had introduced him as "our Gillian's *friend* from Mallory Hall," with a meaningful wink, but the woman had not reacted.

Their homecoming had not been a surprise, for many of the pilgrims had returned to their homes in York before the trio had arrived, spreading the news of King Henry's seeming capitulation to the Pilgrimage of Grace. The little girls had been noisily excited to see Gillian and their grandaunt again, whooping and jumping as they ran out into the street to greet them. Their mother had followed more slowly, wiping her hands on her apron as she came. Margaret seemed to be striving to smooth over her expression. Elizabeth Easington had mellowed while she was away—perhaps she would be perceptive enough to allow Margaret to continue running the household.

It was clear that Miles had easily won the hearts of the three children. "Ah, Mistress Gillian," said Faith, one of the twins, "Sir Miles is so handsome, like a dashing *chevalier* in a romance! Are you going to wed him?"

Gillian could not stop the crimson flush that rose instantly to her cheeks, but was saved from making a reply by the timely intervention of her elderly employer, who tartly told her great-niece to cease her impertinence.

By dawn of the following day—after a near sleepless night—she knew what her answer to Miles must be. Perhaps she was a fool, but she loved Miles Raven and knew her only course was to trust in the love she believed she had seen shining from his pale blue eyes.

The two or three weeks before Miles was due to return would last forever! For a moment she pondered the possibility of hiring an escort and journeying to court on her own, but it was too impractical. She only had a few shillings saved from her meager wages, and there were many ruffians on the road in the aftermath of the pilgrimage. She knew no one she could trust. Nor did she know where the king was keeping court at this time of the year. What if she arrived at Greenwich, only to find the court was at Windsor or one of his other palaces? Even if she found Miles easily, how would it look? Nay, such behavior reminded her too closely of what Lady Celia Pettingham had done. No, she would wait patiently for his return, spending the intervening time caring for her elderly employer and her family, and planning the way in which she would tell him that she had wanted more than anything to be his bride.

Miles trotted his horse through the Holbein Gate of the palace at Whitehall, glad that soon he would be warming his chilled bones by a fire. Winter had descended in dead earnest upon the realm, and it promised to be one of intense cold. Already the Thames, by which the palace was built, was frozen solid.

Thank God Gillian was back under a roof, he thought. Leaving her, not knowing if she would decide to trust her heart and agree to be his wife when he returned, had been the hardest thing he had ever done. He had had to fight the urge to snatch her up across his saddlebow and gallop off with her to the nearest priest and forcibly marry her.

Later, passing through the Long Gallery, he was startled to encounter Lady Celia, strolling with her hand on the arm of none other than Sir Oliver Lang.

She was dressed all in black, from a black velvet French hood to black kid slippers. Only in her pale ivory complexion did she differ in coloring from the late queen, Anne Boleyn. For her to chance resembling that unfortunate woman, someone important to her must have died. He bowed low in greeting.

"Lady Celia, I see you wear mourning," he said carefully. "I pray 'tis not for your father, the marquis?"

"Nay," Celia said, her mouth looking pinched, her eyes lackluster. "'Tis for dear Reginald, unfortunately."

For a moment Miles was blank. Reginald? Then he remembered the fat, balding marquis that Celia had been sporting like a trophy on her arm only weeks ago.

"Craningbourne, her betrothed," Lang snarled.

He ignored Lang. "I'm truly sorry to hear such tragic news. You seemed so happy."

"I was," she sniffed, her eyes glistening in response to his sympathy. "He was carried off by an ague suffered when he went to help suppress the rebels at Lincoln."

"Yes ... *Some* of His Majesty's men died serving him, not sniffing around rebel skirts," said Lang, determined not to be disregarded.

Miles's eyes, which had been full of genuine compassion for Celia at her loss, were cold as he flicked them over Lang. "Celia, if there's anything I can do, please—"

"I shall be at hand to comfort the lady," Lang announced, stepping forward as if to interpose himself between Celia and Raven.

With the death of the marquis, Lang obviously found reason to hope that the wealthy and beautiful Lady Celia Pettingham might look to him. "Very well," murmured Miles, inwardly relieved. "Your servant, Lady Celia."

Celia watched him as he made his way down the gallery from them, waiting until Miles was out of earshot before asking about the accusation Lang had made about Raven's conduct during the campaign.

"Sweetheart, you aren't... That is, you don't cherish any *fondness* for Raven any longer, do you?"

"Nay." She shook her head emphatically, her dark gaze bright with the malice she felt constantly now that fate had deprived her of Reginald, the Marquis of Craningbourne. He had been rich as Croesus, and now a nephew, not she, would enjoy his wealth.

"Well, then, I have found the means to revenge you against Miles, to bring him low."

They didn't begin their campaign at once. But after Miles left court, just before it removed downriver to Greenwich to celebrate the twelve days of Christmas with the king's honored guest, the former rebel Robert Aske, they began to make pointed remarks about Sir Miles Raven, one of King Henry's trusted knights, who loved a traitor to the realm.

It was Christmas Eve in York. The children, Faith, Hope and Grace, could barely contain their excitement as they watched Gillian take the mince pies from the oven. Each pie was shaped in a rectangle to symbolize the manger, and was adorned with a little bit of pastry shaped like a baby to represent the Baby Jesus.

"Will you make a dumb cake, Mistress Gillian?" asked Hope, merriment dancing in her eyes.

"What's that?" Gillian said suspiciously. She was not sure their mother would approve of this conversation, and was still fighting the giggle that threatened to break free.

"Well, you make a little cake all by yourself, without saying a word, and carry it to the pantry to cool," Hope said, full of importance. "There you mark it with your initials. At midnight, the man you will marry in the future steals in and marks *his* initials in it. That's how you know who will be your husband."

"Ah, how interesting," was all Gillian could say. She hadn't discussed her decision to marry Miles with the rest of the household, but she was sure it was obvious to every-

one from her cheerfulness and the little carols she found
herself humming.

"She doesn't need to make a cake, silly," Faith said.
"Mistress Gillian already knows she's going to marry Sir
Miles!"

"Girls! I'm certain Mistress Gillian is tired of your impertinence!" Their mother, entering the kitchen, reproved
them sternly, ignoring Gillian's gesture indicating she did
not mind. Margaret had evidently been standing just outside the room and had heard much, if not all, of the conversation. "Perhaps you had better go practice your
stitchery and leave Mistress Gillian to her work. Sew well,
or you'll not get to see the play when the mummers come!"

The girls scrambled for their room. No one wanted to
miss the traditional visit by the players, who were men of
the neighborhood, or the wassail that would be served afterward.

Gillian sighed as Margaret followed to supervise her
daughters' work. She wished the children had not been sent
away. Remembering that only last year she had passed the
Holy Season in much more solemn observance in the convent, Gillian loved the legends they had been reciting for
her. Some of them were barely remembered from her own
childhood at Mallory Hall, such as the fable that all the
animals could speak at midnight, when Christmas began.
Others she had not heard before, such as the fable that evil
spirits temporarily lose their power at midnight.

Truly she had not minded the children's teasing. They
were excited, but they mirrored the giddy tumult within her
own breast at the thought of Miles' coming. She still did not
know when he would arrive. He had promised to come before Twelfth Night, but she didn't know when....

* * *

Elizabeth Easington, her niece and grand-nieces, as well as Gillian and several of the neighbors, were seated in the hall when the masked mummers, led by Father Christmas, made their silent entrance, assembling in front of the hearth.

Mummers were never women, Gillian had been told. The men of the troupe had been practicing their roles since All-hallows Eve. Many of the parts were hereditary, having been played by each man's father before him, and his grandfather before that.

The firelight illumined the players in their traditional costumes—the charlatan-physician, the lawyer, the valiant soldier, Rumour, St. George, who was the hero, and lastly the evil Turkish knight.

The latter was the tallest of the troupe. Gillian found herself staring at the masked figure, comparing his build to that of Miles Raven. Silly wench! she told herself. You're so eager to see your love that you perceive him in every well-formed Yorkshireman!

"I don't recognize that one," whispered Margaret to her aunt.

"Shh, you're not supposed to," Elizabeth hissed.

The play began. Gillian became caught up in the familiar plot, narrated by Father Christmas, in which the heroic St. George is confronted by the villainous Turkish knight, and a fight to the death ensues. Soon the air was filled with the clanging sounds of the mock battle.

After a moment or two, St. George, of course, was victorious, and the Turkish knight fell, slain with a realistic groan that brought squeals from the children. The saintly hero then suffered pangs of remorse at having killed the Turkish knight, and in distress summoned the other characters, none of whom was able to help the matter, though they gave long comical speeches to explain why. St. George moaned sadly, and everyone chuckled.

At last the physician, with his magical elixir, was summoned, and said in stentorian tones, "Take a little of this flip-flop, and pour it down thy tip-top."

Everyone held their breath, waiting for the Turk to revive after quaffing the miracle potion. But here the Turkish knight departed from the usual script. "But e'en St. George cannot help me this night. I must call upon the fairest maiden, with all her might!"

The prone figured raised up on one elbow, the other hand pointing unerringly in Gillian's direction!

"'Tis thee alone, damsel fair, of rosy cheek and golden hair!"

His voice was muffled behind the mask, but nevertheless Gillian thought that she recognized it, and it thrilled her soul.

The "dead" Turkish knight beckoned to her. Gillian looked about her, seeing that the rest of the audience was mystified about this change in the usual play. Clearly, however, they were willing to play along, and urged "the damsel fair" to go up and save the Turk.

Gillian arose on shaky legs and made her way to the physician, who proffered his elixir.

The Turkish knight waited until she had knelt before him and offered the cup before removing his mask and downing the potion in one triumphant gulp.

Gillian gave a shriek of joy as the revived Turkish knight sprang to his feet, sweeping her up in an enthusiastic embrace. 'Twas Miles!

Chapter Twenty-four

"Miles! But how—"

Miles interrupted by kissing her until she was breathless. He seemed oblivious of the interested onlookers, who at last began to applaud as if they didn't mind the untraditional ending to the play. It was several moments before he lifted his mouth from hers.

"The man who usually plays the Turkish knight was well-paid to allow me to take his place," he explained, "so that I could surprise you."

"You certainly did that!"

Behind them, the bowl of steaming wassail had been brought in and cups were being dipped so that all could partake of the spicy beverage. A toast was offered to the lovers, who smiled and blushed before lifting the cups that had been pressed into their hands. Then the toasts came flying thick and fast. "To York, long may it prosper." "To the Pilgrimage of Grace." "To Aske and Lord Darcy." "To the king's health, and the hope of a royal heir in the New Year," and so forth.

While everyone was distracted by the toasts, Miles pulled Gillian into the parlor. It was lit by a single thick candle.

"'Tis quiet in here, at least. I needed to talk to you, wench," he said with a grin, sitting down on a chair with a carved wooden back and pulling her onto his lap. "Now, then—dare I assume from your enthusiastic welcome that you have decided to trust me with your love, dreadful rascal as I am, and agree to my proposal of marriage?"

There was no question of continued coyness, of making him plead. She would never worry again about his fidelity. His love shone in his eyes.

"Yes," she said, allowing him to see the full measure of her devotion in her tender smile as she lowered her lips to his.

"Shall we leave for Sussex, then, the day after tomorrow, my love?" he asked her, moments later.

She nodded. "But I have nothing to wear, Miles. When I left Mallory Hall, I took none of the lovely gowns your sister had helped me sew."

"Linnet is even now stitching your wedding gown," Miles told her, "for she was confident that you would say yes—more confident than I, I must admit, until I kissed you.... Ah, love, you'll make such a beauteous bride."

He pulled her close again, sweeping off the little cap she wore and murmuring over the golden glory of her hair, which now curled over her shoulders. His lips left hers and went on an exploration of the curves of her neck, while his hand cupped and massaged a full breast, stroking it until the nipple hardened and her body ached with desire for him.

"Ah, Miles, I love you so! And I want you," she murmured boldly. They had left the door ajar, and a sliver of light extended into the room. The sounds of the revelers in the hall were faint and diffused.

"Will you come to me tonight, Gillian?" Miles asked her in a husky whisper. He felt her nod. "Would that I could take you now..."

Suddenly the door swung fully open and there was more light in the room. "Oh, there you are, Gillian," said Margaret briskly, and without apology for interrupting the lovers' privacy. "My aunt needs you to assist her to bed— you are still in her employ, are you not, at least for the time being? Then the children must be gotten off to their beds, and there are guests in the hall to be seen to. I cannot do it all myself, you know."

Embarrassed, Gillian had scrambled off Miles's lap before Margaret had finished her orders, but the woman departed, waving a hand as if she did not want to hear any apology.

"Jealous bitch," Miles growled. "Give her no heed, love, you'll soon be gone from here."

Her resentment at the woman had flared and died just as quickly. "Nay, perhaps I'd best do as she says, Miles. I'd not make a scene during the celebration, not when Mistress Easington has been so good to me. Don't judge Mistress Nutting too harshly, Miles. It can't have been easy for her, losing her husband when her children were so young and having her mother die and leave the house to her aunt instead of to her."

"It certainly seems to have soured her temper! But never mind, love. Put this on before you go to do her bidding."

Reaching inside his doublet, he pulled out a small leather pouch and extracted something. In a moment it was shining on her finger, a gold ring with a crest on which a raven clutched a large sapphire in its claws. "Consider yourself betrothed, Gillian Mallory. Now be off with you, so that you can return to me sooner," he commanded her mock sternly, giving her a loving look as he went to join the revelers.

"I'm sorry Margaret meddled in your time with Miles," Elizabeth Easington apologized when Gillian had accompanied her to her bedchamber, though Gillian had not complained. "I told her to leave you two alone, for 'twas lovely to see you happy at last, and I needed no help to my bed!"

"I don't mind, truly, Mistress Easington," Gillian murmured, knowing she would be able to steal away to Miles later.

"You're too kind, my darling girl, and Margaret is a spiteful fool," the old woman retorted tartly, softening the remark by caressing her cheek. "I shall miss you when you go off with your Miles, do you know that? But I'm glad for you, for he'll be good to you, I know."

"We shall visit you often, Mistress Easington, and perhaps you could come up to Mallory Hall, and Kyloe Manor when 'tis finished."

"Northumbria is too far for these old bones to travel anymore, Gillian. After the Pilgrimage of Grace, I am done with bouncing about over rough roads."

Faith, Hope and Grace were not too difficult to cajole into their beds, though the great church bells of York began to peal, announcing midnight, as Gillian tucked them in.

"The devil's knell!" the twins chorused. "Christ is born, the devil is dead!"

"'Tis Christmas! 'Tis Christmas!" shrieked little Grace. Clearly, it would be some time before the children fell asleep.

Downstairs, the party was still going on, for Margaret had kept the wassail bowl full, and the mummers and other neighbors seemed loath to depart while the intoxicating beverage was still plentiful. Miles was still present, but soon left for his pallet in the parlor, yawning hugely and protesting that his journey had left him monstrously fatigued.

If he hoped the guests would get the hint that it was time to leave, he was doomed to disappointment, for it was over an hour before the last of them departed for their own houses and beds. Then the candles lighting the hall had to be doused, the fire banked and the door locked before Gillian could seek her own bed.

An hour later, Gillian was tiptoeing down the dark hall toward the stairs when the door to the girls' chamber suddenly opened.

Margaret, clutching a flickering stub of a candle, jumped back in surprise.

"Gillian! What are you doing, wandering around in the middle of the night in the dark?"

Gillian was glad the shadows hid her blush, though she wanted to retort that it was none of Margaret's affair.

"Ah, I see—you must have heard poor Grace's wailing as I did, and come to aid her. She has a stomachache, poor dear!" the woman said, though her eyes told a different story; the woman knew very well where Gillian had been going, and she was determined to foil her out of pure spite, if she could. "You're so good, Gillian, dear! I was just going for a cup of chamomile to soothe her pain, but she was distressed that I had to leave her and kept calling for you! I was just coming to summon you, actually!"

And so it was that Miles and Gillian were forced to spend the night in separate chambers, Gillian on a hard chair in the nursery, Miles on his pallet in the parlor, each wishing in vain that they were together.

The next thing Gillian knew, beams of morning sunlight were streaming through the eaves window, and Elizabeth Easington was shaking her awake on her chair.

"You poor girl! Up all night with my overcoddled grandniece, were you? She's right as rain this morning, but you look like death! No Christmas morn church service for

you, my girl! 'Tis to bed you're going, and don't worry
about the rest of us!'' the old woman insisted over Gillian's drowsy protests. "All three girls are dressed and ready
to go, and without waking you, you were that tired! Nay,
I'm sure you're sickening for something, you look so pale!
I'd best have Sir Miles stay to see to you, lest you need
aught, for we'll be gone three hours at least, knowing how
the priest loves to give long sermons about Christ's birth!''

The twinkle in the old woman's eyes was unmistakable.
God bless the woman, she had figured out what happened
last night and was determined to give the two lovers some
time alone together!

She had time to get to her own chamber and make her
hasty ablutions before she heard the front door close behind them, and then she heard Miles' tread on the stair.

"We must remember to appoint that good woman god-
mother to our first child,'' Miles said as he came into the
small chamber at the back of the house.

Gillian giggled. "Who may make his appearance just
nine months from this morn, if you're not careful.'' She
drank in the sight of him in the doorway, freshly shaven,
clad in a pristine white shirt open at the neck, showing a few
curling black hairs, and dark hose that hugged the sinewy
curves of his powerful thighs. He smelled of soap and
Hungary water.

"Who wants to be careful after waiting this long? I'd re-
joice to see your belly swelling with my babe, love, and let
the gossips wear out their fingers counting the months and
weeks!''

She held out her arms to him.

Her linen shift did not survive for more than a few moments after Miles joined her on the bed; the lovers were too
hungry to pause while each pulled off garments, and they
tore at each other's clothing with almost frantic need.

After her near-sleepless night, Gillian was astonished at the bolt of energy that shot through her when Miles first touched her. She went wild at the first moment they lay stretched out, touching skin to skin down their entire straining lengths.

Miles had thought there would need to be a period of slow, gentle exploration after so long a time apart, of re-learning each other's needs and delights, but he was wrong. The long deprivation had raised their desire to a fever pitch, and neither had time for gentleness or care. Their mating was almost savage, but utterly satisfying for both.

Their second lovemaking, amazingly soon afterward, was more slow-paced, and contained the joys they had not paused for in that first frantic coming together, soft strok-ing, sweet, drugging kisses that deepened with infinite lei-sureliness, endearments that warmed the heart and, becoming more earthy, set the blood of each on fire.

Limply replete with satisfaction, Gillian went to sleep with Miles curled up against her. Her last drowsy thought was a hope that when Elizabeth Easington and her family returned, they would not find them thus entwined.

Gillian awakened at midafternoon, alone in her bed, feeling refreshed and deliciously happy. The entire house-hold made merry at supper that night, appointing Miles the Lord of Misrule, a role he played with mischievous perfec-tion, declaring Elizabeth Easington the Queen of Love and Beauty, at which the delighted old lady beamed and pinched his cheek lovingly. He ordered Faith, Hope and Grace to wash the dishes, but so winningly did he ask them that they did so with chattering eagerness. Margaret was commanded to sing a love song to the assembled house-hold, and she did so in a reedy, quavering voice, but so fulsome were his compliments afterward that she quite forgot to glare at him. For Gillian he reserved the penance—for sleeping the day away, he said with a twinkle in his silver-blue eyes—of kissing the Lord of Misrule under the mistletoe hung from the doorway. She emerged pink-cheeked and glowing from his embrace under the eyes of the other women.

By the time the meal was over, it had begun to snow, tentatively at first, and then the wind began to howl through the streets of York as the flakes began to fall so fast it seemed that one corner of a giant sheet had been let loose in the heavens, and the snow reserved for the rest of the winter was now descending on Yorkshire.

The next morning, it was clear that there could be no question of traveling that day, and the following days only brought more snow, trapping Miles and Gillian in York.

They were determined not to mind. Miles and Gillian celebrated the Twelve Days of Christmas as only those caught up in the glow of love can do, knowing that as soon as the roads were passable they would leave and go to Ravenwood to celebrate their wedding with Miles' family. Each night, Miles managed to steal into her bedchamber after the household was asleep, making love to her with tender fierceness in the dark hours. Gillian hated the necessity of his leaving her warm bed afterward, but each knew they could hardly sleep together openly under the circumstances. Elizabeth Easington had been wonderfully indulgent, but it was obvious from Margaret's pinched mouth and baleful stare that she resented their contentment. Ah, well, soon they would be away from York and the need for subterfuge over.

Chapter Twenty-five

They were to leave as soon as Gillian finished making her farewells. Yesterday had been Twelfth Night, as the Feast of the Epiphany had come to be called, and during the previous evening the household had enjoyed Twelfth Night cake and the gift giving that hearkened back to the gifts the three wise men had brought the infant Jesus. Miles had given Gillian a golden pendant with the same raven image as on her betrothal ring. Gillian had given him a linen shirt she had made, with blackwork stitched around the collar and cuffs.

She had given Elizabeth Easington a warm woolen shawl, and the three children handstitched caps made out of some scraps of velvet, plus sticks of candy purchased in a shop near Micklegate Bar. She had sewn an embroidered covering for Margaret's prayer book, and the woman had allowed herself to appear pleased by the gift. Her mistress had given her a present—"for your wedding night, my dear"—a night rail of cutwork linen so gossamer fine that it brought a blush to Gillian's cheeks, just thinking about wearing it for Miles.

"Are you about ready to leave, Gillian, love?" Miles called up the stairs as the sun rose over the walls of York.

"I'll just be a minute—"

Her voice was interrupted by a loud, insistent knocking at the front door.

There were two men dressed in royal livery, their green tabards bearing the Tudor rose, the royal insignia.

"Sir Miles Raven? We are sent to summon you immediately to court."

He had not been allowed to take Gillian with him, though he had explained that they were to be married soon. Nay, His Majesty's need of Sir Miles was urgent and he had best fetch his bride from York later.

An hour after arriving at Greenwich, he was arrested by the royal guard "for daring to contract a marriage alliance without consulting His Majesty King Henry VIII, with a suspected rebel and traitor to the crown."

Within hours he had been taken five miles up the Thames to the Tower, where he was lodged without ceremony in a cell with few comforts except a bed and a table. What money he had carried with him had been taken by the constable—"for your meals, sir, as I'm sure ye won't be wanting the common fare," he had been told, though Miles had assured him he would rather eat humble food if he could only have the means to send a message or two. No trial was scheduled at present.

It appeared that Henry wished him to be held incommunicado. Would Gillian think he had abandoned her yet again, and give in to bitterness and despair?

How had Henry even caught wind of his plan to marry Gillian Mallory? Before Miles had returned to York, he had not been certain she would accept him! Suddenly he remembered his encounter with Celia and Lang at Whitehall. Lang must have told Henry not only of Miles' intention to wed, but of the fact that Miles' beloved had been in the Pilgrimage of Grace. Damn his black soul!

But why was the Tudor king interested in the marital alliance of a mere knight with a gentlewoman who had played a negligible part in the Pilgrimage of Grace? Had Lang embroidered the facts so greatly that Gillian seemed to have taken more responsibility in the rebellion than she had?

And how had Henry known where to find him? Had he tricked Thomas into giving the information? He pondered these questions as he stared bleakly out onto Tower Green from the small window that looked out of the Beauchamp Tower, in which he was lodged.

There, on the stretch of green grass below, Anne Boleyn had laid her slender neck across the block before the Calais swordsman who had beheaded her. By the saints, was Henry that offended at not being consulted by Miles about his marital plans, or did he see his subject's love for Gillian as so treasonous that he would require the ultimate penalty? Was Gillian in danger, as well? The thought made him pound his fists against the stone until they were aching and raw, but there was nothing he could do, except curse Henry Tudor in his heart.

His jailer was impervious to flattery and charm, Miles found out as the days went by, and since he held Miles's money, Miles had nothing to bargain with. But then news came from the north that chilled his very soul with its implications.

Aske had returned to Yorkshire, full of good cheer after being subjected to the full force of Henry's charismatic personality, when a revolt broke out in the East Riding. It was led by one Sir Frances Bigod, an anti-Papist knight who had not been one of the Pilgrims of Grace, and who urged the common people not to believe the promises of Henry Tudor brought by Robert Aske.

Alarmed at the very real possibility that this new rebellion would nullify the royal pardon, Aske and Lord Darcy immediately wrote to the king. They had taken no part in Bigod's plot to seize Hull, they said, and asked Henry to send Norfolk with Aske to York to calm the anxious citizens there.

Norfolk went as requested, but not in the spirit of a peacemaker. He marched with the king's banner before him, which meant he had the power to hang rebels without a trial, and he lost no time in doing so. Rotting bodies hanging in chains upon the gallows became a frequent, horrifying sight. It seemed that soon the king's officers must run out of chains with which to hang the condemned and be forced to fall back on ropes.

Gillian had been too preoccupied with wondering why Miles had been summoned away from her to pay much attention when Robert Aske returned to York.

Though many of York's citizens looked suspiciously at the red satin jacket the king had given Aske, and saw him now as Henry Tudor's creature, others such as Elizabeth Easington were encouraged by his report. Excitedly she told the household the following summer would see Queen Jane crowned in Yorkminster, and the king holding a parliament in their very own city! Surely a great period of peace and prosperity was beginning for England, and doubtless Sir Miles Raven would soon return to claim Gillian.

And then the word reached York of Bigod's rebellion and the savage reprisals.

Terror lay over the city like a clammy shroud. Norfolk was coming, and the hangings would begin in York as they had all over the north. Fearful folk, even children, began to don the uniform of the king, a white smock with a red cross on it to show their loyalty to the sovereign.

Gillian had tried in vain to persuade her mistress to leave with her for Mallory Hall. Surely Norfolk and his minions would not pursue them there, but here in York it was known they had been on the Pilgrimage of Grace!

"They can't hang everyone, dear, and I doubt if they're really interested in two women like ourselves. But in any case I'm too old to tear across Yorkshire and into Northumbria in the dead of winter. Perhaps you should go, however," she murmured vaguely.

But how could she flee, leaving the old woman to her fate as if she, Gillian, cared not a fig? Surely, however, it was madness to stay after hearing the stories of atrocity that crept to York from all over the north!

At any moment Miles would return, wouldn't he, and snatch her away from the oncoming danger? But he did not, and she received no message from him. Gillian began to know the paralyzing lassitude that a mouse must experience when it knows itself cornered by a cat.

Then one morning her chance to run no longer existed. Norfolk had arrived in York, and his first action was to close all the gates. The cat had arrived, and all the mice were sealed inside for his pleasure.

Word swept through the ancient, narrow streets of the walled city, but it was scarcely ahead of the duke's men. They went from house to house, pulling out all those within and asking them if they had taken part in the Pilgrimage of Grace.

Many proudly admitted they had, and were ordered to join their fellow pilgrims being herded along under guard. Others, less willing to risk martyrdom, denied it vehemently, showing their tunics blazoned with red crosses, and usually they were believed.

When the pounding began at their door, it was almost a relief. Gillian opened the door. There was an officer of the king standing there in his Tudor livery, flanked by several others in similar dress who held pikes. "In the name of

Henry VIII, King of England, are there any here who marched in the late rebellion known as the Pilgrimage of Grace?"

"I did," she said in a dull, lifeless voice, then moved to close the door quickly behind her before they could see Elizabeth Easington walking to the threshold.

"But wait, sir!" spoke up Margaret behind her, throwing the door open. "We would be known as the King's loyal servants! In truth, there is another here who was a pilgrim." She extended a bony finger to point at her aunt.

Gillian gasped, staring at the triumphant smirk on Margaret's mouth as the king's officer moved forward to take custody of Elizabeth Easington, too. "You would betray your own flesh and blood, an old woman?"

The three children who had been clutching their mother's skirts in fear gaped at her, uncomprehending. Only little Grace dashed forward, wailing, "Great-aunt Elizabeth! Don't go! Mama, don't let them take her and Gillian!" Margaret, however, merely grabbed her youngest daughter by the arm and restrained her from going to the old woman.

Elizabeth Easington squared her shoulders and stood as tall as her widow's hump would allow, facing her niece unblinkingly. "There was no need to be a Judas, Margaret. I would never have allowed them to take Gillian and not myself."

Chapter Twenty-six

"Saints, look at you! You've the eyes of a caged tiger," Thomas Raven said one day in late February. The jailer had just let him into Miles's cell in the Tower.

The two brothers embraced heartily, then stood back to study one another. Thomas was shorter by a handsbreadth, and stockier, though none of his solidity was fat. He had the same midnight-hued thatch of hair, though his was graying slightly at the temples, the same silver-blue eyes. His mouth had a more serious set to it, though, perhaps because he was the heir to the Raven estate with all its attendant responsibilities.

"You've gotten thinner, brother," Thomas added after a moment. "You'd think with nothing to do but sleep and eat His Majesty's excellent cookery, you'd be fat as Christmas goose." His serious gaze belied his teasing tone.

"I think the coins they stole from my pocket have long since given out," Miles said wryly, "for I've noticed the bill of fare has gotten cursed dull. Marry, 'tis good to see you, Thomas! Do you know you're the first visitor they've allowed me in the—what is it, six weeks I've been here? How did you find out where I was? The constable wouldn't allow me to send any word. He must be immune to the Raven charm." He felt he must be grinning like a capering idiot, but it was so good to see a familiar face!

"One question at a time!" Thomas said in mock protest, throwing up his hands. He settled himself in the cell's only chair, throwing his booted legs on the end of the nearby bed. "And as head of the family, 'twill be my question that gets answered first! What did you do, Miles? Make cow eyes at Queen Jane? Tell His Majesty he was getting paunchy? You've always been more daring than I, brother, but I didn't think you foolhardy! Don't worry, Miles, the jailer has been well paid not to eavesdrop," he added at Miles' slightly alarmed expression.

"Nay, of course I did nothing like that." Briefly he told Thomas of what had taken place since he had last been at Ravenwood, and how he believed Sir Oliver Lang and Lady Celia had slandered him to King Henry. "So I have had no idea all this time whether Henry has me here out of Tudor petulance, to teach me a lesson, or if I'm to meet Anne Boleyn's ghost out there," he finished, with a nod of his head indicating Tower Green outside. "And meanwhile, I have no idea what's become of Gillian. I'm about to go mad, not knowing! Have you heard anything?"

"Nay, my contacts in the north haven't answered my inquiries. Perhaps they are in jail themselves," Thomas said.

"Will they let you come again? Perhaps in a week or so you would have heard something." He wanted to ask Thomas to go up to York himself, but he couldn't bring himself to frame the words. Not because his brother would be unwilling, but because he would do it, and Miles couldn't expose him to such danger.

"It won't be necessary for me to return to this dank hole," said his brother with a reassuring smile, pulling a rolled parchment from within his slashed doublet and extending it to Miles. "I have here your release papers, signed by Henry himself."

"What? Why didn't you say so immediately?" Miles had leaped to his feet and was studying the official document. "But why has he done this? Why keep me for weeks without a word and then just let me out?"

"Has Henry VIII done anything since he was first bewitched by Anne Boleyn that was really logical?" Thomas pointed out. "A timely gift of several hundred pounds from the Raven coffers did help, though."

"A bribe—though I've done naught," Miles said with bitterness.

"Of course. But don't question your good fortune, little brother. Take it and run! There's one clause there, however, that you may find objectionable," Thomas said, as Miles went back to scanning the parchment. "Look at the last line or two before the signature."

Miles did so, and after a moment his face darkened and his hand clenched on the paper. "It says I, and the entire Raven family, are to remain in the south until such time as the king deems the rebellious Pilgrimage of Grace has been finally suppressed, that we are not to go to York under any circumstances! What kind of nonsense is this? I have to find Gillian! I have to see if she's been swept up in Norfolk's net and save her if I can! If...if she still lives," he concluded in a hoarse whisper, as if he hardly dare say the words aloud.

Thomas rose, moving quickly for a man of his powerful build, and laid a hand on his brother's shoulder. "Steady, now. Of course you must find her. I never doubted for a moment that you would feel otherwise. You wouldn't be a Raven if you would let a piece of paper or a royal command keep you from the woman you loved. Your gray stallion is waiting in the Tower stables, and I've brought a change of clothes you can put on once you're well away from London. In them, you may not look like Sir Miles Raven, knight of the realm, but there's no use announcing who you are and that you're defying the king's order all the way to York. Once you've found her—'' Miles noticed he did not say *if* he found her ''—don't stop till you're clear across the border into Scotland.''

''Leave England? Forever?''

''Only while Henry lives. Why risk your life again on the whims of that bloated tyrant?''

Miles considered his brother's words for only a moment. ''Because that bloated tyrant may take out his pique on the rest of the Ravens, and I'll not have you and Mother and Linnet paying for the royal temper. Nor will I let Lang run me out of my own country. He's forgotten how vulnerable *he* is.'' Miles's eyes narrowed. ''Nay, if Gillian lives, I'll wed her and we'll live on our northern lands, and King Henry will be content enough to have me there.''

''How, short of a miracle, do you expect to accomplish that, brother?''

Then Miles told him of the terrible gamble he would have to take after he found Gillian.

Gillian turned, shivering, from the narrow, high window she could only peer out of by standing on tiptoe. She had wanted to see if it was still snowing, but she could not avoid seeing the rest of the horrible scenery of the gateway area just inside Micklegate Bar. In plain view stood the gibbet on which eight rotting bodies swung in the March wind, still bound with chains as if to keep the corpses from escaping.

These eight had been victims of Norfolk's severity, and had been picked at random from the hundred or so men and women imprisoned in two large rooms converted to cells. They had been executed before the duke had left York for other places in the North, and the survivors had heard that the same rough justice was being meted out elsewhere.

And now Norfolk had returned to York, and the rumor had flown around the improvised jail that there were to be more executions, that the king's thirst for blood in York had not been satisfied by the previous eight victims.

Will they hang us all? Gillian wondered, pulling the ragged blanket more closely about her. And if they do, will they do it all at once, in one hideous spectacle of death, or draw it out, a few condemned men and women at a time, the better to teach the rebellious north a lesson?

A visitor from the outside, a wife daring enough to come in to see her imprisoned husband, had reported that Norfolk was in the process of hiring juries—that those condemned would go to the gallows convicted by their own neighbors, anxious to prove their overwhelming loyalty to the crown! His Grace was giving preference to those applicants who had arrested relatives, and not because he thought they would render more merciful judgments. So this is how the crown finally would win—by turning brother against brother, son against father. No doubt Margaret Nutting would jump at the chance to serve on such a jury.

If Norfolk dawdled, she doubted that Mistress Easington would live to dangle from the gallows tree. Her elderly mistress had picked up the cough that echoed all through the cells at night, and today she had felt feverish.

'Twas less than a year since Gillian had sat by the side of the prioress of Kyloe and watched her slowly waste away from the lung sickness. She knew the signs. All that was unknown was whether the hangman or the lung sickness would claim the old woman first.

Gillian hoped it was the latter, and that it came more quickly than the prioress's end had. No one should have to die by slowly choking at the end of a rope, listening to the shouts of the crowd. She wished she would fall ill herself, but the resiliency of youth had kept her healthy in spite of the cold, the miserable slop that passed as food, and her despair.

Where was Miles Raven? Where had the king sent him, that he would not have heard what was happening in the north? What a bitter joke, that her love might be carrying out the king's business in France, for example, while an agent of the king executed his betrothed in York!

She turned from the window and made her way through the maze of the supine and sitting forms of her cell mates till she reached Elizabeth Easington.

"I'm sorry, Gillian dear, I've tried, but I just cannot stomach this vile gruel," the old woman said apologetically, coughing again.

"It's all right, mistress, it's hardly worth swallowing anyway."

Gillian had just knelt at Elizabeth Easington's side, intent on feeling her forehead, when the jailer's heavy tread sounded at the door.

"Is there a woman within by name of Gillian Mallory? There be a visitor for ye," the jailer announced.

Her heart began to pump with mad joy. "'Tis Miles, I just know it," she whispered to the old woman. "Oh, Mistress Easington, perhaps he'll be able to get us out—perhaps this very afternoon!"

"I hope so, my dear," the old woman managed.

Her fellow prisoners moved out of her path as she dashed to the door and waited impatiently as the jailer worked the key in the lock.

The sight, when the heavy door stood open, caused her to back away uncertainly from the door. Over the jailer's shoulder she could see a smirking Sir Oliver Lang, and behind him, grinning evilly, George Brunt.

"What do you want, Sir Oliver?" she asked, suspicion obvious in her voice.

"So welcoming," he mocked. "In spite of the fact that I've risked His Grace's displeasure by coming to see you. I serve the Duke of Norfolk, you know, in his capacity as the king's justiciar of the north, so you would do well to speak kindly—"

"The king's hangman, you mean," Gillian retorted. "Jailer, I do not have anything to say to this man." She turned on her heel, intending to go inside the cell, but Lang was quicker.

He grabbed her arm, yanking her to him.

From within the cell, Elizabeth Easington had seen his action and her young friend's expression of fear and loathing.

"Unhand her, you blackguard! Jailer, make him let go of her," the old woman shouted, struggling to her feet. "He's up to no good!"

"He's the duke's man, old meddler! Mind your own affairs!" snarled the jailer, clenching his fist as if he would box the elderly woman's ears.

Elizabeth Easington was not to be put off by the threat of a fist. "I tell you, he's a bad man, and my servant does not want to go with him!"

"And who are you to order anyone about, you harridan! Within a sennight you'll likely be swinging on the gallows!"

The old woman lunged at Lang, avoiding the detaining grasp of the jailer with surprising agility and ignoring Gillian's urging to get back. She had no weapon but her hands;

these she used to pummel and claw at Lang and Brunt in a futile attempt to get them to loose their hold on Gillian.

Gillian, screaming, saw the flash of steel in Brunt's hand a split second before the man buried his dagger in Elizabeth Easington's back. The old woman's screech was cut off in a gurgle of blood. Her eyes stared wildly as her hands scrabbled at the air. Then she fell heavily in the straw, spittle mixed with blood oozing from a corner of her mouth.

A young merchant's wife scrambled to her side, pressing her hand to the old woman's heart. After a minute, she straightened.

There would be no gallows now for Elizabeth Easington.

Gillian froze for a moment, waiting to see what her jailer would do, but he seemed paralyzed with indecision.

"Murderer!" she cried at Brunt, who had backed away, his gaze darting from the dead body at his feet to the jailer and then to Gillian. She struggled in Lang's hold. "Jailer, aren't you going to have him arrested? You saw him murder a frail old woman! And Sir Oliver Lang, here, is just as guilty, for Brunt is his henchman!"

The jailer, a slovenly, unkempt man with blackened teeth, avoided her gaze. "Ye said ye needed to interrogate this prisoner, sir. Go ahead, then."

Gillian resumed her screeching and kicking. Murder had just been done in front of dozens of witnesses, and now the jailer was going to allow this unsavory pair to take her off for God knew what!

"Quiet, wench!" Lang shouted in her ear, then whispered, "or I won't tell you what I know about your lover's disappearance. Yes, I have news of the estimable Sir Miles Raven."

"Miles? What is it? What do you know of him?" she said, trying to see Sir Oliver through her tears.

"Not so fast, mistress. I think we will talk elsewhere," Lang said, nodding toward the dozens of women watching them from within the cell. "My friend the jailer has arranged for a small chamber where we can be...private."

Her flesh crawled as he fixed his insolent stare upon her, studying her uncombed, shoulder-length blond hair and the stained serge dress she had been forced to wear ever since she had been arrested. No doubt she stank, but she didn't care if she offended Lang's hooked nose. Staring at the hated knight, she allowed him to pull her down the corridor.

"This is the jailer's room," Lang explained when she saw the rumpled bed in the corner of the small room. "'Twas the only place I could talk to you, Gillian," he said, speaking soothingly as if to a skittish horse as he walked toward her.

She backed away. "You said you knew of Miles. Where is he? Where has the king sent him? Does he know I am arrested?"

"He may know, but there's absolutely nothing he can do, my dear," Lang said, a gloating smile stealing over his features. He came closer still.

"What do you mean? Where is he?"

"Why, in the Tower, of course, where all His Majesty's enemies reside...until they meet their fates," he said, giving in to wild laughter. "He will pay the price for consorting with a known traitor, that is to say, your lovely self."

"Miles...in the Tower!" Her brain was still reeling with the import of Lang's words when another figure slunk inside the door and slammed it behind him.

"Brunt, you were to wait in the corridor till I called you," Lang said, seizing Gillian as she whirled to face the newcomer.

Brunt sniggered. "Are ye certain ye won't need me t'hold her down, Sir Oliver, while you, uh, take your pleasure of her? I'd enjoy watching a gentleman such as yourself swiving the bitch. Before I humble her, that is."

Hearing Brunt's words, Gillian began to thrash like a madwoman in Lang's arms, trying to wrench her arms free, but Lang's grip was steel.

"That won't be necessary," Lang shouted over his captive's shrieks, controlling the fighting woman within his arms with difficulty. "I've told you you could have her after I did, and you will, but only if you get out and guard the corridor as I ordered!"

Gillian did not pause in her desperate battle to free herself as Brunt sullenly left the room to take his post in the corridor, but both she and Lang were too involved with each other to notice that Brunt left the door open a crack to view Gillian Mallory's humiliation.

Chapter Twenty-seven

The jailer watched, rubbing his grimy hands on his jerkin, as the two men dragged the unwilling girl down the hall. The gentleman had claimed to be in the Duke of Norfolk's service, but in truth his bribe of several pounds had mattered more than anything either of that scurvy pair had said. 'Twas obvious they were more interested in rape than interrogation. Ah, well, the wench was about to die anyway.

The fact that the jailer was so amenable to bribes made it very easy for Miles Raven to obtain the information that the woman he sought was indeed imprisoned in the Micklegate jail. Yes, he would be glad to allow the gentleman to see her, but he would have to wait until the duke's officials were through questioning her.

Something about the leering way he said *questioning* made Miles' hair stand on end.

"Questioning her?" he repeated. "Where? Have they taken her to the duke's headquarters within the city?"

"Nay, sir," the jailer replied in his thick Yorkshire accent. "They wuz in a hurry like, the two of them, and I said they could use my chamber."

"I am of His Grace's staff also," Miles lied smoothly. He had already given a false name. "I was to be present for this, ah, interrogation, but it seems they began without me. Kindly show me to your quarters." When the man hesitated, Raven offered him another guinea.

"Ignore what you may hear," Miles commanded the uncouth fellow. "And forget the fact that I was ever here, or the prisoner, for that matter. The gallows will not miss one innocent woman."

The jailer grinned, picturing the gentleman standing before him interrupting the other two at their sport. That would certainly be setting the cat among the doves, for he didn't believe for a moment the man's story that he was expected!

"Thank ye, sir," he said, accepting the additional bribe. The gent was right, the king's officials would never miss one woman among so many rebels. Then, jerking his head upward in the direction of his quarters, he added, "'Tis just up the stairs and down the corridor to yer right."

Miles climbed the stairs, wanting to be as quiet as possible. He did not know who might be with Gillian; it would be a good idea to take them by surprise. No clinking spurs were clasped to his heels; he had left the golden symbol of his knighthood with Thomas when he had departed London in the plain warm clothes his brother had provided.

The old, creaking wood beneath his feet protested every step, but he need not have worried. The man guarding the door of the jailer's chamber was much too absorbed with what was going on within to hear him stealing up behind him.

Just then, from within the room, came a scream. A woman's scream. Gillian's scream!

Drawing his dagger, he plunged it quickly, cleanly into the man's upper back. The man went down with a soft groan, turning on his side as the death throes convulsed his body. It was Brunt!

There came the sound of a blow and a feminine cry of pain.

Miles threw himself against the door, exploding into the room as he drew his sword. His eyes instantly took in the scene before him, the bed in the corner of the room, on which Gillian, her skirts pushed up to her waist, struggled beneath Sir Oliver Lang. The latter's breeches and small-clothes lay discarded on the floor beside the bed, and his bare buttocks and stiffened manhood were a hideous confirmation of Miles' fears.

"Damn you, Brunt, I said you were to wait your turn," Lang snarled, furious at the interruption. His mouth fell open as he recognized Miles. "Raven! I—"

"I should have known 'twas you and your fool friend Brunt," Miles said. "Prepare to die, as Brunt just did, quickly and unshriven!"

Lang scrambled off Gillian, staring in horror at the long, wicked length of Raven's blade and the death he saw in the other knight's eyes.

"Brunt is dead? And y-you'd k-kill me without g-giving me a chance to defend myself?" Lang stammered in fear. "Because of a rebel wench?"

Miles nodded, drawing from within himself an icy calm. He saw Gillian staring at him as if he was a figure from a dream, and unconsciously he noted her thinness, the piece of straw sticking to her matted hair. There would be time to remedy such things later, after he'd slaughtered this vermin. "I wouldn't let anyone hurt a woman, but yes, especially because it is Gillian."

"Here, take her!" Lang said, gesturing frantically at the huddled woman on the bed. "One wench is much the same as another, after all!"

Lang knew he was a ridiculous sight, standing there half-naked as he faced death. He saw no softening in Raven's eyes, no sign that his opponent would take the woman and let him live. He'd already slain that idiot Brunt, after all. In desperation Lang pulled Gillian to her feet and threw her at Raven, hoping it would buy him enough time to reach the sword propped in the far corner of the room, where he'd left it lest his intended victim reach it while she attempted to resist.

He was inches from the sword when he felt Raven's blade pricking the side of his neck, and went rigid.

"I don't think I care for a sword fight today, Lang. Duels are for gentlemen, which you certainly are not."

He had pushed Gillian gently behind him, not wanting her to see when he slit the scoundrel's throat from ear to ear. No, there would be no knightly combat between himself and this piece of filth—

"Nay, Miles, don't! Don't kill him! He did not...finish! There has been enough death!" she cried, pulling on his sleeve but careful not to hamper his sword arm. She could not have said why she pleaded for Lang's life, except that after the awfulness of seeing Elizabeth Easington slain before her, she could not bear to see another human being die.

There was a dreadful moment in which she thought he would go ahead anyway, and plunge the point of his sword into the soft, jowly flesh of Lang's neck. "Please, Miles! We can tie and gag him, and be away before he can free himself."

"Very well," Miles said at last, leaving his sword point touching Lang's neck, "though there was never a pig who deserved more to die for what he nearly did to you."

He found some coiled rope on the jailer's table and tied Lang securely until he was trussed up like a slain boar. Whether the rope was the jailer's or Lang and Brunt had anticipated a worse fight with their prisoner, he didn't know. "I know you'll eventually be freed from these bonds, Lang, but before you come protesting to court over your treatment, remember the day that I came upon you and her late Majesty Queen Anne Boleyn in a highly compromising position. I intend to tell King Henry, Lang—though the Lord knows I should have told him years ago and saved him and the realm from much grief. I think it would be, shall we say, advantageous for you to take yourself from England, wouldn't you agree?"

Lang glared at Miles, hatred glistening from his eyes.

"Damn you, Raven," he ground out.

"Doubtless I will be," Miles countered, almost cheerfully. "But 'twill make me satisfied to see you exiled in disgrace. You're getting off lightly, you know."

"You'll never get away with it. King Henry will—"

"I think I've heard enough," Miles commented, and knocked him unconscious with a doubled-up fist.

He turned to Gillian, gazing at her fully for the first time, seeing the torn bodice of her gown, the bruise on her right cheek, the scratches on her neck, the puffiness of her lower lip.

"I should have killed him," he said, as he opened his arms and pulled her into his comforting embrace.

Gillian immediately began to weep, and for a few moments he just let her, stroking her shaking shoulders. "Soft, now, sweetheart," he soothed her. "There's nothing more to fear. The jailer's been well paid to let you go." Then a new thought struck him. "Where is the old woman? Was Mistress Easington arrested with you?"

Her sobs increased. "They killed her... when she tried to prevent them taking me from the cell!"

"'Tis just one more reason I should have killed Lang," Miles said. "Now I must get you out of here."

"Miles . . . is there no way we can free them—the rest of the prisoners?" she asked in a soft voice, her blue eyes pleading. "None of them—the women or the men—are truly rebels, none would harm a hair on Henry Tudor's head."

"No more than you are," he agreed, his eyes bleak at the thought of what he must say. "But there are guards without, and the town is full of Norfolk's men. We shall be very lucky to get ourselves free and our names cleared. I'm sorry, my love. I wish I could help them, as well."

They gazed soberly at one another for a long moment, then she squeezed his hand to show him she understood. "Then what must we do next?"

Chapter Twenty-eight

Gillian gasped in horror as they passed the unmoving, contorted figure of Brunt, still lying in the corridor with the dagger buried between his shoulder blades. She shuddered as Miles pulled the dagger from the corpse, and after wiping the congealed blood on the dead man's doublet, put it back in his belt. At least he would never torment poor Mag again, she reminded herself.

Miles marched Gillian out into the street, past the lounging guards, her hands bound in back of her as if she was a prisoner.

"This woman goes to be questioned by His Grace himself," he had announced, marching her in the direction of the duke's headquarters in the center of the city until they were out of sight of Micklegate Bar. Then he had directed her quickly down a side street.

There, in a tavern courtyard, being guarded by a ragged youth, were two horses—one of them Miles's gray stallion, the other her own black mare!

"Sultana!" she exclaimed, going forward to embrace her mare's dark neck. "But how—"

"I just went to the stable in back of Mistress Easington's home—I didn't know about her being in jail then, of course—and took her. No one was about, and I didn't want to take the time to explain to anyone."

"'Twas a very good thing you did not," she said. Quickly, as he assisted her to mount, she explained how Elizabeth Easington had been betrayed by Margaret.

Miles' face darkened. "Damned devious woman. I suppose she'll be relieved to know her claim to the house is now uncontested."

Gillian stared down the narrow street, biting her lip. "What must her children think of her..." Then a new thought struck her. "Miles—Lang told me the king had you held in the Tower! Is that true?"

"Aye. I lay there for weeks, thanks to the slander of Lang and Celia. It seems they told His Majesty all about my relationship with the seditious rebel that you supposedly are. I'll warrant they embroidered the truth till 'twas well-nigh unrecognizable!" His mouth twisted wryly. "I never knew if I was to die or be freed until my brother came with my release. Thomas paid a hefty fine on my behalf, and I suppose Henry thought he'd taught me a lesson. Did you think I'd forgotten my promise, sweetheart?" he asked her, studying the beautiful but thin face and the tangled, lackluster hair.

Her blue eyes clouded. "A few times," she admitted, "but most days I figured that you had been sent away, too far to know about what was happening to me until 'twas too late. And here I did not know you were in just as much danger.... Oh, Miles, had I known you were in the Tower—!" She shivered.

"You look like a princess," Miles reassured her several days later, chafing her hand between the two of his, "but you feel like a maid with cold hands."

"I can't help it, Miles, I'm so frightened, imagining what will happen if what we tell the king does not please him." Nervously Gillian adjusted the necklace of gold and pearls that was bordered by folds of the sheer linen bodice, then adjusted the set of the pleated linen headdress. The brocade-trimmed gown of Tudor green with its quilted underskirt belled around her as she fidgeted.

The clothes were Linnet's, borrowed from a wardrobe in the Ravens' London lodgings. They had stopped there to refresh themselves and change from their humble clothing of disguise before going on to Greenwich.

Miles had advised Gillian to choose the demurest of his sister's gowns. "King Henry is in love with Jane Seymour, though she'll never rule him as Anne did, and she's a simple, meek woman, completely the opposite of the glamorous Boleyn. If you seem like one such as Queen Jane, well dressed but not seductively so, nor ascetic as old Queen Catherine, 'twill be harder to think of you as some religious rebel."

Miles, however, had dressed as befitted his station as a knight of the realm, as if to remind Henry that he had been one of his inner circle, a trusted courtier and friend, rather than one who plotted against him. His short charcoal-gray coat boasted a squirrel-fur-trimmed collar, with padded sleeves and fur-trimmed cuffs turned back halfway to his elbows, showing the frill at his wrists. Beneath it, his doublet and breeches were of black, emphasizing the contrast between his dark hair and silver-blue eyes. The doublet was slashed to show the shirt puffed out in vertical rows down his chest. Set on top of the thick, midnight-hued hair was a flat black velvet cap decorated with a gold medallion in front and a feather on the side.

Suddenly the door between the Presence Chamber and the anteroom in which they waited opened. A short man wearing a gold chain of office stepped out, peering at them silhouetted against a mullioned window. "Sir Miles, Mistress Mallory, His Majesty will see you now."

This is it, Miles thought, with a sudden welling of dread. There was no going back. Gillian walked slightly ahead of him, her head held proudly, the skirt of her gown swaying slightly. She appeared to have banished fear to her innermost depths for this encounter.

All at once, he wished he could call Gillian back and they could flee down the palace corridors and down the Thames. Surely a life in exile was not too great a price to pay for her safety! What kind of fool full of bombast and arrogance had he been, to tell her with such assurance that what they would tell King Henry would placate him? The king was an unpredictable tyrant, apt to do anything on a whim! It was too late now to admit he might have been wrong. Miles breathed a wordless prayer.

"Arise, Mistress Mallory, that we may see you," came the distant voice like a warm embrace in the chill air. There was a faint musical quality to his speech, a reminder that the Tudors were originally a Welsh family.

Gillian stared up at the man clothed in white, gold-trimmed brocade sitting on his throne. He was massive; at his shoulders and thighs, the flesh strained the seams of his costly doublet. A matching halo-brimmed bonnet studded with topaz sat atop thinning hair of ginger mixed with gray; beneath that was a jowly, florid face bordered by a short beard and blue eyes half-hidden by folds of flesh. Though what she saw was a man past his prime and older than his years through the effects of overindulgence, Gillian felt the force of Henry Tudor's personality.

A hand with pudgy, beringed fingers lifted from the arm of the throne and beckoned her forward. She went, though her feet did not feel the floor beneath her.

Henry Tudor spoke again. "Mistress Mallory, we would make you known to our beloved wife, Queen Jane."

Gillian had been so absorbed by the brocade-clad colossus that she had failed to see the woman who sat beside him, her carved throne slightly shorter than her royal husband's. Hastily, Gillian made a second curtsy.

Jane Seymour was a pale mouse of a woman next to her magnificent husband, in spite of the gown of mulberry velvet and the necklace of gold and rubies, both of which should have brought some color to her face. The wisps of hair that showed beneath her hood were a lifeless ash blond.

Her lips were thin and bloodless. Only her eyes looked alive, though Gillian could not discern their hue, and these glanced nervously at her spouse before looking at Gillian. When Jane Seymour saw that King Henry did not look upset, her lips twitched at Gillian in what may have been meant as an encouraging smile. She did not, however, speak, and Gillian found herself wondering what kind of voice she had.

"Charming, charming..." King Henry said. Up close, even a murmur from this huge man had a booming quality to it, yet the voice was still pleasant to the ears. He was speaking of her, yet Gillian found the description fit the king. There was something hypnotizing, sirenlike about the force of this man's charm. No wonder Robert Aske had returned convinced of this man's sincerity after spending Christmas with him!

"Wife, can you believe this woman was once a nun, a holy dame in a convent, a bride of Christ?" Henry in-

quired. She dared not correct Henry to tell him that she had
never taken her final vows.

Queen Jane answered softly, but whether in assent or
disbelief was unclear. It was unimportant to Henry Tudor.
"Look at her beauty, her slender yet womanly form! Surely
we did the male sex a favor by liberating her from her ster-
ile conventual existence! Did we not, Sir Miles?"

"I feel so, Your Majesty," came Miles' voice from behind her. How Gillian wished she could seize his hand and
hold on to it!

"And did you, mistress, realize at once the benefit of the
great *favor* you had been vouchsafed by our royal decree?"

Here was treacherous ground indeed! Did she dare to
admit her true feelings? Those penetrating eyes, so small in
that heavy face, nevertheless missed nothing.

"Not immediately, Your Majesty," she said. Inwardly
she trembled, but she was pleased to find that her voice did
not quaver but came through clearly.

King Henry quirked a royal brow. "Not immediately?
Yet you had been given a pension, mistress. Surely you were
not entirely bereft." The king sounded faintly reproach-
ful.

"Your Majesty, if I might speak—"

"Not yet, Sir Miles, not yet. Mistress Mallory has a
voice," King Henry said, raising a preemptive hand. He
looked at Gillian.

Her knees had finally stopped shaking. "Nay, Sire, I did
not, for the convent priest had stolen it for his own use, and
we did not know we were to receive it. Many of the younger
women were able to go back to their families, but about a
dozen, mostly older women, went out seeking another
convent. I . . . I don't know what happened to them, Sire."

"And you, mistress?"

"I remained at the priory. I was nursing the prioress, who was dying."

"And when she died, you were quite alone in the wilds of Northumberland," Henry concluded for her. "And were you very angry at us, mistress?" he asked her in a deceptively mild tone.

His words were quicksand, waiting to trap her, yet rebellion surged through her. She would not lie to this man, not because she feared he would discern it, but because it was beneath her!

"Aye, Sire, in that month I had to watch her die and wonder what I would do, whether I would starve before I became a thief or sold my body, I was angry. I had no family. As I saw it, my king had decreed the only way of life I had ever known was over, but had not given me the means to make an honest living."

"Yet you did not know of the bounty I had extended to the displaced monks and nuns," Henry pointed out.

"Nay, Sire."

She kept her head high and her eyes looking steadily into the king's. Then Henry threw back his head and let out a great peal of laughter.

"Here is no cringing sheep, but a young lioness! And then what happened, mistress?"

"Then Sir Miles, coming to take possession of his property, found me, and I discovered within the convent certain papers that revealed me to be the heiress of a small manor known as Mallory Hall, which lies upon Budle Bay."

"So you learned you were not, indeed, destitute at all. I understand you began to run the estate, and let lodgings to Sir Miles, who began to fall in love with you," King Henry said, chuckling as he saw her eyes widen. "Oh, yes, mistress, I know a great many things about my subjects. And as you fell in love with my handsome knight, did you lose your anger at your sovereign?"

"I began to become reconciled with the idea of a life in the world, Your Majesty," she said, fighting the blush that threatened to rise at the thought of the way the passion Miles had inspired in her had helped with her adjustment.

King Henry shifted his massive bulk and darted a look at his queen. "And so you were becoming content with your lot, happy with a woman's proper place in the world, about to marry a handsome knight of the realm and bear his babes in wifely obedience. How then did you fall into the snare of rebellion, marching against us in unlawful insurrection with those misguided fools in the Pilgrimage of Grace? Furthermore, how did you beguile my trusted *friend*—" he nodded meaningfully at Miles "—to join in your disobedience, so that not even a stay in the Tower has sobered him, causing him to go to York against our express order to foolishly rescue you from the inevitable consequence of your folly? Did you not tremble to bring about the downfall of this good knight, foolish woman?"

In the space of a few sentences, Henry Tudor had transformed himself from the genial, rotund questioner to a raging thunderstorm of fury. His face was flushed, his eyes piggishly small and mean. Gillian felt an icy cold fist close around her heart.

"Sire, I never meant any rebellion against you. I went along on the Pilgrimage of Grace because my employer, Mistress Elizabeth Easington, wanted to go. She was an old woman and I wanted to see her cared for."

"Your employer? What need had you, mistress of a manor, for an employer?"

She had the feeling he knew the answer, that he was just playing with her as a cat does a mouse. "I . . . I had left my manor after a quarrel with Sir Miles."

"By this time, you had agreed to wed Sir Miles, had you not?"

"Aye, Your Majesty. But I—" She was about to tell him that she had believed Sir Miles previously betrothed, and therefore ineligible, but he cut her off.

"You show a damnable pattern of defiance against the overlordship of a male, be he your king or your future lord," Henry snarled. "No doubt that was drummed into you in that unnatural atmosphere of a convent, in which a woman is ruler, against all natural law. Woman was born to be meek and obedient to a man, bound to obey and serve, eh, my queen?" Henry patted the hand of Jane, who just looked at him and nodded, puppetlike.

With the abyss yawning before her, Gillian still found it in her to pity the woman on the throne next to King Henry. Even though she was queen, how subservient she must have to be to survive with this unpredictable man who had banished one woman, the wife of his youth, to a lonely death, and sent another to the block! Miles would never have wanted such a woman!

There seemed to be nothing she could say that would not further enrage the king, so she remained silent.

"And you, Sir Miles, you ignored the daughters of our finest men to contract an alliance with this wench?"

Miles stepped forward, taking Gillian's hand as if in answer to her prayer. In the face of the king's anger, his action caused Queen Jane to give a small gasp.

Gillian closed her eyes, savoring the warmth and strength she felt flowing from Miles into her. If she went straight from this room to the gallows, the touch of the man she loved would stay with her forever.

"Sire, I loved her for her goodness, her steadfastness and her determination. Qualities that should adorn the finest ladies of your realm."

"And yet she left you to march with the rebels," King Henry needled.

"She thought me already obligated to a lady, Sire, and therefore a deceiver and a seducer. She left before I could tell her the truth. I believe she would not have been caught up in the Pilgrimage of Grace otherwise—though if she had not gone on it, I might not have found her again. As soon as I did find her, however, we, ah, settled our differences and planned to wed. Your Majesty, I would vouch that Gillian Mallory has learned from her errors and would be a gentle, true wife to me, as modeled by Her Majesty."

Gillian felt a distinct increase in the pressure of Miles' fingers, warning her not to disagree.

"You planned to marry, without consulting your sovereign, a woman involved in insurrection! Against our specific instructions you took that woman from jail, where she and others faced punishment for their crimes. Fortunately we have been kept informed by our *loyal* subjects. Come forward, Lady Celia."

Chapter Twenty-nine

When had Lady Celia stolen into the back of the Presence Chamber? She glided forward, smirking in triumph. Miles noted that she still wore black, no doubt to make herself a more sympathetic figure as one in mourning.

"Dear lady, you have kept us informed of the nature of our Sir Miles' behavior, how he seduced you, then cruelly left you for this woman before us. Gallantly, you went on with your life, only to be cheated by Death, when the Marquis of Craningbourne died untimely early. You felt it your obligation to tell us that Sir Miles' new *amour* was a woman who felt no loyalty to her king."

Celia faced Miles and Gillian, her eyes glittering with hatred, then inclined her head to Henry Tudor. "I did, Your Majesty, though it grieved me, due to the love I confess I still felt for Sir Miles. I was angry on Your Majesty's behalf, since you trusted him with your royal friendship."

"Speaking of trust, Your Majesty," Miles spoke up, "I wonder if Lady Celia would trust her fellow accuser so much if she knew he came to Mistress Mallory's prison cell in York with the intent of rape."

Celia's tinkling laughter had a brittle, shrill quality to it. "And what if he did? She is a rebel trollop, after all." But her face had gone sickly pallid under the natural ivory of her complexion.

Miles paused, looking at Celia from the top of her black hood to her elegant, black slipper-shod toes. "Yes, Your Majesty, Sir Oliver Lang took Gillian from her cell with the object of forcing his lust, and that of his henchman, one George Brunt, on her, a lust he had nurtured ever since he met her and found she did not return his feelings. I wonder what Lady Celia would say if she knew Sir Oliver permitted the slaying of a helpless old woman, Elizabeth Easington, who tried to prevent it from happening? I arrived in time to prevent the rape, but not the murder of that poor old woman, and yes, Your Majesty—I will admit I took Gillian Mallory from the jail, not waiting to see the verdict of the duke's court, for I trusted no other mercy but that of my king."

Miles looked deeply into the skeptical eyes of Henry Tudor, willing him to believe his words. He dared not look away, even for an instant. Everything rode on this moment.

"Is this true, Mistress Mallory?" inquired King Henry.

"Yes, Sire. I was on the point of being violated by Sir Oliver Lang when Sir Miles rescued me."

"And what did you do to the man who was about to defile the woman you love, Sir Miles?"

"I tied him up, Your Majesty."

"You did not kill him? A man in the very act of a brutish crime?" Henry retorted doubtfully. Clearly he doubted the accusation of rape, since Sir Oliver had not been killed by his accuser.

Gillian spoke up before Miles could open his mouth. "I would not allow it, Your Majesty." Her voice was even and strong. "It had already been necessary to kill George Brunt, the brutish lout who had stabbed Elizabeth Easington to death. I said there had been enough killing."

"You subdued Sir Oliver Lang and brought this woman to me?" Henry said to Miles. "Surely, Lady Celia, if Sir Miles' and Mistress Gillian's story is not true, your friend Sir Oliver would have come hotfoot down to us from York, protesting his innocence."

But Lady Celia was not wholly defeated yet. "As they have said, the henchman committed the murder, not Sir Oliver, and only they claim he sanctioned the act. Once done, well, the old woman was all but condemned to die anyway, was she not? And as for Sir Oliver forcing himself on this woman, well, you can see for yourself, Sire—she is a tempting baggage, is she not?" Daringly, before Gillian could see what she intended, Celia reached out and pulled the linen headdress from Gillian's head, pointing at the honey-blond curls that tumbled free from confinement. "Look at the glorious golden hair, that seductive, pouting mouth, that enticing body! What man would not find her tempting?" Celia pleaded, glancing sidelong at the king.

It was a bold move, calculated to appeal to a man who had been a voluptuary at Venus' temple since his youth. Henry Tudor wet his lips as he stared at her without her modest head covering, and Gillian felt suddenly naked. Beside him, Queen Jane stirred uneasily.

"Men will be men, eh, Lady Celia?" Miles said sardonically. "Perhaps... But I wonder at a woman who bestows her affections on a man who would force another woman, a helpless prisoner?"

Celia gave another high-pitched laugh. "Who says it was rape? Perhaps Mistress Mallory saw a way to buy herself off the gallows, Sir Miles."

King Henry seemed to consider that possibility. Miles saw that he would have to use his final weapon.

"Perhaps Sir Oliver did not come to court, protesting his innocence in this affair, because he is guilty of a much more heinous crime—that of treason," Miles said, turning his gaze from Celia to King Henry as he finished speaking.

"Eh? Treason? Make yourself clear, Sir Miles," the king commanded.

Miles dared a glance at Celia. If it was possible, Celia looked even paler than she had before. Obviously Lang had admitted the truth to her, perhaps even boasted about it.

Miles took a deep breath. "I mean, Your Majesty, that Sir Oliver Lang is guilty of carnal knowledge of the late Queen Anne Boleyn. This has been defined in a court of law as treason, has it not?"

Henry's eyes narrowed. "Yes, that is treason—as is the concealing of that knowledge. Just how long have you known about Lang's actions, Sir Miles?"

The small murmurs, the rustles of brocade and velvet and silk as men and women shifted their position in the Presence Chamber, stopped. It hardly seemed that anyone in the chamber, save the king, dared to breathe.

"Since it happened, Your Majesty. I...I came upon them accidentally." *There. I have said it. I have admitted I knew that Lang cuckolded Henry, who was planning to marry Anne as soon as he could, and I did not tell him. I have as good as laid my own head on the block. But please, please, let my blood be enough and let Gillian be safe!*

Henry gave a bellow of rage, the veins standing out on his neck. "And why did you not come straight to me with your tale, Sir Miles? Was Sir Oliver such a close friend then, that you valued his neck over your sovereign's honor?" His eyes looked like a maddened boar's.

Miles opened his mouth to speak, but Queen Jane was quicker. "Dear My Lord, for shame! 'Tis obvious Sir Miles did what he did, not for any desire to conceal wrongdoings, but out of love for you, not wanting to cause you pain! You were in love, Your Majesty! Could you have borne the pain such knowledge would have caused you, even if you could have believed it then?''

Miles felt his jaw drop in amazement at the little queen's bravery. For Jane Seymour to have publicly disputed with her husband, and to have reminded Henry that once he had been so besotted with her bewitching predecessor that he could not see the evil beneath Anne's charming exterior, was bold indeed.

Henry's high color drained, and he went as white as his doublet.

O Jesu, Gillian thought, Queen Jane will die alongside Miles and me, poor woman!

Henry continued to look at the woman beside him, who met his gaze calmly, not flinching, though she knew it possible her royal spouse might strike her in front of everyone. The last time she had challenged his authority, when she had begged him to let the monasteries reopen, he had reminded her of the fate of Anne Boleyn.

"You dare much," he said at last.

"Nay, Sire. I but remind you of motives that you may not have considered. Sir Miles has ever been loyal to you, my lord husband."

Henry dropped his eyes from Jane's to study her body, imagining it as it had been last night when he had lain with her. It had been a month since he had last felt well enough to act the husband, due to the chronic pain in his ulcerous leg. Was it his imagination, or had her breasts been a little fuller than before, her belly a bit rounder? Could she be, even now, *enceinte* with his son? Surely, at last, it was so! And if it was true, the last thing he wanted to do was upset her by becoming angry with her and condemning the knight and woman before him to death! Surely his son would get a firmer hold in Jane's womb if she was made happy by his royal clemency. After all, he was going to pardon a few of the rebels anyway, even some of the leaders.

If Raven was guilty of anything, surely it was only of misjudgment in the matter of the Boleyn woman, he thought, wincing at the memory of Anne's betrayals—and of defying his king to free the woman.

"Lady Celia," the king announced in a booming, peremptory tone, "I suggest you inform Sir Oliver Lang, wherever he may be lurking, that he is not welcome in England any more. His estates are forfeit. The day we see that treacherous weasel's face again, that day he lays his head upon the block!"

His tone made it plain that Lady Celia Pettingham was no longer welcome at court, either, and she backed out of the room with indecent haste, her eyes flashing with impotent fury. Henry Tudor turned to Gillian.

"Mistress Mallory, is it possible you could become as meek and mild as my beloved queen, obedient to your lord husband, if we were to pardon you?"

Gillian could scarcely breathe, her heart was hammering so fast. She could not resist a look at Queen Jane, however.

The two women's eyes met, and Jane Seymour knew she was no more like this woman than a pigeon was a swan. She had had her moment of daring, in which she had soared close enough to the sun to singe her feathers, and it was enough.

"Yes, Your Majesty. I have never meant to be anything but your obedient subject." *Though I can never forgive much you have done, you will not live forever, and I will pray your heir will be a better ruler.* "All I have ever wanted, once the convent was closed to me, was to be the loving wife of Sir Miles Raven, and to bear his babes." Her eyes left the king's, and gazed steadfastly into Miles' proud silver-blue ones. She knew Miles realized that she would never be meek and mild, nor did he want her to be. Probably Henry Tudor knew it, too.

"And you, Sir Miles, can you keep this lovely subject of ours from the path of trouble?"

Miles smiled at his beloved Gillian, but his face was solemn when he turned to answer his king.

"With Your Majesty's loving rule of his wife as example, Sire, I'm certain I can."

"Then let there be no further delay!" Henry boomed, raising his arms as he stood. "Ready the chapel, and let us stand as witnesses to the solemnizing of your vows! Someone call a priest!"

Epilogue

By midsummer, all traces of the unrest following the Pilgrimage of Grace had been vanquished. Robert Aske was hung in chains in his city of York. Many of the other leaders also died as a result of their belief in this tragic cause. Others were pardoned, seemingly at random, but hundreds of commoners deemed rebels were hung without formal trials.

Queen Jane was indeed pregnant, and delivered her child, the king's only son, Edward, on October 12, 1537. During her pregnancy, her every whim had been indulged, particularly in regard to rich food, and she took part in her son's christening ceremony within a few days of the long, difficult birth. Within ten days, she was dead, the victim of childbed fever, and Henry was once again looking for a wife.

Lady Celia Pettingham joined her co-conspirator Sir Oliver Lang in York, and after telling him of the disastrous events at Greenwich that had resulted in his banishment, followed by the pardoning and restoring to favor of Sir Miles Raven and Gillian Mallory and their immediate wedding, Celia and Lang left England together. Lang preferred Scotland, but Celia, imagining Scotland a barbaric land full of uncultured barbarians, insisted on France. Although she was disgraced now, she had an eye to the future. At present there was only Lang to protect her from the world, but if they lived in France, who knew when a wealthy, aristocratic *duc* or *comte* might take her away from a mere knight?

Sir Miles had been given Belford Abbey by the king as a wedding present, making him at a stroke of the royal pen one of the wealthiest landowners in northern England. All this mattered little to Sir Miles and Lady Gillian Raven. They turned the abbey into a home for displaced gentlewomen, most of whom had been nuns before the dissolution of the monasteries. Within a year of its beginning, Kyloe Manor was finished, one of the most beautiful manor houses in Northumbria. Sir Miles and Lady Gillian moved into it, accompanied by their first child, a son. But they spent equal time, especially during the busy times of sheep raising, spring and fall, at Mallory Hall.

Of necessity the shepherd, Jock, began spending more time at the Hall to assist the widow Mag Brunt with the burdensome task of running the house when Lady Gillian was absent. Mag seemed to bloom in her widowhood, the weight of years dropping from her now that George Brunt was no longer around to plague her life. It wasn't long before Jock noticed, and asked the bonny widow to marry him, promising to be a good father to her three boys and her little girl.

Miles eventually provided the king with the promised colt sired by Cloud, which was given to his son, Edward, for Henry's riding days were over. Chronically ill for the rest of his life, Henry never made it to Kyloe Manor for the grouse shooting.

Henry VIII was to live until 1547, divorcing his fourth wife, beheading his fifth—a cousin to Anne Boleyn—being survived by his sixth. Two of his eternal complaints were that he could never lure Sir Miles and Lady Raven down to court from their beloved Northumbria often enough, and that, try as he might, he could never find the happiness that those two found in their marriage.

* * * * *

Harlequin® Historical

FIRST IMPRESSIONS THAT ARE SURE TO ENDURE!

MARCH MADNESS

It's March Madness time again! Each year, Harlequin Historicals picks the best and brightest new stars in historical romance and brings them to you in one exciting month!

The Heart's Desire by Gayle Wilson—When the hunt for a spy pairs a cynical duke with a determined young woman, caution is thrown to the wind in one night of passion.

Rain Shadow by Cheryl St.John—A widower in need of a wife falls in love with the wrong woman, an Indian-raised sharp-shooter more suited to a Wild West show than to a farm.

My Lord Beaumont by Madris Dupree—Adventure abounds in this tale about a rakish nobleman who learns a lesson in love when he rescues a young stowaway.

Capture by Emily French—The story of a courageous woman who is captured by Algonquin Indians, and the warrior whose dreams foretell her part in an ancient prophecy.

Four exciting historicals by four promising new authors who are certain to become your favorites. Look for them wherever Harlequin Historicals are sold. Don't be left behind!

HHM94

**Fifty red-blooded, white-hot, true-blue hunks
from every State in the Union!**

Look for MEN MADE IN AMERICA! Written by some of our most poplar authors, these stories feature fifty of the strongest, sexiest men, each from a different state in the union!

Two titles available every other month at your favorite retail outlet.

In January, look for:

DREAM COME TRUE by Ann Major (Florida)
WAY OF THE WILLOW by Linda Shaw (Georgia)

In March, look for:

TANGLED LIES by Anne Stuart (Hawaii)
ROGUE'S VALLEY by Kathleen Creighton (Idaho)

You won't be able to resist MEN MADE IN AMERICA!

If you missed your state or would like to order any other states that have already been published, send your name, address, zip or postal code along with a check or money order (please do not send cash) for $3.59 for each book, plus 75¢ postage and handling ($1.00 in Canada), payable to Harlequin Reader Service, to:

In the U.S.

3010 Walden Avenue
P.O. Box 1369
Buffalo, NY 14269-1369

In Canada

P.O. Box 609
Fort Erie, Ontario
L2A 5X3

Please specify book title(s) with your order.
Canadian residents add applicable federal and provincial taxes.

MEN194

**A SON OF BRITAIN, A DAUGHTER OF ROME.
ENEMIES BY BIRTH, LOVERS BY DESTINY.**

LYNN BARTLETT

DEFY THE EAGLE

From bestselling author Lynn Bartlett comes this tale of epic passion
and ancient rebellion. Jilana, the daughter of a Roman merchant,
and Caddaric, rebel warrior of Britain, are caught in the clash of two
cultures amid one of the greatest eras in history.

Coming in February 1994
from Harlequin Historicals

Don't miss it! Available wherever Harlequin Books are sold.

HHB1G1

My Valentine 1994

Celebrate the most romantic day of the year with
MY VALENTINE 1994
a collection of original stories, written by
four of Harlequin's most popular authors...

**MARGOT DALTON
MURIEL JENSEN
MARISA CARROLL
KAREN YOUNG**

*Available in February, wherever
Harlequin Books are sold.*

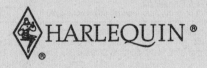

HARLEQUIN ®

VAL94

HARLEQUIN®

Don't miss these Harlequin favorites by some of our most distin-
guished authors!
And now, you can receive a discount by ordering two or more titles!

HT#25409	THE NIGHT IN SHINING ARMOR by JoAnn Ross	$2.99	☐
HT#25471	LOVESTORM by JoAnn Ross	$2.99	☐
HP#11463	THE WEDDING by Emma Darcy	$2.89	☐
HP#11592	THE LAST GRAND PASSION by Emma Darcy	$2.99	☐
HR#03188	DOUBLY DELICIOUS by Emma Goldrick	$2.89	☐
HR#03248	SAFE IN MY HEART by Leigh Michaels	$2.89	☐
HS#70464	CHILDREN OF THE HEART by Sally Garrett	$3.25	☐
HS#70524	STRING OF MIRACLES by Sally Garrett	$3.39	☐
HS#70500	THE SILENCE OF MIDNIGHT by Karen Young	$3.39	☐
HI#22178	SCHOOL FOR SPIES by Vickie York	$2.79	☐
HI#22212	DANGEROUS VINTAGE by Laura Pender	$2.89	☐
HI#22219	TORCH JOB by Patricia Rosemoor	$2.89	☐
HAR#16459	MACKENZIE'S BABY by Anne McAllister	$3.39	☐
HAR#16466	A COWBOY FOR CHRISTMAS by Anne McAllister	$3.39	☐
HAR#16462	THE PIRATE AND HIS LADY by Margaret St. George	$3.39	☐
HAR#16477	THE LAST REAL MAN by Rebecca Flanders	$3.39	☐
HH#28704	A CORNER OF HEAVEN by Theresa Michaels	$3.99	☐
HH#28707	LIGHT ON THE MOUNTAIN by Maura Seger	$3.99	☐

Harlequin Promotional Titles

#83247	YESTERDAY COMES TOMORROW by Rebecca Flanders	$4.99	☐
#83257	MY VALENTINE 1993	$4.99	☐
	(short-story collection featuring Anne Stuart, Judith Arnold, Anne McAllister, Linda Randall Wisdom)		

(limited quantities available on certain titles)

	AMOUNT	$
DEDUCT:	**10% DISCOUNT FOR 2+ BOOKS**	$
ADD:	**POSTAGE & HANDLING**	$
	($1.00 for one book, 50¢ for each additional)	
	APPLICABLE TAXES*	$ _____
	TOTAL PAYABLE	$ _____
	(check or money order—please do not send cash)	

To order, complete this form and send it, along with a check or money order for the
total above, payable to Harlequin Books, to: **In the U.S.:** 3010 Walden Avenue,
P.O. Box 9047, Buffalo, NY 14269-9047; **In Canada:** P.O. Box 613, Fort Erie, Ontario,
L2A 5X3.

Name: _____

Address: _____ City: _____

State/Prov.: _____ Zip/Postal Code: _____

*New York residents remit applicable sales taxes.
Canadian residents remit applicable GST and provincial taxes.

HBACK-JM